A Perilous Pose

Sibyl heard her fiancé, the incomparable Lord Buckingham, enter the house.

Quickly she turned to Robert Medland. "Now! You must kiss me, Robert," she whispered.

"This is the nicest part of your corkbrained scheme, my dear," Robert murmured against her lips as he proceeded to obey her injunction.

Sibyl believed she could control what a mere kiss would do to her. After all, hadn't even the legendary Buckingham's superbly skilled lips left her cold? But now she found that she was playing with fire— and that more than her reputation could go up in smoke. . . .

EMILY HENDRICKSON lives at Lake Tahoe, Nevada, with her retired airline pilot husband. Of all the many places she has traveled to around the world, England is her favorite and a natural choice as a setting for her novels. Although writing claims most of her time, she enjoys gardening, watercolors, and sewing for her grand-daughters as well as the occasional trip with her husband.

SIGNET REGENCY ROMANCE
COMING IN AUGUST 1991

Irene Saunders
Talk Of The Town

Margaret Westhaven
Country Dance

Barbara Allister
A Love Match

Laura Matthews
The Seventh Suitor

A
Scandalous
Suggestion

by

Emily Hendrickson

A SIGNET BOOK

SIGNET
Published by the Penguin Group
Penguin Books USA Inc., 375 Hudson Street,
New York, New York, 10014, U.S.A.
Penguin Books Ltd, 27 Wrights Lane, London W8 5TZ, England
Penguin Books Australia Ltd, Ringwood, Victoria, Australia
Penguin Books Canada Ltd, 2801 John Street,
Markham, Ontario, Canada L3R 1B4
Penguin Books (N.Z.) Ltd, 182-190 Wairau Road,
Auckland 10, New Zealand

Penguin Books Ltd, Registered Offices:
Harmondsworth, Middlesex, England

First published by Signet, an imprint of New American Library,
a division of Penguin Books USA Inc.

First Printing, July, 1991

10 9 8 7 6 5 4 3 2 1

 REGISTERED TRADEMARK—MARCA REGISTRADA

PRINTED IN THE UNITED STATES OF AMERICA

1

THE THAMES LAPPED against the shore, the tide beginning to turn, pulling things better not noticed along with it. One of the royal swans paddled past her, ignoring most of what lay beneath the surface. The sight of the elegant bird added to the unreality of the scene before her.

Sibyl Eagleton tugged her heavy shawl more closely about her, staring across the far side of the river where buildings rose like ghostly specters in the early morning mist. It was a dream world with menacing spires on a silver fog.

What a silly fool she was, to be sure. Last night had been an utter disaster. Poor Mama, she had nurtured such high hopes and now was so disappointed. And to think Sibyl had ended up half concealed behind a potted palm.

All the shopping for pretty clothes, the entire trip to London for her come-out, what a sad waste. She had truly enjoyed getting new things, as any girl would, but to what end?

It was not as though Sibyl had not warned her parents. She had pleaded with them, for she was quite comfortable at home, and had not wished to travel to London in the first place. The very thought of all the Society people, with their odd priorities and peculiar starts, made her shy away from parties and the like. Had it not been for the threat of Alfred Norton, she'd have insisted on staying home.

The kindest thing one might say about Alfred was that he was a nodcock. He rather frightened Sibyl. He had come upon her in the garden, breathing fumes of ale, bad teeth, and garlic in her face until she reeled. And he had demanded that she marry him, for he obviously considered himself to be the best catch in all of Mablethorpe—a squire's only son with great prospects. Perhaps he was. That did not mean she would wed him. She shuddered at the very thought and took a step closer to the river.

"I would not do that were I you. The water is cold and dirty, not fit for a bath."

Sibyl spun around, frightened at the voice so close to her. She had been sure she was alone here. She had expected the mists and early hour to discourage most people. This was not in the commercial area, nor were there likely to be hawkers and sellers about. She had thought herself to be safe.

"I do not intend to, sir." She stared at him, her gaze caught in his. Even in the misty light she could note his soft gray eyes, so understanding and kind. He was not as tall as some, but she thought him just right. He had strong features and a solid, trim build. There was nothing of the dandy about him.

"Just plain mister will do . . . Miss?"

"Just miss," she decided. No names. "And thank you for your concern." She could detect the gentility in his speech, and certainly his clothes were of the latest cut and finest fabrics. That gray coat was undoubtedly made by a master tailor, so well did it fit. "Although, I confess, the river would solve quite a few problems." She turned to look down again at the swirling dark waters.

"Is that why you are here? To flee from your problems? How could a pretty young miss like you have such serious dilemmas? I would have wagered the worst of them was deciding what gown to wear, or which beau to accept." He joined her to lean against the ramshackle railing, watching her rather than the river.

"You sound like my stepmama. It is not that simple. For example, last evening I went to an assembly," she confided, not pausing to consider that she was able to discuss such a painful subject with a total stranger. "Once there I was introduced to a perfectly acceptable young man. At least, I suppose he was. He asked me to dance. I knew how," she assured this man.

Her feet performed a few of the steps quite unconsciously before she recalled where she was. "What I do not know how to do is converse. My tongue was tied in knots. He rattled off various names I suppose I ought to know, and parties, none of which I had attended. When the dance was over, he escaped, and in a way, so did I. Never in the history of assemblies has a young woman had so many torn flouces. And," she peeped up at him, her eyes alive with mischief, "I had not one flounce on my gown."

She firmed her mouth. "If that is a sample of the young men from whom I am expected to choose, I want none of them. I believe I shall remain a spinster. Potted palms are a deal more companionable. They do not expect answers to stupid questions."

He gave a rather endearing chuckle, and her heart warmed to this man, this stranger in the mists.

"Silly girl. He was nothing but a sad fribble, if that is all he could manage to say to a lovely young miss at her first assembly. Come, let me give you an example."

He bowed most elegantly. She curtsied, frowning slightly in bewilderment.

He extended his hand to her, a charming grin tilting his well-shaped mouth. She took one look into those beautiful gray eyes and accepted his gloved hand. Then he began to hum a melody she recognized. She joined him to make a soft duet.

In and out and around they went, through delicate patterns, following one of the dances Sibyl had learned. Seeming satisfied she would hum the tune, he said, "Lovely weather we are having for this time of year, what?" He gave a significant glance at the fog, one that made her smile.

"Lovely," she said breathlessly. "Never have I seen a more misty mist."

"Not half as lovely as the lady in my arms."

"Oh, fie, sir, what flummery." She giggled, her soft eyes lighting up with delight at this nonsense.

"I shall compose an ode to your languishing blue eyes, or perhaps that rosebud mouth." He gave her a considering look, then said, "No, your innocent expression, like that of a newly-opened flower. Ah, but then, that beautiful English complexion must merit a few lines. It glows like the finest satin, petal soft, begging to be kissed."

"Oh, sir, you go too far!" She laughed as he whirled her around in perfect meter, her voice ringing out in sheer joy. It seemed like such a long time since she had laughed at such foolery.

"And then the gentleman ought to reserve a second dance,

no more, mind you. He should follow your progress with hungry eyes, watching with many sighs as others beg for your attention. Soon, you ought to have a veritable train of young men, officers, gentlemen of title, all at your beck and call.''

"What, no prince? I insist. I have dreamed of living in a castle on a hill," she declared with a mocking, imperious manner. She smiled then, her gaze softening, and said, "I have no need for titles. My new uncle is an earl, and although kindly, strikes me quite silent when we meet."

"I shall tell you a secret. Underneath all those fine clothes, they are all much the same. Next time you go to a ball, or something of that sort, just think how each of the people you meet would look in his or her nightrail."

"Sir," she declared, trying not to laugh, "what a shocking thing to say."

"It does work." Those eyes twinkled down at her with great charm, and she wondered what lady was so fortunate as to receive his homage.

"Does it, indeed?" She pushed the image of this man arrayed in a nightrail from her mind with great difficulty, returning her attention to the river. "It never stops, does it? How I should like to get on a boat and sail and sail far away from here. I have never been on a boat, but I suspect it would be intriguing."

"Farther down river there are boats one may take to places like Margate and Gravesend." He pointed to a pier that could barely be seen through the rising mist. It was a distant gray smear on the river's edge.

"That sounds like an enchanting prospect—especially at this moment, as I am. Graves end. Rather gloomy, I believe." She shuddered at the depressing thoughts that flooded into her mind.

"None of that. I promise all will get better. You must make an effort, and suspect there are others equally alarmed at the snobs of Society. Try again."

His smile was terribly appealing, she decided in a fit of great charity with the stranger. Now, had she someone like him . . . But, someone like him was undoubtedly spoken for by one of those elegant society women who put her in such a quake.

"You sound like my stepmama. She reads tea leaves, you see. In my cup she saw a musical note, which foretells good luck. She also saw a moon, which means a love interest. According to her, the castle she saw means security and safety. For all I know, it could mean nothing more than I might have the good luck to be carried off to a castle on a moonlit night by my true love." She gave a reflective sigh, then turned her face toward his. "Do you believe in such things, sir?"

He also sighed, and looked as though he wanted to reassure her that all the good things would come true.

"Never mind. I can see it is difficult for you. Perhaps you may meet her one day. If you do, ask for tea, then have her read the leaves in your cup. I fear she has been dreadfully accurate. Although one never knows how events will turn out precisely, you know."

"That is a truism. If you talk like this to your young gentlemen, they will be enchanted. Your stepmama will have them standing in line to have their fortunes read."

Sibyl chuckled. "I do not know if that will give me the splendid match she wants."

"Come, the mist is rising. You must go home before anyone sees you." He stretched out an arm, to escort her up the bank, she supposed.

"You have seen me. I feel I may trust you not to say a word, however. Do you suppose there are ghosts in the mist that whisper secrets?" She accepted his hand and assistance up the steps until they stood on the walkway. Behind them the parliament buildings loomed, ghostly shapes picked out by a filtered sun.

"Promise me one thing." He had grown quite intent, his face assuming a serious mien, like one about to give a lecture. "Never come here again like this. You were fortunate this time, that I saw you. Another time you might not be so lucky."

As he spoke two young men staggered down the street, obviously three sheets to the wind. Yet they espied her, making horrid suggestions that caused her cheeks to flame, even if she did not understand them completely.

When the two had turned a corner, her stranger from the mist gave her a serious look. "An excellent object lesson. You see what I mean, I collect?"

"I do," she replied in a small voice.

"Where do you live?"

She gave him an alarmed look, wondering if the man she thought so nice was something else.

Apparently he correctly interpreted her wide-eyed stare, for he chuckled. "I want only to take you a part of the way, to assure myself you come to no harm. My carriage is waiting over there." He gestured toward his curricle, where a handsome pair of grays were being walked by his groom.

She gave her stranger a tremulous smile, suddenly aware that she felt safe with him, totally safe. She almost chuckled at that thought, for she suspected most gentlemen would not think it a compliment for a woman to say he made her feel so.

Although he did have a devilish twinkle in those gray eyes at times. And his laugh had a wicked little catch to it at odd moments. How peculiar that she should feel so close to him. They were spirits of the mist, kindred spirits. Perhaps they would be wafted away?

She agreed to his offer, as the path across the park and the streets to Cranswick House would likely be filling with vendors now. She walked with him to the curricle. Once seated, they began to go in the general direction of Mayfair. He handled the ribbons with a casual skill she admired.

"I live this way, I believe. At least that building seems familiar," she pointed out as they reached the corner of Piccadilly and Half Moon Street. They wound their way along until South Audley.

"You walked all this way?"

"I am a country girl, you know. I suppose that is why I went out this morning, I could not bear to be cooped up in a building when I am used to wandering about in the lanes and byways."

The streets had been eerily silent on this Sunday morning. Fog had muffled the sound of the church bells. Now the cries of London were ringing out, the muffin man, the milk maid, and all the others who roamed the streets hawking their wares, the discordant music of the city.

They had driven along in companionable silence. He abruptly broke it. "I am frightened quite out of my skin to think what might have happened to you this morning. Promise me you will never, never consider such a trek again!"

"I gather it is more serious than I dreamed," she said contritely, some of his anger penetrating with effect. "I am not so foolish as to ignore your advice. I promise." The memory of the words hurled by those two castaway men would linger in her mind for some time.

His look of approval was not noted by her, for she concentrated on looking at each corner as they turned to proceed along South Audley.

At last she saw the church ahead, one she recognized as being close to her house. "You may leave me here, sir. And I thank you. I was most fortunate to meet such a gallant gentleman."

He took her hand, holding it lightly in his while he searched her face. He could see a brown curl teasing him from under the shawl. Her eyes were too trusting, her face too innocent. How would she cope with a come-out in this sometimes cruel society? "Perhaps we may meet again?"

"Perhaps," she agreed, thinking it highly unlikely. "Thank you again for your kindness, sir." She stepped from the curricle, then looked back at him.

"Not at all," he smiled, "fair maid of the mist." He saluted her, then flicked his whip lightly above the horses. The carriage moved on down the street.

She slipped inside the church for a moment, listening to the strains of the early service choir. Her heart was performing such peculiar antics, ones she had not known before and suspected a little.

In his curricle, the gentleman continued to the corner, then hurried in the direction of his home on Mount Street, his fatigue returning with a vengeance now. After being up all night, he almost wondered if the enchanting and innocent angel of the mists was nothing more than an illusion. Nothing was to be seen of her as he glanced back, and he wondered who she was and if he might see her again. He ought to have persisted in knowing her name, yet in the confines of Society, he doubtless could find her if he so chose. She was young and pretty, delightfully naive in her trusting, virginal manner. He was very glad he had happened along and caught sight of what he imagined to be a contemplated suicide. She might not be in that same state of innocence at this moment, had he not stopped. His look became grim.

"La, Sibyl, where have you been? Do not tell me you have wandered about in the little park in the square again?" Lady Lavinia Eagleton impatiently questioned the charming girl who now stood hesitantly in the breakfast room doorway. Becoming a stepmother had brought a number of surprises, not the least of which was discovering a miss who did not long for a London come-out.

"All right, Mama, I shall not tell you. I am a bit homesick for the country." She resolved not to say anything regarding her early-morning expedition. As it was, the entire thing had become more like a dream. Her poor stepmama would be horrified beyond belief, and Sibyl would be hedged around with further constraints. She felt confident that the stranger would say nothing, for indeed what could he say? She doubted if she would ever see him again.

Lady Lavinia watched Sibyl take a chair opposite to where she sat, contrition flooding over her. "I must tell you how sorry I am for last evening, dear girl. I ought not to have sat chatting with old friends. I was terribly remiss in my duties and I intend to make up for it."

Sibyl gave her an alarmed look. "How, pray tell? By taking me to another of those tedious assemblies where I may be insulted by another sprig of nobility? I did not care for my introduction, you may be sure." She ought not to have spoken so plainly, indeed, she was sorry to cause any wounds, but she could not wish for more embarrassment.

"Oh, dear, this is not at all how I envisioned it." Lady Lavinia glanced up to welcome her dearest brother. "William, do tell this silly girl that she must not give up after one assembly."

The dignified Earl of Cranswick was a remarkably well-preserved gentleman who greatly reminded Sibyl of her cousin George, his son. The earl had lived alone at Cranswick House since the death of his beloved wife following the birth of their daughter, the delightful Samantha. Presumably he had not felt the need to marry again.

Sibyl had heard snippets of gossip. He lived a somewhat rackety life, a member of the Carlton House set, a friend of the Prince Regent. A life of gay dissipation had not left its mark on Lord Cranswick. His chestnut hair and sherry-brown eyes were as vivid as his son's. His figure was trim and manner quite elegant. She was not surprised at the tales of his conquests among the fair set. He promptly turned Sibyl into that tongue-tied mouse she complained of to the stranger.

"What happened?" His look down that aristocratic nose sent Sibyl's heart plunging.

"Well," Lady Lavinia explained virtuously, "we went to the Stanley assembly. After one dance with the Wingfield boy, she rather faded away into the woodwork."

"Actually, it was a potted palm," Sibyl inserted wryly, forgetting to be intimidated by the earl in the interest of accuracy.

"Wingfield? If he is anything like his father, the lad is a stuffed prig."

Sibyl laughed for the first time since leaving the stranger. "I should say that probably suits him well, sir. He seemed a bit fond of titles and important places." She looked down at her teacup. "I had thought to take ourselves back to Mablethorpe and restore your house to peace and quiet," she said by way of apology for interrupting what must be a highly agreeable life for a bachelor.

"Rubbish," the earl declared, his eyes lighting with amusement at this young miss. "I believe I have had quite enough of peace and quiet for a while. Stay and do as my sister suggests. I think it hardly fair to judge Society on the basis of the Wingfield boy."

Lady Lavinia glanced with relief at her husband as he entered the room. Here, most clearly, was an excellent reinforcement for her argument.

"Henry, Sibyl is not persuaded in the least to make another attempt. It is all my fault," she burst out, suddenly rushing from the room in a flutter of white and pink draperies, her morning cap askew and a white handkerchief at the ready in her hand.

"Now, now," Lord Eagleton, formerly a general in his majesty's army, said as he followed his new wife out the door, his commanding manner deserting him in the face of womanly tears.

"And they wonder why I have not remarried." The earl

poured another cup of coffee, then accepted a plate of his favorite foods from his butler.

Sibyl tilted her head, studying this much more human person. "It seems to me that we are in much the same pickle. I want to retreat to the country, you want to stay as you are."

He glanced up at her, the surprise clear on his face. "I suppose you might say that," he agreed reluctantly. "Was it actually so bad?"

"Horrid," she seconded with growing amusement. Seen in the light of morning, the event had lost some of its humiliation. That alteration along with the kind words from the stranger made it seem less terrible. He had teased her from the mood that had settled on her like some bleak, funereal cloak.

"What you must do is acquire something unusual," the earl declared, punctuating his words with the stab of his fork. "I know a lady who had a pink poodle," he added by way of being helpful.

"I play the pianoforte and do the tiresome bit of embroidery. I should like to do something different," she said with a wistful air. "But not, I think, a pink poodle. Nor a tan terrier."

"A diversion," he supplied, waving his fork in the air. "One not done by every young woman, something to set you apart."

"That is precisely what I do not like—to be set apart."

"Collect something," he urged, then reapplied himself to his beef, the subject seeming closed as far as he was concerned.

"Collect? You mean like seashells or butterflies?"

"Butterflies," he nodded. "Just the ticket. I shall watch with interest to see what happens."

"Say nothing of this to Mama for the present, sir," Sibyl requested. "I believe I should like her to do a bit of considering first. I am not totally reconciled to this stay in the city. I should not wish another Mr. Wingfield, if you please."

"God forbid," he agreed.

"And," she added as an afterthought, "I shall give the matter of butterflies some consideration." Sibyl lingered, wishing she might ask him if he knew the identity of the stranger from the mists. But she had no name, and she doubted her romanticized description would be a bit of help. Melting gray eyes, a figure just the right height for her, and manners fit for a king were hardly to produce recognition on the earl's part.

"Do," said the earl, then swallowed that last bite of a hearty breakfast. "You ride, of course."

"Papa brought my mare to Town with us."

"Good. Take one of my grooms with you when you go out. London is less kind and not at all forgiving of a lapse, should you err."

She watched him leave the room, her little pink tongue nervously teasing the upper lip while she thought over the scene by the river. She could trust the stranger of the mists, she was sure of it. Nevertheless, she rose from her chair and wandered about the lower floor in an abstracted state, wishing she had been more prudent.

The house was intimidating, although the manor house in Mablethorpe was pleasant in its Tudor way. Cranswick House rose five stories, with a fine portico in front. She thought it the finest house on the square, which said a great deal, for the area seemed a most excellent address.

The first floor had many tall windows across the front. She floated up the stairs, then went to look out one of them, watching the earl ride off to the park on his chestnut gelding.

Fiddling with the ribbons on her pale blue muslin, she wondered what she ought to do. Should she actually collect butterflies? What a nonsensical notion, to be sure. Yet was it? It would give her something to pursue while in town. Certainly, it would offer a subject for conversation, a safe, neutral topic while navigating the dance floor.

And if they raised an eyebrow at her, she would look down her nose just as the earl had done. She walked over to a tall, gold-framed looking glass above the fireplace. There, she practiced until she dissolved in laughter.

"I am glad you are in better humor, puss," her father said from the doorway. "Your mama is most upset."

Contrite, for she truly was a tender-hearted girl, Sibyl quickly hastened to his side. "She did leave me, but I doubtless would have found the potted palm in any event."

"It is my fault, for keeping you at that remote spot for so long." His remorse tore at Sibyl.

"But, Papa, that is where I met Marianna, the lady who captured George's heart. Had I not been at Miss Chudleigh's school, you would not have met Mama. None of your new happiness would exist. It is best I learn to live with her desire to see me launched. But I warn you, if they are all such fribbles, I shall return to Mablethorpe. And," she added, "I shall not wed Albert."

"Never," Lord Eagleton agreed. "Perhaps I can find a way to introduce you to a few fine young men."

He turned to wander down the stairs, leaving Sibyl curious as to what was going on in his mind. She would far rather have the selecting of her future husband left to her own hands. But, she was an heiress, a matter they chose to keep concealed for the moment. One hint of money and the men at point-non-plus would be after her in a flash.

Her papa wanted to see her well-fixed, with a good husband. She just hoped the entire family could agree on the man selected.

Deciding to do as the earl suggested, she went up to her room to change into her habit, after sending word to the stables for her mare and a groom to go with them.

The habit shirt with its lace ruff reconciled her to the severe cut of her blue riding dress. With its simple lines, she had but one petticoat beneath and wore pink drawers that she had been assured were the latest rage of the *ton*.

The groom rode close enough to give her directions to the park, and the best place to ride. He was a kindly man, yet he did not offer the sort of company she would have truly enjoyed. Once they were on a path, he remained silent, only occasionally pointing out a person for her.

It was a lonely ride, as she knew no one. The earl was nowhere in sight. It served to highlight the difference in coming to London.

"There be the hussars, miss. Capital group of riders," offered the groom as Sibyl turned her head to watch the smartly dressed men riding toward the Horse Guards.

Her papa would undoubtedly know some of these men, or, more likely, they would know him. Yet that did her little good now. How dashing they looked.

Not far from where she rode, she observed a lady gowned in pink flirting with a handsome gentleman. Not the man of the mists, she noted after checking.

Turning her mare in the direction of Cranswick House, she

said, "I believe I shall go back. It is not at all like home."

The groom looked askance at her remark, probably wondering how any young miss might take exception to the wonders of Hyde Park. She doubted if he had ever left the city. He couldn't know how delightful a dash across a field might be, instead of this staid place.

Lady Lavinia watched the drooping figure of her stepdaughter from her bedroom window. Sighing with apprehension that her plans were sailing out to sea on an empty boat, she wondered what she could do. Having Sibyl make her come-out was not going to be as simple as she had hoped. Would that she not make a mull of it. She got one last glimpse of Sibyl before she rode through to the mews. Lavinia wondered frantically what in the world she was going to do to salvage the situation.

2

LADY LAVINIA PONDERED the previous night while at her morning toilette. Her tea leaves had never been so wrong before. She did not precisely slump—for no true lady ever did such a thing—but she wilted slightly. What "good luck" could there be for a girl who spent the evening hidden behind a palm frond? And how on earth might she come to find her "love" when no gentleman could possibly see her?

Lavinia sighed wistfully, and began to wonder if perhaps she had been grossly mistaken in her efforts to give Sibyl a Season. Still, the girl was a dear, tender-hearted little thing. What a pity there was not someone who needed tending, for she would see to it in a trice.

Rising from her dressing table and dismissing Purdy with an absent wave of her hand, Lavinia wandered to the window of the charming room she had lived in when a girl in this house. What memories flooded back when she looked about her.

Gathering her gray velvet cloak from the chair by her door, she left her room and slowly marched down the stairs. After permitting Bentley to assist her with the cloak, she strolled from the house, lost in thought.

The butler watched her depart with a shake of his head, as though most disapproving of her independence but resigned to it.

From her window overlooking the square, Sibyl took note of Lady Lavinia and suspected the reason for the solitary walk so unfashionably early in the morning. Her stepmama was unhappy, that much Sibyl could guess. And well she might be. It was not enough for Lady Lavinia to see her old friends and enjoy the delights of a London Season once again. Sibyl must shine.

Allowing the curtain to slip from her fingers, Sibyl crossed to change out of her habit. Once dressed in a violet gown tied with purple ribbons, she dropped on the bench at the foot of her bed. She pulled at the crocheted lace that covered the top of the bed with an absent hand, then sighed.

Why was it so important for her to have a splendid come-out? Wouldn't it do as well for her to meet some quiet gentleman she might actually converse with, who would truly enjoy her music and share her love for beautiful things? Someone like the gentleman of the mists? She really wished she had asked his name. Yet it would have been most improper for them to have exchanged such. One must be properly introduced.

Lord Cranswick's suggestion about collecting butterflies, a thing that would never have occurred to her, returned. Was it so silly? She had always enjoyed the pretty creatures. Would it not prove interesting to make such a collection, discover what varieties might be found here? She instantly resolved to do just that. But, she reassured herself, it was not merely to make herself "noticed" or "different." If she pursued this, it would be because she wanted to enjoy the pleasure of it.

First, she would find a good guide book to London. Then she would locate a net to catch those delightful butterflies. Perhaps it might prove to be great fun!

Bestirring herself to action, she quickly and neatly arranged her hair in a knot of soft curls on the back of her head, then dug in her wardrobe for a pretty bonnet.

She would take one of the maids, as she knew she must, but it would be one who could hold her tongue. While there was nothing improper about obtaining a guidebook to the city, a net presented a greater problem. Maybe the guidebook might be of help? Embroidery was far more acceptable as an occupation for one's time. The problem with that was that Sibyl was bored to flinders with embroidery.

Bentley advised her that the maid most likely to suit her purposes would be Annie, the little upstairs maid who had helped Sibyl at night. "Quiet and obedient, our Annie is, miss. She has never been one to relate a bit of gossip from abovestairs."

Annie dutifully followed Sibyl to Hatchards, where an excellent guide to London was quickly purchased. Titled *Picture of London,* it listed all the interesting sights of the city in great detail. Sibyl agreed with the general description of London for the most part. The principal streets were wide and airy, as the book said. The book failed to mention the smells or noise, however. She found it reassuring that there were numerous beadles, watchmen, and patrols, even if she had never seen one about. There had been no evidence of such this morning when those two foxed young men had jeered at her. The warning against asking directions of a person in the street seemed hardly necessary. Sibyl was loathe to approach any stranger for such assistance.

Rather, she inquired of the clerk. He, in turn, inquired of someone else. In a few minutes, Sibyl accepted a written direction to a not-too-distant shop where the long-handled net she required could be obtained.

A wide-eyed Annie watched all this strange business quite as mute as a fish.

At last, her mission accomplished, Sibyl found a hackney and told the jarvey to take them back to Grosvenor Square.

Lady Lavinia was thinking of another path to take in her plans for Sibyl. She had slipped into the little church on South Audley with a heavy heart, sliding onto a rear pew while she pondered her problem.

As she was gazing blankly off into space in the general direction of the altar, a tentative voice reached through her abstractions.

"Lavinia Mayne, is that really you I see?"

Abruptly startled from her musings, Lavinia rose from the pew to encounter an instantly familiar face. "Delia, how lovely to find my dear friend. I did not see you last evening," she chided, the way one can only with one who has been a bosom bow. "Where do you reside now? Do you and Charles still live near here?"

"Charles died several years ago, Lavinia." The genial, round face clouded over for a moment, then she continued, "It was just as well, for I vow he would have had us in dun territory had he not," she honestly admitted. While it was plain she had regarded her husband with fondness, she evidently had not been blind to his addiction to gaming.

"I am sorry, Delia. Come, this is no proper place for us to chat. We are residing with my brother at his house. Can you spare an hour for tea?" Lavinia persuasively tucked Delia's arm close to her, propelling the amused lady out the church door with discreet speed.

"Who is the rest of your 'we,' Lavinia? The last I heard you were caring for William's children up in Yorkshire." Delia easily adjusted her step to Lavinia's quick one.

"They are married, and so am I," Lavinia declared with rosy pleasure. "My dear Henry is Baron Eagleton now, but was a general when we met." As briefly as possible, Lavinia told the story of meeting General Eagleton, and some of what had passed, concluding with the trip to London.

"But? You have a problem, I perceive, for I recall that expression well," Delia said as they walked up the steps to the imposing structure on Grosvenor Square. It had changed some since she and Lavinia had been girls. The scent of sandalwood mingled with roses greeted them, witness that the earl liked his abode to be most pleasant. Lavinia's brother, the Earl of Cranswick, had his own crowd and her path rarely crossed with his nowadays. Once she had admired him as a fine figure of a man. He still was.

Lavinia handed her cloak to Bentley, requesting tea to be brought to her sitting room before leading Delia up the broad stairs to the private apartment she shared with Henry. Fortunately, he was out and about his business—not that she wouldn't be pleased to introduce him, but Delia had always possessed excellent sense. Lavinia had need of such today without having any roundaboutation.

"Henry has a dear little daughter, his Sibyl, whom we brought to Town for her come-out. The only rub is that the girl is rather shy. I confess, I am at my wit's end."

"She doesn't want to attend the balls and parties of the *ton*?" Delia inquired with understanding sympathy.

"Last night she hid behind a palm frond for most of the evening. I was at fault, I know, for I permitted the joy of returning to Society to obscure my duty. She kept appearing before me, murmuring little things that sounded fine until I considered them later. Oh, Delia, I feel utterly wretched!"

"I know what you mean," the refined Mrs. Medland said, her bond with her girlhood friend strengthened by this confession. "My son, Robert, is a quiet sort, although not precisely what I would call shy. He declares himself bored with the *ton,* turns from Almack's with disdain, and refuses to attend the balls and assemblies. Even without a title he has a respectable inheritance so that he is considered a decent catch by the mamas. Although he has no need to hunt for an heiress, he utterly declines to look for one—or for a wife of any kind, for that matter. He spends a good deal of time racing his yacht when he is not absorbed in his study of nature."

The two women exchanged looks of commiseration which slowly grew to speculation while Bentley brought in the tray of tea things. A goodly assortment of pastries were included, as Bentley had noticed that Lady Lavinia had ignored her breakfast.

"Are you thinking what I am?" Lavinia inquired after they were once again alone. She poured out steaming tea for each, then offered the delicate pastries to her friend before hungrily attacking one with dainty greed. Plotting required sustenance.

"I am thinking we might find a way to bring our two young people together," Delia Medland replied with a show of delight.

"Precisely," Lavinia answered, nodding her head once with strong agreement, while slipping a second pastry onto her plate.

"How? Does Sibyl have any special interests we might utilize?" Delia nibbled on a delectable tart, while hope began to shine in her eyes.

"She plays the pianoforte with skill and feeling, if I do say so. Not the sort of rubbish we have to listen to most of the time, but true musicality. However," Lavinia sighed with resignation, "I doubt she would play for strangers."

"Other interests?" Delia persisted.

"William said he suggested she collect butterflies and she seems to enjoy paintings. Perhaps a trip to the British Museum or the Royal Academy might be in order? And, of course, she rides," Lavinia added as an afterthought.

"All have potential, especially the butterflies. So few young women enjoy nature. Since she likes music, you must come to the musicale at my house this evening. I have found the most delightful performers of high quality. You will hear no tedious music there, I promise."

"How kind of you, but still . . ." Lavinia pondered the suggestion, then nodded with hesitant agreement.

"Offer her a treat. After last evening, she may feel constrained to attend with you." Delia anxiously searched her friend's face.

"But how to encourage the two?"

"That is not as simple," Delia admitted. "She is a tender-hearted young miss, from your talk of her. Could you hint that Robert is retiring and needing someone to help him? What young woman does not secretly long to be of aid to a handsome but shy man? We need not reveal he merely enjoys his quiet. Racing that yacht provides thrills enough, but solitary ones."

"Robert is handsome, eh? Not surprising when you recall Charles—you, too, for that matter. I must say that Sibyl is not only sweet in nature, but a pretty girl as well."

There was a scratching at the door, and when bid, the young lady under discussion entered the room. She curtsied to her mama and the guest most properly. Graceful and charming, judged Delia of her possible daughter-in-law, if all went well. The introductions were cautious but pleasant.

Sibyl was still flushed from her journey about town. She smiled at the ladies, then accepted a cup of tea, recalling her breakfast had been scanty at best. At first, conversation was general.

"Mrs. Medland has kindly invited us to her musicale, dear girl," Lavinia announced at last to Sibyl. "She tells me she has some interesting talent for us to hear. I know how fond you are of good music, so I accepted."

"Actually, I have hopes you might assist me as well," Delia confided to the young woman seated near her. Sibyl's manners were exquisite, and her voice had a soft, dulcet quality that was most pleasing to the ears. From where she sat, Delia could detect the lovely scent of lily of the valley, no doubt a fragrance from the shop of the celebrated perfumer, Floris. The girl indeed charmed.

"I should be happy to help you, ma'am, though I fail to see

how I may." Sibyl politely turned her attention from her mama to the guest, a kind-looking lady with soft brown hair peeping from beneath her cap and bonnet, and possessing a pair of lovely gray eyes which instantly reminded Sibyl of another fine pair of gray eyes.

"I have persuaded my son, Robert, to join me this evening, but I fear he will not do so happily. He prefers his books."

Her curiosity aroused, Sibyl properly inquired, "Dear ma'am, surely any son of a lady such as you would be an asset to Society, books or no." Sibyl's fine brows drew together in consideration of such a problem while her pink mouth pursed in sympathetic understanding for one who did not care for Society.

Lavinia darted a pleased glance at Delia, observing the delicate lift of an eyebrow that told her the compliment had been well received.

"He is a most honorable young man, to be sure, and has been a great comfort to me since the loss of my husband. But he is far too retiring. I begin to despair of his ever making an eligible connection. If, perhaps, you could help him, persuade him to talk a bit, join the party, as it were? He needs to be drawn out of himself and his books."

Sibyl studied the attractive gray eyes, with the appeal of a worried mother so eloquently revealed in them. While she was pleased to attend the musicale with the promise of excellent entertainment, she was less happy to consider persuading a gentleman from his tranquil habits.

Yet, she could not ignore the hope in those eyes. Mrs. Medland looked at Sibyl as woman to woman, requesting assistance with the knowledge that the person she asked was adult enough to perform the task to hand.

Sibyl nodded. "I shall do as you wish, although I cannot promise success. I can only take pity on him and talk as I wish someone would converse with me." Sibyl knew conversation to be the most difficult thing for her to accomplish.

For Sibyl, this was a great deal to offer and Lavinia sensed it at once. She gazed at her friend, hoping that she would also draw the same conclusion.

"Most agreeable of you. I am so happy that I found you this morning, Lavinia, my dearest friend. We shall have a delightful

Season, one denied me years ago, for you must recall that after I was betrothed to Charles, my papa removed me to the country. You are not the only one who wishes to enjoy this Season.''

After bidding Lady Lavinia a fond good-bye for the nonce, Delia hurried to her charming residence on Mount Street. Her son was at home, a thing not in the least surprising.

"Robert, you have remembered the musicale this evening, have you not?'' She smiled wanly, if a bit anxiously, at her son.

"I do, although I have planned to slip into the library after the guests arrive. Do you mind?'' His half-smile revealed he knew his mother most tolerant of his preference for quiet in which to read and study.

"Very much, my dear. I have particular need of your services this evening. Do you recall my mentioning Lady Lavinia Mayne? Sister of Cranswick? She is in Town, married now to Baron Eagleton. Her pretty little stepdaughter is making her come-out this year.''

Robert gave his mother a guarded look. In his experience, women worried about those pretty buds of Society only when the girl was a total antidote. ''And?''

"I have persuaded her to attend this evening, for the girl is a fine pianist and adores music, but she is horribly shy. I hoped you would make her feel at ease, just for this evening. Lavinia is such a dear creature and I know she worries about her little lamb.''

"Hmpf,'' Robert muttered, liking the prospect less and less. Then he recalled his misty lady, and felt compassion for the young girl thrown on Society.''

"I met her at Lavinia's just now,'' continued Delia, ignoring her son's lack of enthusiasm. ''She's a taking girl. Oh, not your style at all, of course. But she has soft brown hair pulled back from a fine oval face, and sensitive blue eyes with a pert little nose that is rather sweet. She would not put you to the blush with your friends, I think. Not very tall, thank heaven. It would be difficult if she were a Long-Meg.''

Robert was exceedingly conscious that he had not quite the height of some of his friends. He gave his mother a look that told her he suspected the miss was to be short.

His eyes became thoughtful. "And what do you know of my style, mother?"

"Oh," she said in an uncomfortable way, "I see and hear, you know."

"I see," was his dry rejoinder. "Well, you ask little enough of me. I expect I can tolerate the company of a green girl for one evening. Although I hope my credit can stand it." He bestowed a lazy grin on his mother of the sort calculated sufficient to set any young woman's heart to a rapid beat, then returned to his papers.

She had succeeded! What a relief. It would have been humiliating had she been required to acknowledge the immediate defeat of their plans to Lavinia and be the recipient of her gentle teasing.

When evening arrived, Sibyl presented herself in the main drawing room with more than a few trepidations. Now that the business of acquiring gowns and all the other necessary things was behind them, there was no excuse to avoid the invitations that had begun to flow into Cranswick House. She must steel herself and hope that potted palms were plentiful in the city.

The earl had listened with a tolerant ear to the tale his sister had spun. Upon seeing the sweet vision in celestial blue, wearing an evening cap of blue and silver and dainty pearls of the finest quality about her neck, he decided he would also take in the musicale. It might be amusing to see what young Robert Medland would make of this turn of events. This young girl was not in the usual order at all.

Lord Eagleton beamed at his pride and joy. "Don't you look a treat. Capital! I vow, not another will hold a candle to you tonight."

"Oh, Papa," she said with proper modesty. She twinkled a smile at him, causing the earl to revise Robert Medland's chances by a considerable amount. "I'll wager you would say that to all your daughters, had you been blessed with more of them."

"They would have to be prime ones to outshine you, puss."

She appeared to discount her father's doting words. Yet the

earl suspected they had made her feel better about the coming evening.

Lavinia raised an expressive brow when told her brother would join them. "I declare, between the two of you, I shall be the most fortunate lady at the musicale." She beamed at them both, then nudged Henry toward the door.

Robert watched the approach of Cranswick and his party with a few qualms. The older woman with the white wispy hair and the discreet plumes waving in the air must be his sister, Lady Lavinia Eagleton, with the baron on her other side. His face looked familiar, then Robert recalled he had been a general serving in France before being invalided home. He looked fit enough now, and obviously proud of the young girl who drifted along at his side. At last Robert's gaze shifted fully to the young girl he was to pay gentle court to tonight.

This exquisite creature was the girl who was being puffed off in his direction? It was none other than his lady of the mists. Their eyes met, the shock of recognition instant.

She could not acknowledge having met him before. That way lay danger. It was best to pretend they were strangers, for in a manner of speaking, they were.

When she came up to him, prettily presenting her hand and dipping an elegant curtsy, worthy of a duchess at the very least, Robert wished to guard his tongue. What best to say when presented by his mother? Mrs. Medland performed her duty, turning reluctantly to her next guest.

Apparently quite as aware of the pitfalls about them as he, Sibyl quietly said, "I am so happy to meet you. Your mama is a very dear lady. It was such a pleasure to meet her today."

The simple speech charmed him to his heart. He bowed over the daintiest hand he could recall in some time, indeed, since this morning. "I'm delighted, Miss Eagleton."

She blushed. "I believe your mama exaggerated a trifle to me. She described you as retiring. She obviously does not know of your penchant for assisting unknown ladies on the brink of the river."

"You had no difficulty in getting home? How did your day go?" He had worried about her off and on during the following hours.

"No problem, as the church is close to Cranswick House. I went for a ride later. It was dreadfully dull, but I enjoyed it nonetheless." She flashed him a look that revealed the morning scene was still as vivid to her as it was for him. She quickly sought a chair and flushed when he abandoned the receiving line to join her.

The music was wonderful. The pianist was extremely talented and played several Bach airs with a sensitivity she seemed to appreciate.

Robert watched her eager little face with an intent gaze. She was totally absorbed in the music. There were none of those flirtatious glances, accidental touchings, or dropped fans he had come to expect of young ladies. Rather, she sat quietly, her hands modestly folded in her lap, and listened. It was a rare quality in any woman, Robert knew. For such a young woman, she possessed a remarkably restful nature. He wondered how she would like the opera.

"Oh," she sighed in delight as the music ended, "that was lovely. Your mother is prodigiously clever to find such talent."

He thought of the tidy sum paid to the performer and knew there wasn't a pianist in town who would refuse to grace the select gathering at Mrs. Medland's house on Mount Street when she held her musicales.

"I don't suppose you have been to the opera as yet?"

"No." She shook her head, endangering the tiny evening cap of silver and blue pinned atop it.

"Would you join a party I am arranging for the performance of Mozart that is coming up soon? Your parents as well, of course?"

"That would be most charming, sir." Her melting look of pleasure held Robert still for a moment before he began to explain about the singer who would perform next.

From where he sat, Cranswick could watch with great interest the progress across the room. It had been worth the attendance to an affair he would usually have scorned. Although he had to admit that the pianist was a notch above anything he had heard in some time. And the glowing hostess was another surprise.

Delia Medland had taken off her blacks some years ago, but she had lived quietly, not meeting the rather fast group Cranswick had frolicked with these last years. Pity. She was an attractive woman. Not his sort in the least, mind you, but rather pretty nonetheless. Tonight, dressed in that silvery thing that lit her eyes with a peculiar glow, she really was . . . pretty.

From where she surveyed the room—William Mayne, the Earl of Cranswick, in particular—Delia considered what a shame it was that such a handsome man should be such a rackety one. He was tall and slender, possessed of a fine address and a pair of extremely handsome legs. But what a naughty man. She had heard whispers of his mistress, his high living. He dashed about with the Regent's set. Indeed, he might be the most eligible man alive, but she couldn't give him a second look. Delia ignored the fact that she had watched him for the past hour. Surreptitiously, of course.

Crossing the rear of the drawing room that had been cleared of nearly all but the necessary chairs and the musical instruments, she joined him. "I am surprised to see you here this evening, Lord Cranswick. I was unaware you cared for musicales."

"I'll confess that when I saw my sister's stepdaughter, I had a notion to see her impact on your Robert, over there. Quite something to watch." He raised an expressive brow.

"Lavinia told you of our plans?" Delia was not pleased to have the earl know of the scheme she had made with his sister. It made it seem tawdry, somehow, like something those odious matchmakers might do who spared nothing to see their child wed to the highest and best possible.

"I shan't say a word, if you are worried about such," he replied.

"I didn't think you would, sir."

"You are looking uncommonly well. The years have been exceedingly kind to you. Obviously, you have avoided my rackety sort of life." His admiring gaze was pleasing.

"It does not look to have harmed you."

"Mother," Robert said as he walked up to where they stood, "I should like to form a party for the opera. Do you think Lord and Lady Eagleton would consent to go with Miss Eagleton and myself? And perhaps you would like to join us?" he added to both of them politely.

Delia gave the earl an uncomfortable look.

The earl spoke up at that point. "I collect you speak of the Mozart thing coming up? I have a particularly fine box, and I would deem it a great pleasure if you would be my guests for dinner first, then we could all attend together."

Roses bloomed on Delia Medland's cheeks as she flashed him a challenging look. "Thank you, sir, we should be happy to accept." She knew Lavinia would be delighted, for entirely different reasons.

Robert looked at his parent, then at Cranswick, frowning at the very notion that occurred to him. Palpably absurd, old man, he told himself. He crossed the room to acquaint Lord and Lady Eagleton with the plans, then rejoined Sibyl, informing her as well.

He was greatly pleased. He would be able to spend time with his delightful lady of the mists, perhaps help her along? Surely a delightful cause.

3

SIBYL HAD NEVER been the dithering sort. At the moment one might be forgiven if such were the impression. One minute she was in alt at the opportunity to attend the coming Mozart production at the Opera House, the next she considered the group of which she would be a part and she found her trepidations rising.

" 'Tis not of great import, my dear," Lady Lavinia murmured as Sibyl left off her practicing at the pianoforte to gaze out the window of the morning room with pensive eyes. "We are friends, you see."

Sibyl nodded. She knew they were all friends, more or less, but she was in a quandary over Mr. Medland. He was most handsome and possessed exquisite manners, but he also knew things about her no one else did. While she felt he would not reveal her improper foray to the banks of the Thames, she did not know him all that well. Perhaps he might think it quite all right were he to tease her about the matter.

The garden caught her eye. As yet she had not found an opportunity to try her hand at chasing after butterflies. The idea amused her. It offered a pleasant contrast to Society's doings and a relief from her worries.

For it seemed London was one daunting experience after another. Sibyl knew she must seek to overcome this tendency to retreat from the problems of life.

A small sigh of resignation escaped. Medland. What was she to do? Keep an eye on the man? He made it easy for her. Just witness how he had leaped to offer the evening at the opera. And to a reserved gentleman such as he was, that could be no small thing. Part of her wished to believe he was honorable, trustworthy. Another part recalled that wicked chuckle, that devilish twinkle in his eyes as they had danced in the mist upon the bank of the Thames.

Sibyl began to look forward to the opera with greater enthusiasm, especially when the cloud-white gown of delicate silk sarcenet spangled with diamante arrived from the dressmaker. It had a proper neckline for a young miss, not shockingly low, and clung to her slender figure with flattering grace.

"I shall instruct Annie to dress your hair looped into a chignon to the back with careless curls over your brow. I have some pearls that will look perfect wreathed in your hair. You shall be an entrancing combination of the innocence of pearls with the finesse of the diamante." Lavinia clasped her hands together as she considered the impact of Sibyl on the senses of Robert Medland. If the vision of her stepdaughter rigged fine as fivepence in this charming get-up didn't send him reeling, he might as well go aloft to his maker.

In the intervening days, Sibyl rode daily in the park, dressed in the new habit of blue wool cloth with the pretty ruff at her neck. She was alone, but for the groom. She had not met any young ladies as yet, something she hoped to remedy soon. What a pity Mrs. Medland did not have a daughter.

After hearing of the solitary rides and detecting the nuance of longing in Sibyl's voice, Lady Lavinia had a talk with her husband. General Lord Eagleton was quick off the mark and at once acquiesced to his lady's suggestion.

On her next ride out, her father accompanied her, his military bearing most admirable. As they rode through the clusters of horses and carriages that thronged the park of an afternoon, Sibly felt a measure of growing assurance. Her papa was so distinguished.

A group of young officers recognized the general. Before she knew it, Sibyl found herself introduced. A Captain Ransom paid her particular regard, his brown eyes warmly admiring.

"You are acquiring quite an entourage, Sibyl," her papa commented the second time they rode out. "I shan't be wanted in the future, with so handsome a collection of beaux."

"Papa," Sibyl demurred with commendable modesty, "what utter rubbish. They think that because I'm your daughter, you might pass along a kind word to someone in a high place were they to catch your eye in a favorable way."

"Plain speaking indeed, but I suspect you state it wrongly,

puss. Henceforth, I shall ride early in the morning and we shall see who is right.'' He offered her a companionable grin and she had to be content with his words.

He was right, of course, much to Sibyl's secret delight. While she thought the soldiers bordering on a group of fribbles, it was great fun to listen to their nonsense. Therefore, she smiled at all and listened with flattering charm to the tales and boastings with no discernible partiality to any one of the young men.

Robert Medland took note of the group from where he rode. He observed that while the young men jostled about the pretty Miss Eagleton, she seemed to keep a proper distance from them all. Then he observed a captain seemed to rate a special smile. Robert trotted over to join them. As her particular friend, he owed it to her to check this young man out.

Sibyl had caught sight of the elusive Mr. Medland from afar. She welcomed him with a smile, first beaming an apolgetic look to Captain Ransom. Mr. Medland seemed determined to edge into place on her right, nudging the captain from the favored spot.

Captain Ransom checked his timepiece, then suggested they had best return to their barracks. The officers bid flattering farewell to Sibyl, nodded politely to Robert, then cantered off to the west.

''You have made conquests, Miss Eagleton.'' Mr. Medland threw a glacial look after the happy-go-lucky group of young men. ''You are like a butterfly surrounded by bright flowers. Or is it weeds?'' He looked rather disgruntled.

Sibyl laughed, a soft, musical sound that captivated the ear. ''Nonsense.'' While Papa thought them fine, he would look elsewhere for his daughter's husband, she knew that. She suspected he had wanted to provide her with company on her rides, and as long as she behaved herself, she imagined it was innocent enough. ''Do you disapprove of my company?''

''Your father would never countenance a union between you and one of those young men.'' He stared after the departing officers. ''However charming, most are without the needful. If you wish to please your parents, look higher than such as those hussars. Save that innocent sparkle for those worthy of it.''

She considered her gloves a moment, then raised sapphire

eyes to meet his gaze. "It is a harmless diversion, sir." She thought back to the delightful gentleman she had met by the river, his sound counsel, his caring. He was far more heroic than those prancing, boastful soldiers. Mr. Medland possessed qualities above them. She gave him a resigned but friendly smile.

"I gather you have said nothing of our encounter that morning and I do thank you. My stepmama would be furious with me if she knew." She wanted to say something to remind him that she hoped for continued silence.

His eyes flashed with a momentary anger. "A gentleman would never tattle, Miss Eagleton." Then his gaze softened. "I am sorry, I ought not rail at you, for goodness knows you have enough to contend with. I do not think anyone suspects we have met previous to the musicale. That was not so very difficult, was it?"

"You helped me a good deal. With music there is little need for conversation." She did not add that she felt most at ease with him.

"I shall do my utmost to keep your secret."

Her eyes danced at the notion of a secret with Mr. Medland. Not wishing to push herself forward, she stopped, then said to him, "I ought to be returning home as well. Until later." She had no intention of presuming on their initial meeting. For all she knew, he might be sorry he had stopped in the mist to chat with her that morning.

Her eyes grew wistful as a backward glance saw Mr. Medland ride off alone through the sun-dappled green of the Park. She watched as he paused to speak with a lady in pink silk trimmed with rows of ruffles. The lady twirled a pagoda parasol while smiling flirtatiously at him from the seat of her stylish carriage. He might be retiring, but apparently there were other women who found him attractive in spite of his lack of title. Beautiful women. Whatever had made his mama think he needed help?

At last the night arrived. Lavinia had heard the Mozart production was totally sold out. Everyone who claimed a place in the *ton* planned to attend dressed in their finest. Long-suffering gentlemen, her husband most likely one of them, hoped to be able to find a congenial friend with whom they could chat when the opera got boring, as it was bound to do. Ladies prepared to enchant, and perhaps to listen. Lady Eagleton said nothing of this aspect of the occasion to Sibyl, fearing an attack of nerves or worse. She had been relieved to discover that no potted palms had been used to decorate the private boxes of the opera. That would have been the outside of enough, and totally upset her plans for the night.

When Sibyl hesitantly entered the drawing room the Earl of Cranswick and Mr. Medland were there, Mrs. Medland having gone to Lavinia's room for an extra pin.

Robert stared at the vision in a delicate white gown that shimmered and sparkled as though she was an ethereal being. Pearls were woven through the soft brown hair with a charming effect. From the crown of her glossy hair to the tip of her white Denmark satin slippers, she was very lovely. One gloved hand held a dainty reticule of white satin. It idly swung back and forth, the only sign of possible nerves.

The earl was vastly amused at the sight of the dumbstruck male at his side. How well he recalled the first sight of his wife in her evening glory. It had knocked him off his pins. Though it *had* been a long, long time ago. Seeing Delia as a very mature woman had made him realize just how long it had been. It was time and enough . . .

Sibyl faltered in her steps at this silent reception, then said, "Good evening, gentlemen. The others are not here?"

Taking pity on a young woman obviously not accustomed to the effect of her delicate beauty on a susceptible man, the earl informed her, "They will be here shortly. Your mother is helping Mrs. Medland with her gown, something about a pin, I believe." His attitude implied he disbelieved that supposition.

"Well, Medland, Cranswick, nice evening." The general entered, then paused as he beheld his daughter. "Very nice. Your mama has done a fine job of it, puss."

This reserved encomium was greeted by a rosy blush of pleasure from Sibyl. "Thank you, Papa." She was happy her papa was approving, yet slightly embarrassed he had to say anything in front of Mr. Medland, who, if you must know, had done nothing but stare at her until she longed to peep into a looking glass to check her face for spots.

They were saved from further awkwardness by the arrival of the other ladies. The six went down to dinner in a mood of congeniality.

What a change Robert Medland's table manners were from Albert Norton's, Sibyl observed, as he deftly managed the food on his plate. It was a pleasure to observe a true gentleman. How fortunate she was to have him as a friend.

When the earl announced that they would depart for the opera directly after their meal, Sibyl was startled from her contemplations with the notion that while she might be moderately full, she had no idea what she had eaten!

"Did I tell you yet how lovely you look, Miss Eagleton?" Robert said in an undertone meant for her ears alone. He assisted her up into the Medland town carriage. Lord and Lady Eagleton rode with Robert and Sibyl while Mrs. Medland found herself joining the earl in his barouche.

Sibyl flashed Mr. Medland a tremulous smile that forgave him for his earlier staring. "How kind, sir. I did so want to shine for Papa's sake, you know. He sets such store on my doing well this Season that it quite puts me in a quake." The understanding smile from Mr. Medland went a long way to add to Sibyl's assurance.

Once the group was settled, the two carriages set off for the opera at a proper clip.

The earl glanced at the lady by his side. How lucky it was that Lavinia had implored that he take them in for the Season. Without realizing it, he had become jaded, bored with his life. Having young Sibyl around had made him aware what he had missed by not insisting that his daughter join him for a Season, although he couldn't find fault with her choice of husband. His hoydenish Samantha had flatly refused a London Season, preferring her life in Yorkshire.

Seeing the proud look flash cross Eagleton's face when he beheld his pretty daughter had brought a stab of envy, the earl confessed to himself. He turned to Mrs. Medland. "Are you pleased so far, madam?"

She cautiously replied, "That depends on what you mean."

He chuckled, a rather endearing, rich sound to one who had

been widowed for some years. "Why, on your hopes for your son and my niece-by-marriage."

Delia made a moue of chagrin, which he fortunately could not see in the faint light within the carriage. "None of that, please. We hope, and have suggested they help one another. That is all, sirrah."

"I see. You missed seeing your son's face when the pretty Sibyl walked into the drawing room. What a pity." Again that chuckle. It wasn't precisely devilish, but bordered on wicked, to be sure.

"Really? That sounds promising. One has high hopes for a son, especially. I feel sure you know what I mean."

"I missed all that, madam. Left it up to Lavinia to raise both of my offspring." The amusement had gone from his voice. In its place was definite regret.

Even a less perceptive woman than Delia Medland could have heard the note of sorrow in his voice. She grew silent and no further conversation took place.

When the carriages finally pulled up before the Opera House, Sibyl stepped down, unable to refrain from staring about her a trifle. A discreet nudge from her stepmama brought her to her senses. A proper lady did not goggle like some country serving girl. Not that Sibyl felt far above that status, what with the glittering gowns on the arriving women, and the elegant gentlemen, for the most part dressed in sober evening black.

Her modestly downcast eyes prevented her from noticing her own effect upon the *ton*. Mrs. Drummond-Burrell, that high-stickler of Society, had taken notice of the unassuming young woman with the lovely manners and shy mien who had the good fortune to be escorted by none other than that charming Robert Medland. Turning to her husband, she said, "I believe I see Lady Lavinia Mayne here tonight. There, her brother and Mrs. Medland are joining her party. Pretty little gel with Medland. Wonder who she is? Wait until I see Sally tomorrow," the lady concluded with the pleased expression of one who is first to note an *on-dit* of worth.

"How charming," breathed Sibyl to herself as she entered the earl's box in the second tier just above the stage. The view was excellent. She took the seat by the front of the box that the earl urged her to accept, all the while scarcely removing her gaze from the crowd that was rapidly filling the theater. She decided there must be several thousand in the audience by the time the curtains rose for the performance.

Catalani was in magnificent voice. Possessing such power of expression, it was quite understandable that she be so extravagantly paid, Sibyl decided when informed of the fine salary the singer received.

Sibyl was enchanted by the entire cast of performers. She was less than pleased by the behavior of the dandies and fops who strolled about in the pit, rattling their fancy canes and making a great show of popping the lids on their snuffboxes, all the while chattering loud enough to disturb the dead. Certainly it was necessary at times to strain to hear the singers.

"Can nothing be done?" she whispered to the man at her side.

Robert cast a disgusted look at the occupants of the pit and shook his head. "The owner tried. He built a foyer in hopes of attracting them, but they continue as you see."

She leaned forward to better view the stage, the lights catching the diamante on her gown. Her face was flushed with her happiness. Eyes sparkling, she turned to Mr. Medland.

"It is excessively wonderful, you know. In a way, it brings to mind the unreal quality I felt that morning, watching the mist rise, feeling it was but a dream."

Robert leaned toward her to better hear her soft words. "You enjoy a touch of the magical, then? Fairy tales?"

"Fie, sir, would you have me confess I long to be swept away by my prince?" Her eyes met his in shared laughter. "I vowed to be practical, you know."

"There are times one must be otherwise. Do you know, I feel as though we are old friends," he commented suddenly. "It must be that we have shared an experience out of time. Since our families are close, I believe we might dispense with a few of the formalities. Will you call me Robert?" At her shy nod, he smiled. "And I shall call you Sibyl, my maid of the mists."

Sibyl returned her gaze to the stage for the conclusion of the current scene. Her heart beat faster, and her cheeks felt almost hot. Was it the opera? Or most likely his presence so close to her side?

* * *

Across the stage, Montague, Viscount Buckingham, took note of the Divine Vision smiling at Mr. Medland. When the intermission came, he had already left his box to make his way around to the other side. As the earl opened the door to escort Delia Medland for a stroll, he nearly fell over the impressive figure of Viscount Buckingham.

"Pardon me, sir. I should like to pay my respects to the young lady in your party if I may?"

The earl gave a distant nod, then handed the lovely Mrs. Medland into the hall. They shortly disappeared from view.

When the viscount entered the box, he saw his first impression had been but a mere nothing compared to the Vision up close. How dainty! How exquisite! The shy beauty was magnificent. He would bestow a smile and perhaps a bit of conversation on her. Ladies were usually quite thrilled to receive his attention.

He ignored the black look from Medland when that gentleman became aware of his presence. Rather, Buckingham strolled forward, with what he liked to conceive of as a droll smile on his lips. "Oh, Divine Vision, that I may know your name," he declaimed in charming accents.

The young lady turned a startled face to him.

"My daughter is Miss Sibyl Eagleton, sirrah," General Lord Eagleton said in a dangerously quiet voice.

Not listening to the hint in the older gentleman's words, indeed, not even looking at his face, Viscount Buckingham nodded in his superior manner and bowed to Sibyl. "Sibyl, a name worthy of a goddess. Montague, Viscount Buckingham, at your service, oh, angel."

"Please, sir, won't you join us for a while? There is a chair." Her cheeks pink, she gestured to the one vacated by Mrs. Medland next to her own.

Buckingham thought of his skin-tight pantaloons and denied himself the pleasure.

"We stay with my brother, the Earl of Cranswick, Lord Buckingham." Lady Lavinia gazed at the newcomer in a speculative manner.

"I trust you attend Almack's next Wednesday evening? I have not seen you there, although the Season is still in its infancy."

This time he had the presence of mind to consult with Lady Lavinia.

"I daresay we shall," the good lady replied in an imperturbable manner.

Sibyl held her breath at this tarradiddle. How her stepmama expected to acquire those vouchers in the space between Saturday night and Wednesday was more than Sibyl could figure out. One simply did not ask for such a thing unless a cit or a mushroom, she had been told, and they always failed.

The viscount bowed over Sibyl's hand, declaring he would be desolate until he saw her again, then left.

Sibyl caught Robert's glare at Lord Buckingham as the viscount departed. Why he should feel so toward the pleasant man, she couldn't see. Accordingly, she frowned at Robert, giving him a look of censure.

"The viscount seems to be a charming gentleman, does he not?" Sibyl inquired. "Perhaps I may have to revise my thoughts regarding a title. I wonder if he will call?" The last was whispered to herself.

Robert's reply was cut off by the return of the earl and Mrs. Medland, and the resumption of the opera.

Sibyl decided she liked the Mozart opera very well, especially the orchestral parts. She found Catalani a trifle tedious after some time. "Does she never stop smiling?" she asked Mrs. Medland in a soft aside.

That lady exchanged an understanding look, saying, "I understand that while she might throw tantrums behind the curtain, she always smiles on stage."

"How excessively odd," Sibyl murmured in reply. She glanced across the stage to the boxes on the other side to catch sight of Viscount Buckingham. He was staring at her in a most obvious manner, one she found secretly exciting.

They departed the theater without confronting the viscount once again. Sibyl was sorry not to view the urbane gentleman. His manners were so wonderful and he certainly was handsome. Perhaps they would acquire—through some magic—those vouchers for Almack's and see him again? Or he might even come to call! She curved her mouth in a secret little smile at the very thought of receiving such a visitor.

Taking note of the tender smile, Robert wished the viscount to China, for her protection, of course, and decided he had best warn Miss Eagleton what manner of man Buckingham was.

"Well, puss, are you pleased with this foray into Society?" asked her father, his face a genial contrast to Robert's glower.

"I cannot believe that we are to get vouchers by Wednesday, dearest Mama." Sibyl so forgot herself to speak before Robert of the thing uppermost in her mind.

"We shall," Lavinia announced with complacency. The dim light prevented them from seeing the frown on her forehead.

The carriage drive home was extremely silent for all.

Sibyl took little side glances at Robert, wondering what prompted his annoyance with Lord Buckingham.

Once they arrived, Robert handed Sibyl down from the carriage with excellent courtesy. He escorted her into the entry hall, along with her parents, correctly bowing to her, saying, "I shall call upon you tomorrow, Sibyl. I should like to converse with you about the, er, opera."

Sibyl dropped her gaze, murmuring words to the effect that she would be pleased to see him. Then, after a proper curtsy, she gracefully drifted up the stairs in a flurry of silken skirts following her stepmama. The delicate scent of sandalwood and roses swirled about Robert where he stood in the hall, watching her until she disappeared around the top of the stairs.

"Until tomorrow, my boy," the earl said in a low voice, having just come in after seeing Mrs. Medland safely to her door.

Feeling slightly foolish to be caught staring after a chit not long out of the schoolroom and one he was quite certain would not be destined for any man less than a peer, Robert flushed a light red. It was fortunate the healthy tan he had acquired while boating admirably concealed his rise in color. "Sir. I wish to thank you once again for your gracious hospitality and the visit to the opera. I feel sure my mother appreciated the treat, and I think," he cast a glance up the staircase once again, "Miss Eagleton did as well."

"Not at all, my boy. Until tomorrow?"

Robert took himself off at once, blessing the proximity of the two houses. He had charged his driver to head for his mews earlier. He was able to march through the dimly lit street to his house on Mount Street while wearing a frown of enormous proportions with no one the wiser.

Morning saw Robert gloomily surveying the earl's morning room with little hope of making himself clear to Sibyl. He knew Buckingham. The man was a regular here-and-thereian, not precisely a cad, for his intentions were not pretense in the beginning, but he was not the sort a man wishes to see attach himself to a friend. And that was what Sibyl was . . . a friend.

The reason for his gloom increased when he studied the elaborate bouquet of roses brought in by the butler. One peek at the card revealed Buckingham's writing. He didn't need to read the blasted thing. It was probably full of poetic praises to her beauty. Rubbish.

"Robert, good morning." Sibyl stood poised at the door like a fawn ready to dash off at the slightest hint of danger. She wore a pretty blue gown that clung nicely.

"Good morning, Sibyl." His cravat was too tight and the room must be extremely warm for a spring day. Didn't people usually stop the fires this time of year?

"You wished to speak with me?" She drifted near the window beyond which a sulfur-yellow butterfly took wing.

"It is about Buckingham. I don't think you ought to see him," he blurted out with all the finesse of a country clod. Where the gift of speech he used while serving his government had gone he didn't know.

Immediately, her back stiffened. "I fail to see why you should be concerned if he pays a call or," she glanced at the roses, "sends me flowers."

Robert wished he had sent a posy, an enormous arrangement that would put Buckingham's nosegay in the pale. "You do not understand. He sees a lovely young girl and promptly falls in love with her, or thinks he does. He courts her for a time, then she does some little thing that irks him, and he walks away from her. Just like that! The man's a dissembler, not to be trusted."

Sibly gave Robert a dubious look while extracting the note from the enormous bouquet of roses. Disregarding the rule of Society that forbade such behavior, she unfolded it, reading it in spite of the disapproval emanating from him.

Her smile charmed him. "I am his goddess." She beamed at Robert, delight dancing in her eyes. "I have never been a goddess before."

Seeing it was a hopeless case, he crossed to the door. What woman wouldn't like to be a goddess, confound it? "Never say I didn't try," he muttered.

Her pleasure dimmed as he marched from the room, his look of disapproval chilling the air long after he had gone. So Lord Buckingham loved and left, did he? Well, she would change all that. Just you wait and see, Mr. Robert Medland, she vowed, it will be different with me.

4

WHEN LORD BUCKINGHAM came to call, it was with the elegance worthy of a royal duke at the very least. If some suspected the viscount considered himself just a touch above those few gentlemen, it was not spoken about.

He bowed correctly to Lady Lavinia, then took Miss Eagleton's hand to bestow a kiss a mere fraction of an inch above it. There was not the slightest hint of impropriety in his behavior, a point that appeared to find great favor with Lady Lavinia. Obviously, his address was all she could wish for her dearest stepdaughter.

She had searched her teacup for omens following her breakfast. A net on the bottom of her cup told her that there would be a safe ending to a period of anxiety. The scattering of dots meant money. But that was all. Not much guidance in the matters of the heart. Yet this young man seemed all that was sincere. Time would reveal his inner feelings and intentions. Many a gentleman started like this, then faded away into the mists of fine ideals.

"I have come to beg your company on a drive in the park," Lord Buckingham said in precisely the correct intonation. He looked very handsome and dashing in a dark blue coat and buff breeches above shining boots.

Sibyl dimpled a sweet smile at him. She properly turned to look to her stepmama for guidance. "May I?"

"I shall inform Annie to join you directly," Lavinia decided swiftly. Her hopes for Robert Medland had come to precious little. Oh, he had seemed most struck last evening at the opera, when he guarded Sibyl like a hen with her only chick, but it seemed he had exchanged words with Sibyl this morning that had quite put her in a pother. Lavinia believed him to be no more than a friend. That was all well and good, but a girl rarely married her friend.

"I had best wear my pelisse," Sibyl said, darting a glance at Lord Buckingham. "With my presentation coming soon, it would not do to catch an inflammation of the lungs, or worse." The muslins such as Sibyl wore this morning had little substance to them. She executed a dainty curtsy before taking leave to fetch her pelisse. Shortly she returned, demurely attired in a blue pelisse and a bonnet trimmed in the same color ribbon, with silk bellflowers in an artful arrangement in the brim.

The two young people left the house in perfect accord, followed by an awed Annie.

Sibyl cast an admiring glance at the noble elegance of his lordship.

Buckingham silently applauded how well Miss Eagleton looked next to him. Her blue pelisse exactly complimented his blue coat.

"What a delightful day. Truly, I believe this spring's flowers to be most colorful. Do you not agree?" Sibyl relaxed, as much as a proper young miss did, against the excellent padding of the squabs, for in truth, this carriage was of the very finest.

"Would that I could find a flower to reflect the glory of your eyes, Miss Eagleton." He bestowed a careful smile on the demure, lovely young lady.

She did not offer him the freedom of her first name as she had done Robert Medland. She was not conscious of comparing the two gentlemen, nevertheless she did.

"La, sir, you put me to the blush," Sibyl gently reproved him, yet a twinkle lurked in her lovely eyes. Robert was a fine, intelligent man, but he did not make her feel so delicately feminine.

"You are a veritable goddess, Miss Eagleton. Your charms place me in transports of delight that so admirable a young woman would condescend to join me for a drive."

This humble speech brought a puzzled frown to her brow when she peeped at him from beneath the brim of her bonnet. He seemed not the least humble in aspect, although she had to admit he had nothing at all to be modest about. How Robert might say he was a here-and-thereian was scandalous, as far as Sibyl was concerned. Indeed, she felt quite puffed up with the honor of being seen driving through the park seated next to this Nonpareil in his elegant equipage. He was a Peerless, an Incomparable, she decided, feeling greatly in charity with him.

Mrs. Drummond-Burrell approached in her very grand carriage. She nodded ever so slightly in response to the correct bow from Lord Buckingham.

Knowing the power this lady held, Sibyl blushed and bestowed a hesitant smile. Then she recalled the rash words spoken by her dearest mama last night and bowed her head. Vouchers, for heaven's sake.

There was nothing in Mrs. Drummond-Burrell's mien to reveal whether or not she approved of Sibyl. However, since Buckingham was most proper, even if given to frequent changes of the heart as Robert claimed, it could be her faint smile reflected the hope he had settled on the True One to claim his feelings. That her august organ of circulation could nourish such a hope was an improbable, but a charming thought, Sibyl decided ruefully.

As the imperious lady in the noble carriage drove off, most likely to a meeting of the patronesses, she left in her wake a shaking young woman.

"Even if she does not say much, she is impressive, is she not?" Sibyl felt slightly dazed by the inspection she had undergone. She knew full well that if that same lady was impressed with herself it might mean the salvation of her adored stepmama. Whatever had possessed Mama to declare that they would be present at Almack's? And on the following Wednesday? It left so little time to plan how best to attain that goal.

"With your excellent connections, she could scarcely be less than taken with you, sweet goddess." His glance of approval conveyed a touch of possessiveness that brought Sibyl's heart to a flutter.

She blushed at his words. While it might be fine to read such lavish praise penned in a note, it was rather shocking to hear it spoken to her while in a carriage on a drive through the park. Annie was dismissed from mind, even though she perched on the rear seat with the groom.

"Please, I beg of you, Lord Buckingham, such sentiments will go to my head," Sibyl demurely decried.

"I think not," he murmured by way of reply. He bore the expression of one who prided himself on his judgment of the fair sex. He had searched long to find a lady who matched his high standards. It seemed to him that Miss Eagleton might be The One.

The drive continued with the polite words of newly acquainted and hopeful lovers. At least Sibyl was hopeful.

At her side, Lord Buckingham looked assured that his addresses would be well received.

Along Rotten Row there were many who watched the stately progress of the shiny black barouche. Robert Medland sat astride his chestnut, glowering at the sight coming toward him. He shook his head in disgust. Yet could he really blame the young girl barely out of the schoolroom if she was flattered by such attentions? He didn't believe in showering such flattery as he suspected now rained down on her head. Robert was convinced a woman ought to see at once what a fine fellow he was, accepting him as he appeared and his regard as genuine without silly words.

"Mr. Medland," Miss Eagleton said with great propriety as he approached, not forgetting for one moment the words that had been exchanged that morning. Her nod was worthy of Mrs. Drummond-Burrell at her most haughty.

He bowed, an ironic twist to his mouth as he considered the lovely vision seated in Buckingham's barouche. "Good day, Miss Eagleton, Buckingham. I do believe we are in for a spot of rain, if I don't miss my guess."

Sibyl imagined he rarely did. She sniffed slightly to give the impression she really did not care for his opinion in the least. Friend though he might be, he did not have the right to chose her suitors. She thought Lord Buckingham charming.

The fine nuances of hostility between the others seemed to escape Lord Buckingham's detection as he drew himself up to a more noble bearing. He took out his immaculate handkerchief and brushed off a speck of lint from his breeches, then gave Medland a scant smile of superiority. "I doubt it, old fellow. I mean to say, those clouds do not look the sort, don't you know." The conversation rapidly went downhill from there.

Shortly, with a barely civil nod, Mr. Medland excused himself with a few murmured words, riding off along the Row to join a lady in a smart black habit.

In her one backward glance, Sibly took note of the gauze veil wrapped about the rider's throat, the smart tilt of her black beaver hat, and the jaunty, yet perfect, seat of her mount. Of course Robert might be interested in some woman. That it bothered Sibyl far more than it ought neatly escaped her.

Swallowing her ire, Sibyl said in a chilly voice, "How nice it is to see one's friends in the park."

"Truly. And you behaved with utmost decorum, Miss Eagleton. Such a rare grace for one so young, I vow." His approval brought a measure of comfort to her.

Studying the neatly gloved hands in her lap, Sibyl wondered how he might feel if he knew of her desire to chase after butterflies. He would undoubtedly think it frivolous, an unworthy pastime for a lady. Yet she would like to try it. She decided she would pursue her course, whether he liked it or not.

When the barouche drew up to the house on Grosvenor Square, Viscount Buckingham escorted Sibyl into the entry with polished manners. A fine drizzle began to fall on the city in spite of Lord Buckingham's estimation of the clouds. His dismay with the clouds was patently clear.

Lady Lavinia happened to come from the rear of the house as they entered. "My dears," she urged in her persuasive way, "do join Mrs. Medland and me for tea. She has just now arrived." Lady Lavinia had the smug expression of one who had just succeeded where others were certain she would fail on her face, which made Sibyl wonder what she had been doing.

The look of caution Sibyl returned to her mama was unseen by his lordship. He bowed, most correctly, and accompanied the ladies to the drawing room where an elaborate tea awaited them.

Mrs. Medland viewed the arrival of the couple with a bland look that revealed nothing of her possible inner reaction. Her fingers tightened slightly on the handle of her teacup and she took a deep breath, the kind one does when holding in one's harsh opnion.

"I see it has begun to rain," Lady Lavinia declared in a vexed voice. "Dear me, as if we do not get enough of that element.

Join me on the sofa, dear Lord Buckingham.'' She directed him to a place at her side, then waved Sibyl to a nearby chair.

Taking the one closest to Mrs. Medland, Sibyl gave the lady a hesitant smile. What had she thought about her driving out with Lord Buckingham?

Lord Buckingham responded to the gentle queries from Lady Lavinia with geatest goodwill. The epitome of the Society gentleman, he sat at admirable ease conversing about the latest *on-dits*, the state of the weather, and the Napoleon exile. The latter was touched upon only lightly, as it was considered a ''deep'' subject by many.

''I saw your son while driving in the Park, ma'am. He,'' Sibyl swallowed, then dared to speak again, ''was with a prodigiously lovely lady. She looked very dashing in her black habit and beaver hat, with the prettiest length of white gauze drifting from around her neck.''

Mrs. Medland's thoughtful smile possibly reflected her reservations. ''I fear I do not know her. I say nothing to him, of course,'' she confided. ''I do never wish to be thought an overbearing mother.''

''I feel certain that you could never be such. Like my own dearest stepmama, you are precisely to-a-pin right.''

Mrs. Medland assumed a pleased expression and appeared to sip her tea with greater pleasure.

At the proper moment, Lord Buckingham rose, bowed exquisitely, then took his departure. Sibyl watched him leave. How fortunate she was to inspire so correct a gentleman to such heights of admiration. She gathered up her pelisse, removed her bonnet, and was about to go to her room when her stepmother stayed her departure.

''Sibyl, my love, I have news.''

Her manner alerted Sibyl to something of import. ''Pray tell, what can it be to bring that gleam to your eyes?'' She crossed to stand by Lady Lavinia.

The well-pleased expression sat nicely on Lavinia's face as she contemplated the other two women. ''I had a surprising visitor earlier, just before Delia arrived. 'Twas Mrs. Drummond-Burrell, no less. And,'' Lavinia paused with great effect, ''she left vouchers for Almack's! She had a fine impression of you, my dear. Said you were a modest little gel with fine manners.''

Sibyl slowly sank down upon the nearest chair, her mouth agape, eyes wide with astonishment.

"By all that is wonderful, I am amazed," Mrs. Medland declared, pleasure for her friend evident. "I felt reasonably certain they would come eventually, but I knew you wanted them soon. I saw Sally Jersey yesterday, but had little opportunity to suggest your names. Bless Mrs. Drummond-Burrell. I never thought she would rise so high in my estimation."

"I saw a net in the bottom of my teacup this morning. I had a feeling about today, that it would prove to be a good one."

"A net in your teacup!" Delia exclaimed. "What is this?"

"Mama reads the tea leaves," Sibyl replied by way of explanation. "She has had the most amazing success!"

"Good gracious," Delia said, her fascination with this aspect of her old friend clear. "Could you read the leaves in my cup, do you think?" She held out her cup, offering it to Lavinia with eager curiosity.

Liking nothing better than to try her skill, Lavinia accepted the cup, studying the interior with avid eyes. In moments, she gave Delia a rather odd look. "There is a cherry in the bottom of your cup surrounded by dots. The many dots mean money, quite a lot of it. The cherry signifies an emotional awakening—a first love, you might say. I'm afraid I cannot explain why a widow might have such an omen. But then, I have no notion of your attachment to Charles. Nor do I expect it is something you wish to discuss." She gave Sibyl a significant glance, which the young lady heeded at once.

"Excuse me, I must take my things to my room." She hurried from the room after a proper curtsy.

The soft murmur of voices faded as Sibyl ran up the stairs. Annie was there, fussing over her gowns. She quickly took the pelisse from Sibyl, hung it up, stowed the bonnet, then slipped from the room. Sibyl changed from her light muslin gown to a dress of blue kerseymere for warmth. It might be spring, but the house was cool. She had no desire to take a chill.

Grosvenor Square was bare of pedestrians as the rain grew heavier. Sibyl stood by the window, watching the carriages crisscross around the perimeter, the horses splashing up water with each hoof as they trotted along, seemingly oblivious to their wetting. The garden in the center looked crisp and green. The earl possessed a key to the gate, and Sibyl had walked inside once, but did not like it overmuch.

Had Robert made it safely to wherever he stabled his horse? And the lady he had favored with his company? Sibyl then thought of Lord Buckingham. He must have dashed to make his barouche. The coachman would have raised the hood and a waterproofed covering would be placed across Lord Buckingham's lap. But one could take a damping in such a carriage, nonetheless. It was to be hoped he did not take sick.

Turning from the window, she strolled back to the bench at the foot of the bed. What gentleman would her parents find to be her husband? So far, she had met Robert Medland, Captain Ransom, and Viscount Buckingham. She suspected her mama favored the last man, even if Robert's mother was a dear friend. If her parents had their way, she would not be returning to live with them. Rather, she would be off to a new home. It was oddly unsettling.

She rose to restlessly pace about the room until she decided it better to utilize her energy by practicing on the pianoforte. Leaving her room, she whisked herself down the stairs, aware of the soft flow of voices still coming from the drawing room as she crossed the landing on that floor.

"I had no idea your life had been such a sad trial, Delia," Lady Lavinia said with a commiserating pat on Delia's arm.

" 'Tis not a thing of which one speaks to merely anyone, Lavinia." Mrs. Medland wore a look of patient resignation.

Lavinia did not immediately reply, being deeply in thought. She had noticed some rather odd behavior in her brother of late that would bear watching. Perhaps she could manage to read his tea leaves as well?

The tea pot was replenished by Bentley and the ladies continued their chat while the rain beat against the windows and a fire sent out a warming glow into the room.

Sibyl looked up as the door to the morning room opened. The

person announced was most unexpected. "Robert!" she exclaimed, unable to conceal her surprise. She hardly thought to see him out in such a nasty rain.

"I came to fetch Mother. She walked over, and with the rain she needs the carriage to come home." As an excuse it lacked originality, for anyone might know the earl's carriage would be at Mrs. Medland's disposal in inclement weather.

"She is upstairs in a comfortable coze with my mama." Rising from her stool at the musical instrument, Sibyl crossed to stare out the window, wondering where the butterflies went when it rained. She was very conscious of his presence in the room, his watching eyes.

"You have been practicing, I gather. I could hear you as I came along the hall. I wish you had not stopped. You play very well, you know, Miss Eagleton." He took a step closer to her.

"I thought we were friends. I said you might call me Sibyl," she hastily replied before recalling she had not intended to permit that familiarity again.

"Hm, yes. I shall try to remember that." His glance was amused. "Music is fine company for a rainy day. I imagine you embroider as well?" He strolled across the room to join her by the window. The soft blue kerseymere gown she wore invited a man's hands to touch. He quickly stifled that notion.

The guilty expression that crossed her face caught his attention. "Or do you have another interest?"

"I have thought about one I should like to try. Embroidery can be so tedious. I think it would be delightful to find something to do while out of doors in the fresh air," she said slowly, trying to sort out her own thoughts on the matter as she spoke. "I have bought a net for to catch butterflies."

He blinked with evident surprise at her revelation. It was a most unusual desire for a young girl—anyone, for that matter. He could scarce believe she shared his interests.

"Why?" He leaned against the sill of the window to better study her face, curious.

"I admire lovely objects, creatures. I should like to have a collection, perhaps travel about England finding the various kinds of butterflies and moths that inhabit our country. Do you think me very strange?"

"Not at all. Perhaps I can be of service to you. Do you have a book? You did not mention such."

"No," she replied. "I looked for one and told the clerk at the bookshop what I wanted. He thought me daft, I feel sure." She gave Robert an impish smile, one he thought rather charming. "I suppose I am, actually. I would be forever in your debt if you could but locate a book on these insects for me. I need to know how to preserve them, too. So many things to learn." She bubbled with enthusiasm such as he hadn't seen in her before.

Robert hadn't the faintest idea why he had sought her out after seeing her driving with that smug Buckingham fellow. The romantic, impetuous stuff Buckingham was apt to spout was the sort of rubbish a green girl might like, Robert supposed. Still, she seemed such a fine young thing and he had this odd urge to take care of her. Lord knew she needed someone. Her father was off to the war office more often than not, offering his excellent advice. That totty-headed Lady Lavinia was a dear woman, but decidedly a bit odd. This request presented him with an opportunity to do her a service while keeping an eye on her.

"I should be pleased to find you that book."

"What an admirable gentleman you are, to be sure. How will I ever thank you enough?" Sibyl beamed a smile at Robert that lit up the room with its brilliance. "You are most kind, when I probably do not deserve it in the least. Come, we shall slip upstairs and perhaps find a cup of tea left in the pot. Mind you, not a word of this to my dear mama. I suspect she would have the vapors at the very least. I do not know if she would approve my gamboling across Hyde Park to hunt for elusive butterflies."

He had the pleasant feeling of being about ten feet tall when she gazed at him with her heart in her eyes like that. He paused at the door and cleared his throat. "About this morning, I am sorry if I intruded upon what is none of my affair."

Her charity with him increased at this handsome apology. "What a prodigiously nice thing to say. But I shan't forget all you do for me." She looked into his kind gray eyes, thinking they reminded her of a bubbling spring where she was used to go for reflections and restoration of her spirit.

They stood thus, staring into each other's eyes, until a footman passing in the hall happened to make a noise.

Robert cleared his throat once again, then offered his arm. "Shall we?"

"By all means, we shall." She dimpled up at him and he suddenly envied Lord Buckingham.

"Look who I have brought you, Mama," said Sibyl in a gay voice as she entered the room upon Robert's firm arm.

"Lavinia has been telling my future, Robert. Would you like to have your tea leaves read?"

Not quite certain what his mother intended by her arched expression, Robert nodded. "That would indeed be a novelty. I have never had such before."

Lady Lavinia preened slightly, then instructed him what to do. He hastily consumed the tea presented to him, then handed her the cup.

"You have a harp in your cap," Lavinia said softly. "Most interesting."

Robert gave his mother an uncomfortable look, one that told her he was not precisely pleased with this nonsense. "And?"

"A harp is said to mean you will have a happy marriage. Romance is on the way, and you will never want for money."

"Well," he replied in hearty accents, "that is fine, indeed."

"Isn't it, just," echoed Sibyl in a whisper. She did not know in the least why she felt as though a cold wind had swept through the room. She wished this fine man the very best in life, didn't she? So, why should she not be enthusiastic at this promise of romance and happiness for him? Was it because she feared she would not share it? While she fancied Lord Buckingham, perhaps, she also cared for Robert. In a corner of her heart she admitted she cared for him a great deal.

Mrs. Medland rose from the sofa. Robert immediately got to his feet, offering her his arm. "Mother?"

"We had best be going. I had hoped the rain would let up, but it seems to be one of those interminable ones. You brought the carriage?"

"If he didn't, I offer mine, dear lady," the Earl of Cranswick said from the doorway.

With his gaze firmly fixed on his mother, Robert could not

miss the soft bloom on her cheeks. He looked at the earl, saying, "No need, thank you, sir. My carriage awaits without."

"I suspected it might be yours. Never know who I might find here nowadays." He flicked a lazy glance at Sibyl, then turned his attention to Mrs. Medland. "I expect you do not go out this evening in the wet. Would you allow me to call, perhaps?"

"I am promised to Lady Sefton, thank you. Although I believe it would be much nicer to remain at home with good company rather than brave the elements."

At that handsome reply, the earl half-grinned, then said, "In that case, I shall see you there myself. For I pride myself on knowing how to properly care for a lady."

When the earl's gaze turned upon him, Robert acknowledged it with a faint nod. It seemed his mother had a bit of added interest in her life.

Sibyl ran to the window to watch the carriage leave. Water splashed from every step, every movement. Mrs. Medland would be brave indeed to attempt this weather. "Do we remain to home this evening?"

"I believe we shall. I wish to discuss Almack's with your papa. You looked to be in charity with Robert when you came up together?"

"La, Mama, he is a kind friend." Sibyl bore her mama's scrutiny well. "I saw him with a lady in the park today. She was wearing a dashing black habit with a wisp of a veil about her throat."

Sibyl bit her lip in vexation. Robert had every right to pay attention to a lady. And Sibyl felt miserable at the very thought.

But, she recalled, brightening, she had the elegant Lord Buckingham coming to call upon her this evening. He had murmured something to that effect before he left, certain the family would not wish to go out in such nasty weather. She had hopes in that direction.

What a pity Robert Medland thought him so bad. Buckingham made her feel like an enchanted princess when he paid her court. Handsome, ardent, wealthy, what more could a girl want?

5

LADY LAVINIA SNEEZED most violently. Once recovered, she surveyed the masses of flowers in the morning room, recalling that an equal presentation cluttered the tables, indeed, every available surface in Sibyl's bedroom. "He does seem to enjoy showering you with flowers, does he not?" Another sneeze followed this comment.

A soft smile danced across Sibyl's sweet face. "That he does." She sobered as she studied her stepmother. "They seem to give you distress, dear Mama."

"Nonsense," declared that lady with stout resolution. "No mere flower could have such effect."

"I shall have Bentley disburse them throughout the house, except for the ones in my room," Sibyl said, not wishing to upset her stepmother. "I declare, it is like awaking in the middle of a garden. Roses, lilies, bellflowers like on my bonnet—oh, so many different kinds. It took great effort to assemble all of them." Sibyl made a pirouette on her morocco slippers, swinging gracefully around with her arms flung out, her hands up. She took one glance at her stepmother's face and immediately dropped her arms, assuming a more demure pose, yet unable to prevent a grin.

"La, child, what next? I suppose you will be wanting waltzing lessons? You seem to have the grace for it."

"Would that be proper? 'Tis not permitted at Almack's, I know. I would not wish to be exiled from there for participating without approval. Nor should I wish to disgrace myself just before my presentation." An anxious look crept into her eyes. "Do you believe Lord Buckingham might think well of such a daring dance?"

At that moment, Bentley appeared in the door to announce Mr. Medland and his mother. "Delia, my dear. Can you credit all this?" Lavinia gestured toward the lavish display of blooms overflowing vases and baskets that filled the room with color and scent, her face a study in conflicting emotions.

Robert cast a dark look toward the floral offerings. "Lovely," he commented.

"Say it is not like a garden, I dare you," Sibyl challenged. Although she was fascinated by Lord Buckingham, and somewhat overwhelmed by his attentions, a part of her wished Robert might be a teensy bit jealous.

"It is like a garden," he answered dutifully, his sense of humor asserting itself. "You look like a flower yourself, dressed in primrose trimmed with green ribbons."

Sibyl blushed with his kind words. "Do you go out and about the city today, Mr. Medland?" she said with a prim little voice that was defeated by the sparkle of conspiratorial glee in her eyes when her glance met his.

Recalling his promise, Robert nodded. "I do. I expect to be near a bookshop. And I thought we had agreed you are to call me Robert?"

"I was not sure. There are times when you seem most forbidding." Why did he have to be so set against Lord Buckingham? It was not as though Robert did not seem to have a partiality of his own.

"How can you say such a thing? Have I not had your interests at heart from the moment we met?" he replied in a paternal manner, the warm look in his eyes not quite matching his air.

"I do thank you for the assistance and support you give me. Perhaps I ought to solicit your help in collecting?" For a moment the image of Robert running across the park after an elusive Tortoiseshell butterfly flashed in her mind, to be dismissed with a wry smile. Yet, had not Lady Lavinia mentioned he had an interest in nature?

"Robert," demanded Lady Lavinia from across the room in her most persuasive tone, "settle this once and for all. Do we hire a dancing master to come to the house for to teach our Sibyl the waltz, or not? I would not court scandal."

"Princess Lieven encourages it. Although not at Almack's as yet, I feel it a matter of time before they allow the waltz to be performed. The young gentlemen delight in holding their partners in such pleasurable proximity," he said, darting a bland look at Sibyl that she immediately found suspect. "If I may, I shall demonstrate. Mother?" His eyes beckoned, and a little grin tugged at his mouth.

Delia Medland rose at once, crossing to the pianoforte where she promptly began to play a nice little waltz. Robert took Sibyl's hands in his, softly instructing her on what to do, how to place her feet, then counting out the beat for her a few times. Her innate sense of rhythm assisted her natural grace. For a man who professed diffidence with Society, he proved surprisingly knowledgeable about any number of things.

After a short while she drew back slightly to gaze up at him. "I declare sir, this is an amazingly fine dance."

If Robert felt anything special from holding that slim young body so close to him in his arms, he gave none of it away. However, he seemed to inhale with pleasure, most likely the lily of the valley scent Sibyl wore.

"It does have advantages over the minuet, surely." His grin widened as he whirled Sibyl about in a final loop of the room, taking care to avoid the flower arrangements.

"Scandalous looking, if you ask me," Lady Lavinia declared while tapping her feet in time to the three-quarter beat. "I should wonder such high-sticklers as Mrs. Drummond-Burrell and Lady Castlereagh would permit it."

"Ah, but Lady Cowper, Princess Esterhazy, and Lady Sefton, as well as Princess Lieven, would outvote them. And Lady Jersey has her own interest in dance, so I have heard."

Intrigued by this hint, Lady Lavinia begged more information. "Tell us, Robert," she commanded in the nicest possible way.

" 'Tis a rumor, nothing more," he temporized. "Perhaps this Wednesday evening we shall find out something?"

With this, my lady had to be content.

"Do play for us, Sibyl," commanded Lavinia.

Knowing better than to shrink from performing, since Robert and Mrs. Medland were friends, Sibyl walked with trepidation to where the instrument stood half buried in flowers.

Contrary to what Lady Lavinia believed, playing for others did not present the greatest problem. Crossing a room to sit down before the keyboard took the most courage. Once Sibyl lost herself in her music, she went on very well indeed.

Robert experienced amazement, then delight that Sibyl should play so extremely well. Hearing her music through a door while out in the hall did not compare to hearing in person. The toccata from Bach's Well-Tempered Clavier had never sounded quite so pleasing, nor the Scarlatti Capriccio so brilliant. The clarity of her notes and her precise, yet feeling renditions could only reap high praise.

"Brava," accompanied by applause, came from the doorway upon the conclusion of the music.

The alarmed look darted by Sibyl at Lord Buckingham caused Robert to frown. Terror? Hardly. Yet she truly disliked performing for others, it seemed.

"Lord Buckingham, how nice to see you." Sibyl rose from the pianoforte to cross the room in a flurry, her muslin skirt swirling about her legs as she took dainty steps to reach his side. She wished to place as much space as possible between herself and the instrument before another request came.

"I must thank you for the lovely flowers. You are too, too extravagant, sir." She dipped a charming curtsy, beaming up a smile that would melt the hardest of hearts.

Buckingham cast a narrow look at the man who was a possible rival for the affections of his goddess, then smiled. It was a superior sort of smile, one that told his opponent that he would have far to go before he could equal the romantic gestures of masses of flowers. Buckingham tucked Sibyl's dainty hand next to his side, then walked toward Lady Lavinia. He bowed to the lady, then seated Sibyl, joining her on the sofa as close to her as was seemly.

Robert Medland cleared his throat, stiffening in his chair as though presented with a distasteful sight.

Sibyl glanced at Robert, wondering what had brought that considering frown to his brow.

The pleasing design of the morning room permitted visitors to sit close to one another for easy discussion of the topics at hand. Gossip was not a matter to be shouted across a vast space. The conversation flowed easily about the room, Lady Lavinia taking charge as she so often did.

Eventually she reached a new subject. "Tell me, Lord Buckingham, what think you of that dance, the waltz?"

He shrugged ever so slightly—one did not wish to wrinkle one's coat, you know—and replied with haunty negligence, "I daresay it will do well enough. I imagine one must wait for the *grandes dames* at Almack's to rule regarding it. I, for one, do not care to risk their censure."

"It is a pity they must be so despotic. How many worthy young girls are crushed because they do not receive the nod from those women," Delia Medland declared.

"I think the waltz a vastly entertaining dance," ventured Sibyl hesitantly in a moment of silence.

All eyes turned to her slim, retiring figure. For a few minutes, ones that seemed more like hours to Sibyl, no one spoke.

"That it is," Robert Medland replied in a thoughtful voice, one it seemed Buckingham wished not to challenge.

"It is a graceful dance, though I have heard tell that Byron abhors it," added his mother.

"He would," Robert muttered, just loud enough for Sibyl to hear.

She flashed him an amused smile of gratitude for his support. It seemed she might count on his humor to alleviate any stiffness in conversation.

Seeing that his goddess looked favorably upon the dance, Buckingham apparently resolved to learn it. "I confess, I know little enough of the waltz. Do you, Medland?" If he expected his rival to cry off from knowledge of the latest dance craze, he was mistaken.

"I was teaching it to Sibyl shortly before you arrived." The lazy hint of Robert's masculine smile taunted Lord Buckingham.

"Indeed?" Buckingham's accents would have frozen the Thames.

"Mother, if you would be so kind, once again?"

Possibly wondering what her dear son was up to with this business, Mrs. Medland sighed, then seated herself at the pianoforte to begin a more complicated waltz. If Robert wished to display his excellent style, this music would undoubtedly do the trick.

Robert bowed before Sibyl, then took her hand to lead her out in the limited space offered, what with the furniture and those dratted baskets and vases of flowers all over the place.

At first Sibyl had all she could do to concentrate on the steps again. Then, as she relaxed, she grew more confident and leaned back in Robert's arms to gaze at him with pure delight.

When the music stopped, Lord Buckingham arose from the sofa where he had sprawled (having worn skin-tight pantaloons) and said, "The dance does appear to have merit. However, I actually stopped by to see if Miss Eagleton might honor me with a drive in my carriage. The rain has cleared and it is most delightful out." It was clear he had no desire to comment further on the waltzing display he had just witnessed.

A radiant smile dawned on Sibyl's face before being hastily subdued. It was not proper to wish for another gentleman's company when at the side of a friend. She turned to her step-mother, her question in her eyes.

"By all means, my dear." Lady Lavinia exchanged a glance with Delia Medland that told that lady a great deal, none of it particularly pleasing, it seemed.

Bidding the departing Medlands a polite, if hurried, farewell, Sibyl slipped up to her room, then shortly returned to join Buckingham in the entry. Lady Lavinia watched from the top of the stairs as they left the house.

"What a charming day, sir," Sibyl said in her soft voice. "I vow the grass is greener and the flowers prettier here than anywhere in the world." Her enthusiasm appeared to please him for he bestowed a benign smile on her. He watched as she settled happily against the squabs of the open carriage after patting her bonnet.

"Do the Medlands often visit your uncle's home?"

Detecting the note of censure in his voice, Sibyl frowned. Robert was a very good friend; he understood her difficulties with shyness. She certainly had confided more to him than anyone else. Although much of that had been said when she did not know who he was, spoken on that misty morning, there was still a special degree of confidentiality between them. What a pity that Lord Buckingham seemed to dislike Robert.

"They do," she said at last. "Mrs. Medland is a bosombeau of my mama's since her come-out days. And Robert—that is, Mr. Medford—has been most kind to me." Those defensive words seemed so inadequate to describe that kindness. Sibyl thought of how she could communicate so much with Robert just by exchanging a glance. Such expressive gray eyes he had. Beautiful, too.

"It is not difficult to wish to be kind to you, my goddess. Your very demeanor prompts such desires." Lord Buckingham continued in this vein until Sibyl's cheeks were rosy from all the fine phrases couched in poetic verse.

They paused to chat with several of his friends. Sibyl had the rather odd feeling she was a prize he had just won, and he wished to display her for all to see and admire. What a peculiar sensation, to be sure.

On their return to the stately house on Grosvenor Square, he asked, "Do you attend the Queen's Drawing Room this coming Thursday afternoon?"

Sibyl inhaled sharply. She had tried hard to put it from her mind, knowing that if she dwelled on it, she would be terrified long before necessary. "Yes, I do."

"Who goes with you?" His was a very speculative gaze, she noticed. Why such curiosity?

"My parents and Lord Cranswick. The earl is presenting my mama and me. She has not been to Court since she married." The Drawing Rooms were held four times a year, and conferred that special royal seal of approval not to be found elsewhere. No merchants ever attended.

"I see." He beamed a satisfied smile on her. "It shall be an important week—Almack's, your presentation. I am truly pleased." At her look of confusion, he added kindly, "A lady who had been properly presented at court by an earl, accepted at Almack's, and nicely dowered is quite admirable. A man of my consequence must be careful whom he chooses, you see. And you, my goddess, are the ultimate I might desire. Yes, I daresay that one of these days I must have speech with your papa; we can discuss your portion. I trust it is very fine. Perhaps following your come-out ball?"

Sibyl gave him a surprised look. His pale blue eyes seemed greatly in earnest. It seemed he was going to offer for her hand! So soon? His earlier words had been romantic, but now he spoke almost like a man of business. It certainly was not as she had envisioned a proposal of marriage! He approached a marriage as though it were a purchase. What did that make her? she wondered. She felt like a piece of property. Did those flowery words mean he loved her? How she wished he would be simple and direct in his speech—at least this once. Yet she ought not be astonished. From what she had learned, his attitude was quite customary.

"You are too kind, sir. The very thought of being allied with so polished a gentleman can only give one pleasure." Sibyl sought to convince him, while reassuring herself as well. There were too many doubts pushing into her mind. Did she desire a more romantic gentleman? She thought briefly of the man who had talked with her in the mists, his concern so gratifying.

"Most proper sentiments," he said with a handsome smile. He bowed precisely, then left the house.

Sibyl watched him depart, wondering if she would see him at Almack's Wednesday evening.

"Did you have a lovely drive in the park, my dear?" inquired Lady Lavinia as Sibyl drifted into the morning room that Lavinia had adopted for use when not entertaining.

"Yes. Although he confuses me at times. He greatly admires me, or is it that I am worthy of him? Yet I believe I like him, for all that. He is all that is proper." Sibyl sank down on one of the dainty chairs by the rear window overlooking the gardens to stare out at a bed of pansies.

"He is such a suitable gentleman, and of the first stare of elegance. Lest I forget, your presentation dress was delivered while you were gone. 'Tis vastly pretty. Although I might wish the Queen would issue a decree that we could all do away with those ridiculous hoops. I vow I feel like a vast structure while wearing them."

"Must I wear so many feathers?" That had worried Sibyl a great deal. She couldn't imagine how she would cope with the arrangement of white feathers that were to rise from her golden diadem headdress.

Taking a good look at her stepdaughter, Lady Lavinia set aside her embroidery. "We had best practice. It would not do for you to have any problems when making your bows to the Queen." The remainder of the day was spent in learning how to handle the hoop while walking and making the proper curtsy. The arrangement of five short white feathers turned out to be light in weight and little trouble.

"The hoop is by far the worst of it, Mama," Sibyl declared. "I shall have to exert great care when making my way through doors. It is well we are not required to sit."

It seemed the prospect of the presentation had the effect of taking away some of the fears from her first appearance at Almack's. With a light heart, Sibyl dressed in her favorite pale primrose over silver lamé for the evening.

The earl had remained home to oversee the departure. He surprised them all by stating, "I shall go with you, at least for a brief time. I wish to see our Sibyl taken up by Society."

"Sir," Sibyl blushed a rose to complement her gown, then accepted his arm to where the carriage awaited them.

After worrying about whether or not she would trip on her hoop tomorrow, thus disgracing them all, arriving at Almack's seemed a mere nothing. The three patronesses in attendance this evening smiled graciously when they saw Sibyl on the arm of the Earl of Cranswick, a gentleman who rarely graced Almack's with his presence.

"Not so bad, eh?" the earl queried, with a knowing look at his niece as he led her out in the first minuet.

"Thanks to you," she replied with proper modesty, although her words were heartfelt.

Following this initial dance, one that precipitated a rush of young men to her side, she felt adrift and somewhat lost, even if her stepmama gave the nod as to who her next partner might be. And then she saw her friend. The constraint she felt slid away.

"Robert," she said with relief as he drew near. "How excessively lovely it is to see you here." She beamed a smile that seemed to light up the room. Certainly it vied with the candles for brilliance.

"May I take you away from all these young sprouts?"

She looked at her stepmama, who nodded with goodwill.

"How nice it is to dance with someone I know is not after my fortune," she confided as they stepped into place for the country dance.

"So you are aware that you present an opportunity for the gentlemen in dun territory?"

"I may be a bit shy, but there is nothing wrong with my ears or my sight," she replied with spirit, albeit softly.

"And yet, I think you are not so shy anymore," he said, his smile just a bit fixed.

"If I am not, I owe a deal of it to you, my friend." Sibyl cast him a warm look before they went down the pattern of the dance.

There was a hint of bafflement in his eyes when next they joined hands in the dance. Sibyl wondered at it, yet something constrained her from inquiring what it might be.

"I see your poet has arrived," Robert said with a dry expression in his voice.

"How do you know he says lovely poetry to me?" demanded Sibyl as they left the dance area to join her stepmama. Mrs. Medland and the earl had been dancing as well. The four converged on where Lady Lavinia chatted with the baron and several acquaintances.

"He always does."

"Are you implying Lord Buckingham makes a practice of wooing ladies with poetry and flowers?" She glared at him with eyes that flashed her disappointment that he might reveal petty jealousy.

"If your ears and eyes are so acute, take note of what you see and hear when he is about, fair lady," he snapped. Robert bowed, then took himself off to where a blonde lady dressed in delicate pink-spotted satin beamed up at him as though he possessed all the charm and money in the world. It seemed Robert had a fondness for blondes.

Sibyl rubbed her arms as though to rid herself of the chill that had crept over her with his parting words.

"My goodness," Lord Buckingham murmured, his smooth purr soothing her sense of pique.

"I confess, I was wondering if you would attend this evening, sir," she said, her voice a trifle breathless as she turned to face Lord Buckingham. He tended to intimidate her with his splendid address.

"It would not be well done of me to permit any of these cubs access to the lady who suits me so well."

Sibyl accepted his hand to enter the dance. It seemed he brooked no opposition, which flattered her a little. She studied his patent leather pumps with what appeared to be diamond buckles on them. His garb was restrained, but for that sparkle of elegance. Not even Brummell could sport a more magnificently tied cravat. Buckingham's waistcoat was severely cut in white quilted satin, his coat a restrained deep blue. He was a none-such, without match. Surely he would be a kind and generous husband?

"Sir, you frown. Nothing is amiss, I trust?"

"Your uncle pays court to the Widow Medland."

"She is very lovely and kind, sir," replied Sibyl. "I imagine most widows are happy to receive the attentions of an excellent gentleman. For example, there is the lovely Lady Wayford." Both Robert and Lord Buckingham had seen fit to look kindly upon that beautiful lady.

"Good thing her past husband does not know how she squanders his money. A wife should behave in a seemly manner, not seek to outshine her husband, even after his going aloft."

"She dresses discreetly, with perfect taste. Why," Sibyl wondered aloud, "do you censure her?"

"She seeks to rise above herself," he declared with finality.

The dance concluded. Sibyl walked at his side to where her parents waited for her. She found his words puzzling. While she was impressed by being the object of his civilities, there were a few minor things that began to trouble her. He seemed rigid, quite inflexible in his attitude, especially in regard to Lady Wayford.

Lady Jersey motioned to the music director, Mr. Colnet. In moments, all others withdrew from the floor while three ladies and four gentleman joined her to form a pattern. What followed was a dance quite different from the Scotch reels and country dances mostly performed here. One pattern followed another in the foreign dance, graceful, yet most energetic.

"It looks to be more like a ballet than a social dance," said Lady Lavinia. She would never go so far as to utter a word of criticism regarding Lady Jersey within the walls of Almack's. That did not prevent her from exchanging glances with Delia Medland that said volumes about a dance that appeared rather daring.

"What with the waltz and now this new dance, the world is indeed going to pieces," Delia commented to the earl, who had moved next to her when his sister walked away.

Yet they all watched and nearly everyone present vowed to

learn the dance, called the quadrille. If Lady Jersey found it delightful, it must be.

"We'd best leave. 'Tis a busy day on the morrow. Shall we see you there, sir?" Lady Lavinia bestowed a favorable look on the gentleman at Sibyl's side.

Lord Buckingham turned to look down at the other lady. "No, I find the Drawing Rooms vastly boring." His smile took some of the sting from his words.

Sibyl left Almack's with a good deal to ponder. Lord Buckingham had declared his intentions, yet she felt reluctant to tell her stepmother about this important event. Why?

The following afternoon found the entire group from Cranswick House entering St. James's Palace. Sibyl cast an appreciative look about the first room into which they were shown. Fashionable festoon curtains in soft red hung at each window. Exquisite tapestries graced the walls, their colors softly glowing with age. Along one wall that was rapidly becoming obscured by the press of people, neat stools stood in a precise row. Sibyl doubted if she would have to consider sitting down even if permitted. Fortunately, it was a most unlikely event in view of the crowd.

The plumassiers of London had done a brisk business, judging from the vast quantity of large feathers of all colors that nodded and bobbed from atop the feminine heads. Her own mama looked most elegant in a gown of white with red panels and trimmed in gold with a white overskirt. The lappets trailing from her headdress were of the finest lace.

"I still say I feel like I should be stuffed and put on display," Lady Lavinia declared in a soft but affronted voice, her white plumes nodding with her emphasis.

"Now, Livvy," her husband said with a smile. "Since this is your presentation at Court following your marriage, it is only right you be as fine as fivepence."

The curtsy was accomplished with no disaster befalling Sibyl. She was sorry the King could not be present, but knew he was far, far too ill to attend such a social event.

Lady Lavinia gracefully made her curtsy as well.

Once Sibyl was past the ordeal of her presentation to the

Queen, she felt free to look about at all the colorful gowns. Hoops swayed gently as the women moved into the next room, plumes seeming to float about in the air above the collective heads like a meeting of a Society of Avians. She grinned at the very thought.

"You find it amusing? You have indeed made progress in overcoming your fears of Society if you can find humor in a presentation." Robert appeared at her elbow, dressed in the proper Court clothes and looking most handsome. His coat and knee breeches were dark blue and discreetly decorated with silk embroidery, as was his white waistcoat. He carried the regulation *chapeau bras* tucked under his arm, and wore the required small-sword at the proper angle. She had not seen him in a white wig before and thought he looked distinguished. Although he wore black pumps with buckles, there were no diamonds winking up from them. The thought crossed her mind that his legs were uncommonly well-shaped. When she met his gaze, she could feel her cheeks turn warm as if her thoughts might be visible.

She rested her gloved arms on the skirt of her gown, a simple matter given the height and size of the uncomfortable hoop. "I am glad I have seen this, but I confess I will be glad to go home."

"At last you have succeeded in fulfilling all of Buckingham's requirements."

"La, sir, what mean you by such a remark?" Sibyl took care not to exclaim overly loud, but she was incensed that Robert should know of this conversation.

"All the world and his wife knows Buckingham and his needs, miss. He is perhaps a trifle high in the instep." Robert's manner was apologetic, yet Sibyl sensed that he thought he was conveying information to her that she needed to know.

"Then he did not speak to you about it?"

Robert, with the look of one who is torn two ways, replied, "He has made it clear that he considers a wife in view of her ability to compliment him in every way. She must possess the required social assets, not to mention her dowry. I gather you meet all his needs."

"But," she murmured softly, "what about mine?"

Robert gave her a commiserating look, then took his leave, going to visit with a lady charmingly dressed in pink gauze draped over white satin and trimmed with heavy gold fringe. Clusters of pink roses cascaded across the skirt to meet a pink bow of enormous proportions. Sibyl would have wagered that every piece of jewelry the woman possessed was pinned, twined, or fastened to her in some manner. She was exceedingly beautiful.

"Lady Wayford's gown looks as though it required an architect," Lady Lavinia said in a soft aside.

Her brother commented, "Lady Wayford is considered acceptable by many, especially the gentlemen."

"Could we not go, Mama?" For some peculiar reason, the sight of Robert paying attention to the lady in pink bothered Sibyl more than the absence of Lord Buckingham, something she preferred not to consider closely at the moment.

Taking a good look at her girl, the lady quickly agreed and within minutes the four had left the palace.

Sibyl accepted the compliments of her family with a strained smile. Her troubled heart was confused as she considered all that had transpired the past few days. She was flattered that Lord Buckingham would consider her for his wife, for he was polished, perfect, and terribly *tonnish*. But, did he never relax? Was he always so stiff? The only time he had seemed out of character was when he made those comments about Lady Wayford.

The charming dance with Robert on that memorable misty morning returned to her and she fell into a reflective silence. The proud Lord Buckingham would never stoop to such delightful foolishness.

6

"A SHORT COURTSHIP is by far the preferable, I believe. It gives one more time to get acquainted and subjects for conversation for after your marriage." Lady Lavinia placed her embroidery on the table at her side, looking across the room to where her dear Sibyl wandered about like a lost child. "I imagine you will retreat to Lord Buckingham's seat in the country for your honeymoon. No, 'tis best not to prolong these things. I can see you are all a-twitter to marry and settle down with your handsome viscount." She sighed. "I must say, you have done very well, child. His attentions have been most marked. A wealthy viscount for the daughter of a baron? Money aside, he is quite a catch."

Sibyl felt a rising swell of panic. Marriage to Buckingham? Had he already spoken to her papa? He had said he would wait until following her ball. All of a sudden she wished to postpone that event. She was not as convinced of her feelings toward Buckingham as she thought she ought to be. "What has Papa to say about this?"

"If you must know, the viscount has not been to see him as yet." Lady Lavinia frowned at that recollection. "Perhaps Buckingham wishes to allow you to have your ball before he asks for your hand? How thoughtful of him. Of course, once you are married, you may have any number of grand balls and parties, even if they are not given at an establishment such as Cranswick House. There are many girls who would be in alt to have such as you anticipate. Come, dearest, no more Friday faces. It is a lovely day."

Bentley presented himself in the doorway at that moment to announce the Marchioness of Wayford and Mrs. Medland.

If Lady Lavinia thought it odd that Sibyl looked as though she longed to rush from the room, she said nothing about it.

"Delia! What a pleasure to see you." Lavinia rose to greet her friend, then waited with exquisite politeness for Delia to present the young widow.

This was the first time Sibyl had been so close to the marchioness. Not only was she a beautiful blonde, she possessed a petite, dainty figure and a face that could only be described an angelic. Sibyl disliked her before she had even uttered a word.

"Robert has spoken of you both so often, I feel as though we are old friends." Lady Wayford smiled with great charm at Lady Lavinia. Her pink jacconet walking dress beneath her spencer of deep rose velvet was the latest fashion, and gave her the look of a rose in bloom.

Delighted with the young widow, Lady Lavinia insisted the two visitors join Sibyl and herself in refreshments and a prolonged visit.

"I saw you at the Drawing Room on Thursday," twittered Lady Lavinia to Lady Wayford. "It is such an ordeal, is it not? Sibyl feared she would forget one of her cards. It would never do to give one to the page in the Presence Chamber, then not have one for the Lord in Waiting. He would not know what name to announce! Dear girl, she did quite well, I believe. Of course, with my brother as her sponsor, there was no real worry."

Sibyl thought her stepmother's air of concern a bit more than needful, given the circumstances. It was impossible to retreat, although she wished to flee from this sophisticated woman who attracted Robert. Why had Mrs. Medland brought her to visit?

"Did you enjoy your entry into Society, Sibyl?" asked Mrs. Medland with a kindly smile.

"It was not quite as difficult as I feared, ma'am. Robert was so good as to visit with me awhile, calming my nerves," Sibyl replied with a hesitant look from beneath her lashes.

"He does quite well at that, does he not?" Lady Wayford said in what Sibyl thought a patronizing tone. "Naturally, I had attended a Drawing Room with my late husband, God rest his soul. This is the first one since his death. I found Robert's encouragement a great comfort."

Sibyl knew that had the lady been acceptable to Society prior to her marriage, she most likely would have been presented at that time, as well as after her marriage. Apparently, she was not of such high *ton* as she wished to imply. Taking courage from this tiny scrap of knowledge, Sibyl smiled, then said, "Robert is kind to stray dogs and cats, not to mention young women with an attack of nerves. How fortunate we are that he is willing to tend to us all."

The narrow glance of dislike from the widow bothered Sibyl hardly at all. She was content to be demure as was proper. "I can only hope that my papa does as well at the levee he is to attend with the earl next week," Sibyl continued. "As a new baron, it is only proper he go to meet the Prince Regent, our future king." Sibyl's eyes reflected her happiness that her dear parent received recognition. "He has a splendid new coat for the occasion."

"A little bird tells me that Miss Eagleton is about to make the catch of the Season," Lady Wayford stated in her soft voice that reminded Sibyl of treacle, sticky and hard to clean off. "I do hope that she has better luck getting him to the altar than his previous hopeful brides-to-be."

"Whatever do you mean, Lady Wayford?" Sibyl perked up. Was there a hint of scandal in his past? And how could Lady Wayford be so well-informed about these ladies? Of course, gossip did spread through Society like fire in a wood stack.

"It is known that he demands perfection of his bride. She must not disappoint him in any way. He sweeps a woman off her feet with rapturous delight, only to let her drop when she falls short of his ideal. How fortunate you meet his standard, Miss Eagleton."

The dry malice in her voice shocked Sibyl, yet she was unsure how to react. Miss Chudleigh's school had not prepared her for this sort of attack—subtle and snide. Best to behave with propriety, although why the lady would feel so sharply intrigued Sibyl not a little.

"I can only wait to see how the matter goes, I suspect. I have not made a decision as yet. It may be that the viscount does not meet my standards." Sibyl smiled sweetly, then moved to assist her mama with serving the tea.

"Then he has not declared himself?" Lady Wayford

persisted, accepting her teacup with a hand delicately gloved in pink kidskin.

"Now, Aurora, you must not tease our young friend," Delia admonished. "She is likely to believe you are prying. I know you would never do anything so vulgar."

Sibyl permitted a small smile to curve her lips. The "lady" was vulgar beneath all that sugared pink-prettiness. It was small enough comfort.

"I thought that Aurora might know a few young ladies for Sibyl to meet." Mrs. Medland cast a hopeful glance at Lady Wayford, then at Lady Lavinia.

"Sibyl met several charming girls at Almack's the other evening. Did I see you there, Lady Wayford?" Sibyl's step-mother gazed at Lady Wayford with a bland innocence that made Sibyl sit up with an alert gaze. She had seen Robert with a petite blonde in pink, but not Lady Wayford.

The lady compressed her lips in vexation, Sibyl thought. Did it mean she was not so fortunate as to attain vouchers for the seventh heaven of Society? Certainly, Lady Wayford concealed whatever she now felt with an admirable command of her features.

"I was not present Wednesday evening. Lady Bletchworth simply insisted I must attend her soiree, you see." One pink-gloved hand brushed a macaroon crumb from Lady Wayford's skirt. The pink feather that curled from the brim of her hat concealed her face for the moment.

Sibyl might be new to Society, but she was well aware that only those who did not have entrée to Almack's planned a party on the night the assemblies were held.

"Perhaps we shall see you there next week?" Sibyl said in a sympathetic voice. "What a pity that so many charming women are denied entrée by a few select women."

"Sibyl," Lady Lavinia murmured in a warning tone. One never uttered a word against those patronesses unless certain of the faithful friendship of the listening ears.

"I believe I do know of some young women your daughter might find congenial, Lady Lavinia. Perhaps you could join us for a breakfast I am giving come next week?" Lady Wayford offered as she set her teacup down with a decided snap on the table close to her. She gathered her skirt to leave.

Delia Medland rose from her chair, looking grateful that the visit was over.

"Lovely," Lady Lavinia replied, rising to walk with her guests to the entry hall.

"The earl is gone from the house?" Lady Wayford inquired artlessly as the group entered the imposing hall.

Sibyl had trailed behind them, watching the three women. It seemed to her that the beautiful Lady Wayford was casting highly speculative glances about the house. Did she think to aim for the title of Countess of Cranswick? It was not so lofty as marchioness, but it held greater wealth.

Just as Lady Lavinia was about to inform her guests that her brother was absent from home, that gentleman entered the front door. Bentley materialized at his side, accepting the earl's hat and gloves as though they were gifts of rare value.

"What a charming sight, I vow! Four lovely women to greet me." He bowed over the hands of each guest, gave Sibyl a kiss on her cheek, then cast a look at his sister that seemed to inquire what might be afoot.

"I have never had the pleasure of seeing your beautiful home, Lord Cranswick. Truly, it is all I have been told—that is, from what little I have seen," purred Lady Wayford, sounding to Sibyl's ears like a well-fed cat.

To Sibyl's watching eyes, it appeared the earl stiffened slightly. However, his manner remained the same toward Lady Wayford.

"Next time we have an affair here, you must surely attend, dear lady. With Sibyl in town, I intend to do more entertaining. Her ball is coming up before long, unless I miss my guess. Right, Livvy?"

Sibyl faded into the dim recesses of the hall at those words. Her ball. Before then she would have to give great consideration to a future as Lady Buckingham for the rest of her life.

Soon the house was silent as Lord Cranswick went up to his rooms, the visitors went on their way, and Lady Lavinia marched off to her own sitting room to attend to the guest list for Sibyl's ball. Now that the presentation was behind them, the ball was next to come.

In the morning room, Sibyl stared out the window to the gardens in the rear of the house.

"I find you here again." Robert Medland held the door open, surveying Sibyl with what she suspected was amusement.

"Am I not allowed to be pensive, sir?" She curved her lips into a reluctant grin at his expression. Her gaze shifted to his arms, held behind him. "What is this?" she wondered aloud.

"When a lovely young miss begs my assistance I try to comply with all due speed. See what I have found for you." With the air of a magician, Robert brought forth a slim parcel.

Her eyes grew round with surprise. "The book?" She had been hoping for this, for if one were to collect butterflies, one must know what to look for, and how many kinds there were, and other things of that nature.

He nodded, handing it to her. "Open it." He watched while she undid the package, a pleased expression on his face at her delight. "I believe that will help you."

She tossed aside the wrapping paper, then flipped the volume open to discover beautiful illustrations of the butterflies and moths found in England. "Oh, Robert, how lovely! What a dear, thoughtful man you are." After placing the book on the earl's desk, and throwing aside her propriety, she reached up to place a light kiss on Robert's cheek. Then she blushed at her boldness, backing away in pretty confusion.

Robert did not take advantage of the situation, as well he might have. He gave her a soft look, then stepped away from her with apparent reluctance. "I am not your brother, Sibyl."

"Yes, I know." She bowed her head, then turned back to touch the book with restless attention.

"Something is wrong?"

"No. Nothing is wrong. Why should there be? My presentation went as hoped, the ball is shortly to come, and I will soon be well and truly launched. I sound like a frigate," she added in an attempt at dry humor.

"You do not sound very happy."

"I should. I am truly pleased with this, Robert. Permit me to repay you." She went to leave the room, the book held against her chest, her eyes daring him to make an objection to this suggestion.

Robert surveyed her, took a step closer, scolding, "There shall be no talk of repayment. That kiss was all I require. I should like to be with you when you go out collecting sometime. Where shall you try first?"

Sibyl glowed with delight. How nice to have a man at her side who did not make her feel foolish for wanting to engage in such an odd pastime. "Perhaps Hyde Park?" she said, while she flipped the book open to the first pages.

He peered over her shoulder, more closely than proper, mind you, to see the illustrations as well as inhale the lily of the valley scent she wore.

"Brimstone, Tortoiseshell, Orange-tips, Fritillary, and Painted Lady—interesting names and pretty colors." She glanced up at Robert to catch her gaze in his. "These really are exquisite illustrations." They were standing so close. She was exquisitely aware of his proximity.

"Lord Buckingham is here, Miss Eagleton," Bentley declared in stately tones from the doorway.

Sibyl clutched her precious gift to her bosom while taking a step away from Robert. She faced the viscount with a guarded expression on her face. She could not imagine what to say to him. It was improper to be alone in the morning room with Robert, even if he was presenting her with an ordinary object like a book.

"Buckingham," Robert said, coming to her rescue once again. "Nice to see you. I was just about to leave after delivering a small commission to Miss Eagleton." Robert nudged Sibyl toward the door. "If you want to take that parcel up to your room, I feel certain the viscount and I can chat until you return."

Bestowing a look of gratitude on Robert, Sibyl murmured something rather incoherent, then slipped out the door. When she returned, it was to find the viscount the sole possessor of the morning room.

"Mr. Medland left. He took great pains to inform me that his visit was an innocent one, in spite of the nearly closed door." The rather narrow look bestowed on Sibyl made her exceedingly uncomfortable.

"Oh," Sibyl replied breathlessly, "it concerns a little surprise for my stepmama. Birthdays, you know. I want to have something special for her and it must be a secret for now.''

On her dash to her room she had decided that it was important that Buckingham not be upset at the scene he had interrupted. Heaven only knew what he would have thought had he arrived just a little earlier when she was placing that innocent kiss on Robert's cheek. For it had been most innocent. Robert had given her an odiously benign smile of the sort one bestows on a child.

''I hoped you might do me the honor of a drive in the park. The afternoon is cool, but the sun is out and seems likely to improve the day.'' He smiled in his splendid way, making her feel obligated to smile back. Like a looking glass.

''I should like that very much, sir.'' She dipped a hasty curtsy, then went to the hall where Annie waited with a pretty primrose pelisse that complemented Sibyl's brown hair. A chip straw bonnet with pomona green ribbons was tied on her head while she instructed Annie to deliver a message to Lady Lavinia. There was no need to ask permission for the drive with Lord Buckingham. Mama would shoo her out the door in a trice.

In the following few days Sibyl saw much of the viscount and nothing at all of Robert, except at a distance. It seemed he was much taken with Lady Wayford. The Earl of Cranswick also paid the lady some attention. The sight of all this notice appeared to annoy Lord Buckingham, Sibyl observed. What a curious turn of events.

Not that Sibyl was totally occupied with observing all around her. Not in the least.

''You are lovely this evening, my goddess,'' Lord Buckingham said softly as he led Sibyl out into a country dance at the Sefton ball. They had sat out the quadrille, as Lady Lavinia was not yet convinced Sibyl should attempt such a daring dance.

Her gown of blue lutestring with a gold tissue overskirt was pretty, but it hardly made her a goddess, she thought with modesty. Lord Buckingham liked to use poetic phrases. Yet at times she had the feeling they were mere words, not expressing true love, as she wished.

''Fie, sir, you are extravagant with your praise.'' Her cheeks felt warm, she suspected a slight blush the cause.

''You must call me Montague, my dear,'' his lordship said

as they progressed through the movement of the dance with dainty steps.

"It would be unseemly to be so bold, sir. My stepmama believes in propriety."

"Yet you were alone with Medland in the morning room," Lord Buckingham reminded her in a silken voice. It seemed he was never to forget that particular slip.

"I explained that was a secret regarding a present for my stepmama. Promise you will not spoil it for her, sir?" Sibyl did not like to lie to him—or anyone, for that matter. It worried her that she had deceived the man she might marry.

Others came between them, and Sibyl could only be grateful for the respite. Although he seemed to believe her innocent, Buckingham contrived to bring up that episode in the morning room with disturbing frequency. What did he expect her to say?

Of course, he did not know what Robert had brought her. Sibyl had succeeded in pushing from her mind the unpleasant but necessary fact that were she to marry Lord Buckingham, he would discover her interest in collecting butterflies. Once married, she had no right to secrets. He had told her that often enough. Yet she failed to reveal to him what she intended to do. It seemed like such a minor matter. Somehow, she did not feel comfortable opening her heart to him.

"Your uncle seems to be paying court to the lovely Marchioness of Wayford. How clever of her to choose someone of higher rank than a mere commoner."

Sibyl longed to declare to Lord Buckingham that there was nothing in the least common about Robert. He stood above every man she had met! "But she is prodigiously lovely, with exquisite manners," she said in defense of the lady.

"Not perfect, however." His narrow look of contempt toward Lady Wayford was not missed by Sibyl in spite of the rigors of the dance. It was an odd comment for him to make under the circumstances. It certainly gave her cause to wonder.

Had Lady Wayford been one of those woman rejected by the viscount at one time? It would account for her unkind words regarding him. It was nearly impossible to be charitable about a man who had given one encouragement, then a rebuff. It might account for his remarks on her, as well.

Whatever the earl felt toward the beautiful Lady Wayford, Sibyl could only be glad it took the lady from Robert's side. She did not seem the kind of woman Robert deserved. She was too much of everything, which explained nothing at all, had Sibyl given consideration to her muddled thoughts.

When she strolled along at the viscount's side after their second dance of that evening, Sibyl was conscious of a number of glances, most of them curious. She felt the muscles tighten on his arm as he beheld Lady Wayford laughing up at the earl, then at another gentleman who was part of her court.

Without consideration of how Sibyl felt about the matter, he dragged her through a side door, then down some poorly lit steps into the Sefton garden. "Fine evening," he said.

Sibyl repressed a shiver from the breeze that whispered through the trees, and wondered where the usually considerate gentleman she had heretofore seen had gone. "So you say," she said quietly.

"Women like her ought to be banned from polite society," he declared with a hint of anger in his voice.

"Lady Wayford is accepted everywhere, sir. Do I detect an unseemly hostility?"

He did not answer Sibyl, but marched along the neat paths with a peculiar determination. Sibyl did not like the shadows, nor did she feel comfortable alone with him in the near dark, despite all the lanterns about. Their light was paltry at best.

"We should return to my parents, sir," she reminded him. She ought not to have to do such a thing.

The viscount stopped suddenly, taking a look at Sibyl that made her shift uneasily in her dainty satin slippers.

She should not have been surprised when he swooped down to bestow an expert kiss on her mouth. She was. It continued far longer than she wished, although it lasted but a few seconds. "Lord Buckingham, you forget yourself!" she declared in a soft, although angry voice. She pushed against his chest with all her might.

He clasped her hands with his, making her protest still less effective. "My little dove, my goddess. You are so proper. So enchanting," he exclaimed. "*You* shall do me honor, unlike some. I shall not have to wonder where and how you spend your days, shall I?"

She considered it a peculiar way to answer her objections to his kiss. That kiss had been very illuminating for her, helping her to realize a number of things. She was about to say so when Robert materialized out of the gloom. Sibyl turned to him with patent relief. "Robert? Does my stepmother look for me?"

"I did not know you were given to seduction in the gardens, Buckingham. Permit me to restore Miss Eagleton to her concerned parents."

Lord Buckingham gave a vexed bow, allowing Medland to escort his prize back to the house.

"Robert, I must speak with you when possible," Sibyl murmured as they entered the Sefton house in a flurry of blue silk and fine black wool. "I need your advice, but not now, not here. Later?"

"I must go from Town a few days. When I return I shall seek you out at once. It is not urgent, is it?"

"It can wait. I daresay you will think me a peagoose, but I confess I need your help once again." She flashed a rueful look up at him.

"I am flattered you turn to me in your distress, Sibyl." His voice was warm, comforting.

Robert brought her to where her parents waited to leave. He took her cloak from the maid, then wrapped it about her shoulders, noticing how she trembled. Glancing back to where Buckingham now strolled at the side of a friend, Robert's mouth firmed in an angry line.

Within minutes, her cloak cozily drawn around her and her family near, Sibyl left the party. Robert left soon after with only Lady Wayford to mark their departure with curious eyes.

Lady Lavinia pressed Sibyl regarding her feelings nearly every day until Sibyl wished she might flee.

Lord Buckingham ardently sought her company. They rode in the morning, drove out in his carriage in the afternoon, visited his aunt, chatted with a sister—in short, spent a great deal of time together. Still, she recalled his kiss and her reaction to it. How different from Robert's.

She knew how she regarded him, yet she also knew how her parents felt about him. Should she follow her heart, or be a dutiful daughter?

Her ball was fast approaching. There was little doubt in her mind that Lord Buckingham would seek out her papa that evening to ask for her hand in marriage. He often mentioned her portion, not with covetousness, but rather as though it was already his to handle.

"You will trust me to know what is best, my goddess," he too frequently said.

Sibyl was coming to detest that name. Yet it helped her reach her decision. She resolved to break with Lord Buckingham. She could not contemplate marriage with him. Surely her parents would not compel her to wed him?

Unwilling to take a step on her own, she felt it important to discuss with someone older and wiser. Robert.

After several days of being overwhelmed by Lord Buckingham's attentions, she sent off a note to the Medlands' house, hoping Robert had by now returned from wherever he had gone.

When he arrived at Cranswick House, Sibyl was in the morning room at the rear of the ground floor, practicing a new piece of music.

"Not too bad, Sibyl," Robert said from just inside the door. He studied her wan face as he sauntered across the room to the pianoforte. "I arrived home last night. How may I be of assistance to you?"

"You have been gone forever."

"A few days."

"I hope it was nothing serious." Her voice questioned, yet he said nothing about his errand, not even where he had been.

"Tell me what has happened," he urged.

"It is Buckingham. I cannot marry him. I know my dearest stepmama has hopes, and I do not like to dash them away, but I cannot marry him." She dropped her hands into her lap while bestowing a look of utter unhappiness on Robert.

He lounged against a nearby table after taking careful note that no one was about to overhear her confidences. "Why?"

"He is all that is proper, except for that one occasion when you came to my rescue." She gave Robert a half-smile, wondering that she should feel so at ease with him, when there were times she trembled from fright while with the viscount.

"However, he has so many thoughtless moments, inconsiderate little tendencies. He is too preoccupied with himself. He has never inquired about what I do or what I enjoy. He speaks only of what he does, what he intends to do with my money once he gets his control over it. It shall all be for my good, mind you."

"And?" encouraged Robert, looking curious to know what else might spill forth from the agitated young woman.

"He talks a good deal about his future, but I cannot see myself as part of it, no matter how romantic he makes it seem. I fear I cannot give him what he demands of me."

"What do you want to do about it? I suspect your lady stepmother feels sympathy toward him."

"I want . . . " She took a deep breath and raised her eyes to meet his gaze. She appeared timidly determined, her eyes flashing with what she perceived as a bold and daring act. "I want to give him a disgust of me. I want to do something so that he will decry me as not perfect, say I am not his goddess, that I disappoint him beyond redemption."

"My, my," Robert replied thoughtfully. "And where do I come into the scheme of things?" He walked over to check the empty hall, almost closed the door, then crossed to place a gentle hand on her shoulder. "I suspect you have a plan."

"That I do," she responded eagerly, rising from the little padded stool to face him. "I believe you may help me with that part. I want him to see me with another gentleman. Since I think he does not like you very much, you would be ideal. I know I can trust you to find the right manner in which to explode that silly image he has of me. Goddess, indeed."

"We are to behave in such a manner that Buckingham takes off in a huff? Cries off, so to speak?"

"Yes," she cried. "I do not wish to marry the man."

"It might just work," he replied slowly.

"I know what would make him exceedingly angry." Her voice shook a little, yet she forged ahead with her words. "He would be furious to find me in another's arms, being kissed."

"I believe he would at that," Robert said, looking at Sibyl with amused eyes. "And you wish me to perform that deed for you? It would not be difficult? I saw you with Buckingham.

You were not pleased with his kiss, although I have heard praises sung to his expertise.'' Robert folded his arms across his chest, studying her face, watching the emotions playing upon it.

Her voice was soft and low as she slowly answered. "No, I was afraid of him. It was not at all what I had expected a kiss to be. It was as though he claimed me, placed some sort of mark on me, stamping me as his property, as it were. It was not a good feeling."

Robert studied her further, saying nothing.

"Well," she cried at last, wanting to hear some sort of reply, even if he refused. "Will you do it?"

7

"WILL I?" Robert studied Sibyl, wondering if she had any notion what she asked of him.

She looked like a sprite in the morning sun, dressed in a soft muslin gown of spring green tied with delicate knots of daffodil-yellow ribbon below her nicely feminine bosom. Her scrap of a lace morning cap perched on her head like a butterfly about to take wing. Her hands were clutched together, snuggled close to her breast while she watched him with those trusting blue eyes, so open, so sensitive. He wanted to touch that pert little nose, claim more liberties with that delicious mouth than he dared to dream.

Clearing his suddenly obstructed throat, he nodded. "Of course I will help you. Did you truly doubt it?"

Her hands dropped to her side; she moved close to him with a sigh. "Robert, what a dear you are. Steadfast, trustworthy. How would I manage without you to come to my aid when I have troubles? I hope that whatever comes your way, we do not lose this." Actually, now that her eyes were open regarding Lord Buckingham, she had come to realize it was Robert she had grown to love. He had crept into her heart by degrees, until he occupied the whole of it now. Yet a lady did not make the advances, did she?

A faint shadow dropped over Sibyl's eyes as she remembered Lady Wayford. Were the lady in pink to settle for a fine gentleman—without a title, admittedly—she could do no better than Robert. Somehow, Sibyl doubted that Lady Wayford seriously believed she could catch the Earl of Cranswick. He had been on the town since he was a child. No, any lady of sense would opt for Robert Medland. How many men of his estimable character, not to mention his handsome looks, were there to be found in London?

Sibyl leaned her head against Robert's comforting and very broad chest. Tenderly, she added, "Are there any finer words to hear than 'my friend'?" If she wished the words might be different, that wish was nobly pushed to the very back of her mind. If all she might have was friendship, she must satisfy herself with that.

His hand came up to awkwardly pat her slender back. He shook his head in a rueful gesture of resignation, praying for fortitude in dealing with this innocent scamp of a girl.

"I can think of a few," he admitted. Then he dropped his hand as though singed, stepping away from her with reluctant although determined feet. "We must make a few plans. I do not want to make mice-feet of anything you feel so strongly about."

Sibyl reached out to him, a mischievous look on her face, her eyes alive with delight. "True. Come," she drew him to a chair, urging him to be seated while she pulled up a stool close by. "I do not despise Lord Buckingham, you must know. It is that I feel we are not suited for each other. I would not wish to hurt him. Although from what I have observed, his skin appears to be remarkably thick." She tilted her head to one side, placing the lace morning cap in great jeopardy. "I am quite of the mind that some lady did hurt Lord Buckingham at one time. That is why he seeks perfection lest he be disappointed again."

"I imagine it is possible." Robert bestowed a look of growing respect on Sibyl. As young as she might be, she possessed a sensible head on those dainty shoulders. At least most of the time, he amended, thinking of her plans to rid herself of Buckingham's suit.

"Now," she continued, "I suggest we must make it totally believable. Lord Buckingham seems of the opinion that no woman can seek anyone else once he selects her for his own." She wrinkled her little nose in disdain for that notion.

"This evening he is to call for me, to take me to the opera. To tell the truth, I would rather attend a performance at Astley's," she confided in an aside before continuing. "If we contrive to be in the drawing room before he is due to arrive, I trust you can make the, ah, kiss convincing?"

"I have been told I can be most convincing at that particular performance." Although his face retained a bland expression, there was a growing mirth in his eyes she could not fail to note.

Sibyl gave him a narrow look. "This is not the time for levity, sirrah."

The grin he had been trying to hold back broke forth. "I know, I know. You are quite the minx this morning."

"I see." She laughed with a trace of embarrassment. Then she grew reflective. "Can you think of anything that has been overlooked?"

"I could hope he does not call me out."

"He would not! Would he? I think that would be a horrid turn of events, I must say. I shouldn't think you would care for pistols at dawn in the least," she declared with an enchanting nod of her head.

"I believe he prefers swords."

"Oh, dear. I trust you are good at that?" She wrinkled up her forehead, her concern quite clear.

"Passable." He doubted Buckingham would care to test his skill, for it was fairly well known that Robert practiced frequently with Angelo at his Haymarket Room. "I am pleased you show such care for me, *mon ange*. I might wish it to take a slightly different form, however."

"You will not change your mind?" Most alarmed, Sibyl placed her hand over his, her eyes pleading with him.

"No, no, I have said I will. Now, can you think of anything else for this almost-seduction?"

She gave him a reproving look. "As I said, it must be convincing. Although it certainly is not to be a seduction, almost or otherwise," she declared, looking at him with serious eyes. "Do you know, I believe that gentlemen with titles are too daunting for me. Or," she amended, "at least that of a viscount. He is so full of his consequence. Between his title and his money, he overwhelms. Just remember, no seduction."

"It will be all that, perhaps more," he teased. Robert left his chair to check the hall. Seeing it vacant for the moment, he glanced back at Sibyl. "Until this evening. *Aux arms*. The time?"

Sibyl explained when it was that Buckingham promised to

arrive, then allowed Robert to leave with no further words of instruction. How odd that he had used the French phrase to do with war. Did he think this a battle?

"Do I look all right?" Sibyl inquired for perhaps the fifth time in a short while. She checked herself in the looking glass. Were her cheeks a bit too pink with repressed excitement? Was her hair properly in place?

"Yes, miss, you be a real treat," Annie replied softly, her patience seemingly inexhaustible.

"I am pleased with this dress," declared Sibyl with satisfaction. She had selected a delicate raspberry sarcenet gown with an overlay of silver gauze. With it she wore her pearls, thinking they looked innocent enough yet gave the dress a certain air. "Do you know when my parents are to return?"

"They are off to dinner with the earl at Mrs. Medland's. I don't know when they return, miss." Annie was quick to listen to anything said by Lady Lavinia's abigail, Purdy. Not being one to gossip, Annie listened and learned, storing the information for possible need.

"I had best go down now, even though it is early," Sibyl said, mostly to herself, for Annie would have no idea what was afoot, other than that her mistress was in a high state of nerves.

The swish of her gown echoed through the silence of the house. The sounds from the square seemed remote, muted. Sibyl walked quickly along the hall, her skirts whispering about her with the silver gauze shimmering in the dim light. She peered over the stairs to the ground floor far below. Shadows slanted across the tiles; she saw Bentley briefly as he moved toward the front door. Robert?

Hurrying down a flight of stairs, she walked rapidly to the drawing room where she had decided it best to stage their "scene."

Bentley had been carefully primed on what to do. He was to bring Robert up as soon as he came. Then she was to be alerted when Buckingham arrived by means of a dropped platter, one that would have the ring of a gong.

Poor Bentley had looked so pained when she presented her

idea. Like an excellent butler, he was not given to such terrible gaffes. His reluctance did him credit, she assured him. But, she had pleaded, she really needed his help in her grand scheme. Bentley had given her that wounded-spaniel look, and agreed.

"Sibyl? Are you ready? Still determined to go through with your plan?" Robert entered the drawing room, slowly crossing to where Sibyl stood by a sofa as though it might offer support if needed.

"Of course. I have not changed my mind. Lord Buckingham must go, and this is the only way I can think to end his preference for me. I know he simply will not accept that I do not wish to marry him. He is a stubborn man." She studied Robert with discerning eyes. "You look very handsome this evening."

He did. He wore a midnight blue coat of Bath cloth over dove-gray pantaloons. His exquisitely embroidered waistcoat fit him nicely, the slate-gray satin with the touches of blue and yellow most elegant.

"Lord Buckingham can see to his laurels this evening. You will outshine him, I believe." She gave Robert a brave little smile, trying to convince him she had little concern for what lay ahead.

At that moment a crash of horrendous proportions came from the ground floor.

"The signal! You must kiss me, Robert," she whispered.

"This is the nicest part of this corkbrained notion, my dear," Robert murmured against her lips as he gathered her in his arms and proceeded to kiss her most thoroughly.

Her hands found the feel of that Bath cloth coat to be very fine. He smelled good, like a spicy flower. The first touch of his lips on hers startled, then aroused her to press against him with delight in this initial kiss.

She was floating, lost in a mist of sensation from which she wished never to return. His arms felt so strong, so secure, a safe haven for her. What his hands were doing as they gently explored her back, crushing her ever so nicely closer and closer until she thought she must surely faint from these strange desires stirring within her, she did not understand. But she enjoyed it.

Her arms tightened about him. She must cling to him lest she slide to the sofa. She somehow knew she must not yield to that wild impulse. But her heart was pounding crazily, like she had dashed up three flights of stairs.

"Miss Eagleton!" came a horrified voice from the doorway. Lord Buckingham had arrived.

Sibyl found it extremely difficult to tear herself away from that enticing, alluring kiss. It seemed Robert had the same feeling, for he stared down into her eyes with an intense, searching look, as if to see into her very heart and soul.

Slowly she turned, then gasped. For there, standing in the doorway was not only Lord Buckingham, but a startled Lavinia, an amazed Papa, a patently amused Lord Cranswick, and a most curious Mrs. Medland. The latter stood like statues, gawking at the scene in the drawing room as Lord Buckingham advanced upon the pair by the sofa with dignified, yet menacing steps.

"I do not think we counted on this, my sweet," Robert said in a barely audible voice quite close to Sibyl's earl. He retained one arm about her shoulders, for which she was extremely thankful. It was not unlikely she might have collapsed had she not his support.

"No," she murmured in reply. " 'Tis horribly unexpected."

"And so, my dear, what have you to say for yourself?" Lord Buckingham drew closer, glaring at Robert Medland as though he would dearly love to wring his neck. The viscount grasped his quizzing glass in one hand, holding it up as though to inspect an insect with it.

"We forgot ourselves. Robert stopped by to bring me something and we found ourselves alone. 'Tis a simple matter of attraction, sir." Sibyl swallowed at that statement, for who knew how it might be taken. She hoped no one thought to ask what had been brought, for there was nothing in sight.

"Attraction?" The word sounded a bit strangled as Buckingham raised his fist to shake it in Robert's face.

Sibyl took a step forward, her fears forgotten in the face of danger for Robert. "It is not his fault. Although it is not precisely all my fault, either," she added in total honesty. If Lord Buckingham had not been such a mutton-headed nodcock, none of this would have been necessary. Her usual shyness had disappeared somewhere along with that shattering kiss. She felt far more confident and able to deal with this man than she had expected.

"Fault!" shouted Lord Buckingham, his languid air completely gone.

"You are angry, aren't you," Sibyl said thoughtfully and not unsympathetically.

"Angry!" Only the insult to Buckingham's dignity and self-esteem exceeded this incivility.

"You might say something other than repeat what I say, you know." Sibyl gave him an affronted look, wondering how on earth she was to get out of this mess with her skin in one piece.

"What have you done to my shy little flower, my romantic, sensitive girl? I thought her so true, so principled and moral." Montague, Lord Buckingham, ignored Sibyl to demand an explanation from Robert, the supposed culprit of the dastardly deed.

"She is still all that; she is quite unchanged, I trust." Robert glanced down at Sibyl, a question in his eyes.

She wasn't sure how to answer that query. She wasn't even sure what the question was, for pity's sake. Never in her life had she felt more muddled than at this moment. Yet, she was not sorry in the least to have chosen this path. The warmth of that kiss went a long way to sustaining her, even now.

"I imagine you are quite disgusted with me, sir. I vow I cannot blame you in the least." Sibyl tried to look demure and still sort of wanton, if such a thing might be managed.

"Disgusted!"

"You are doing it again," she reminded him, wishing he would simply denounce her and leave the house in high dudgeon.

Lord Buckingham shook his head. "This is utter madness. That my precious one should so disappoint, turn out to be so . . . imperfect!" He raised his gaze from where he had stared at the carpet. "You are not what I believed," he declared sadly.

"I am desolated," Sibyl replied dutifully, though with little conviction. "I feel unworthy of your attentions."

"You could not change?"

She shrugged.

Robert cooperated by pulling her against him, providing Sibyl with the opportunity of languishing against his fine, lean form.

"I see," the viscount declared in disgust. "I never thought my instincts to be so at fault. I hope we do not meet again, Miss Eagleton, Medland. Good-bye." He turned, perceived the fascinated audience with horror, and sniffed quite audibly before stalking through the doorway and down the stairs.

The deed was done.

"Oh dear." Lady Lavinia entered the room at last, seeking out a chair into which she collapsed with charming grace.

Mrs. Medland followed, throwing a bewildered glance at her son.

"I expect there is a sane explanation for all this Cheltenham tragedy we just saw," Lord Eagleton said with an amazingly forbearing manner.

"There is," replied Robert with a sigh. "I do not know if anyone will believe it, but there is."

"I did not wish to marry Lord Buckingham, Papa. Only," she sighed wistfully, remembering Robert's kiss once again, "Lord Buckingham did not accept the hints I gave him. I feared it required something quite drastic."

"I would say that you succeeded very well in your intent," came the dry reply. The baron stood a moment, studying his daughter with puzzled eyes. "It might have been better done had you told me first."

"I am distressed with you, my son. How could you agree to such a disgraceful thing?" cried Delia Medland, ignoring the warning pressure of the earl's hand on her shoulder.

"I cannot believe what we just witnessed," added Lady Lavinia. "To think our sweet little Sibyl would stoop to such behavior. And as for you, Robert Medland. You are beyond the pale!" her ladyship declared in horrified, ringing accents.

Bentley chose that moment to enter the room with a tray of restorative refreshments he undoubtedly had deemed appropriate considering the sounds coming from the room, and knowing the viscount had flounced from the house in high dudgeon.

Sibyl waited until the butler departed. The time gave her strength for what she must needs do. No one was going to attack and blame Robert for her harebrained scheme.

After a fortifying breath, she placed her dainty fists on her hips and faced the group with determined eyes. Her mouth formed an adorable pout.

"I will not hear one word against Robert, do you hear? He is a fine, honorable man, high-principled, trustworthy, and most estimable in character. He is true-blue, Papa. If you searched the earth you could not find a more straightarrow gentleman. He, he . . .'' She faltered, glancing at Robert, then down at the carpet. ''He is not to be censured. Blame me, if you must blame anyone.'' She would like to have placed all blame on that miserable Lord Buckingham, but she doubted if anyone would accept that.

''Very noble, indeed, puss. Well, Medland?'' Lord Eagleton inquired, with more than a trace of the general to be heard in his voice.

''I don't suppose you'd let us go off to Astley's? No? I thought not.'' At the baron's gently quizzical look, Robert added, ''She wants to go there,'' as if that explained everything.

Oddly enough, it appeared to make some sense to the baron, for he gave Robert a commiserating look before shaking his head. ''Not tonight.''

''A glass of brandy, dear fellows?'' offered the earl.

Robert accepted the drink, as did the baron.

Across the room Lady Lavinia poured out the tea into the egg-shell thin cups on the tray with a somewhat shaky hand. ''I need to read those leaves,'' she declared softly to Delia.

Delia Medland had watched the puzzling scene across the room with a confused look. She turned to her friend. ''You think it will help?''

Giving a dark look at the gentlemen who were now deep in discreet conversation, she shrugged. ''I need something.''

Sibyl edged toward her stepmama and the doorway, wishing she might escape to her room. With any luck at all, she'd be ordered there.

''There is a hill in my cup,'' her ladyship declared just loud enough for Delia to hear.

''Is that serious?'' Delia looked askance at Lavinia, possibly wondering if reading tea leaves affected one's sanity.

''It means there are obstacles to progress. I could only wish I knew what,'' Lavinia declared in a musing voice. ''I had such hopes for Lord Buckingham and our little girl. He is all that is recherché in Society, my dear.''

Delia glanced across at her own dear son, a frown creasing her forehead. It was clear she felt her own son not far behind that estimation.

''May I go to my room?'' whispered Sibyl.

"I imagine that is best, though be warned you have not heard the last of this, my girl," her stepmother replied in a repressive way.

Sibyl looked at Robert, catching his gaze as she paused by the door. She sent him a look of apology. She would have liked to speak with him, but doubted if any of the older people in the room would consider that. She hadn't believed how stuffy they all were. That she had changed a great deal since she arrived in London didn't occur to her.

The dash up the stairs to her room was accomplished in jig time. She opened her door, letting herself inside as silently as possible. It would be too difficult to explain to Annie why she was here instead of at the opera.

Fortunately, Annie was belowstairs with the other servants, not expecting to be needed for some time. Sibyl exhaled a grateful sigh that Bentley had kept this all to himself for the moment.

Once her dress was removed and she had slipped into her soft, silken robe, she pulled up a chair so as to watch the square. She wanted to see when Robert left the house. While it was doubtful her papa would do anything uncivilized to Robert, she wanted to make sure he was safe.

At the smart rap on her door, Sibyl drew her robe more closely about her, then bade whoever it was to come in.

Lady Lavinia entered, noting that the dress had been hung up, the room was neat, and her girl was sitting by the window, composed but very subdued.

"That was an exceedingly foolish thing to do."

"I know," Sibyl admitted. "I had tried to tell him—that is, Buckingham—but he would not listen to anything I said. He did all the talking, Mama. I could not slip so much as a word into his conversation, it seemed. Papa was used to say that children should be seen, not heard. I guess Lord Buckingham feels that way about ladies, too."

"Robert offered for your hand." Lady Lavinia studied the view of the square, thus missing the flash of hope that so briefly crossed Sibyl's delicate face.

"What? Did Papa force him to declare? I'll not accept. I believe Robert has other plans in mind than marriage to a green goose like me." A vision in pink and cream lurked always in her memory.

"It was only proper, my love. You do silly things and reap the consequences."

"Mama, say I must not hold him to this," Sibyl pleaded.

"Your papa said it was a very good thing he did, as did my brother, William. However, if you feel thus, I shall not require you to accept him."

Sibyl knew that she would like to say yes more than anything in the world. Robert was the true-blue hero of her girlish dreams, the knight who would carry her off to his castle in the clouds. But she couldn't permit him to make this sacrifice for her. Not when he paid such attentions to Lady Wayford.

"It is my wish not to force him to marry me, Mama. Only think how lowering it would be, to know your husband married you against his wishes. It is not fair to him."

"Sweetly said. Before Robert left he asked if he might take you to Astley's tomorrow. I cannot believe your papa agreed. What is this world coming to, indeed!"

"Indeed," echoed Sibyl, in vain glancing out the window to see Robert. He was gone. However, she would see him tomorrow evening. They would be friends again, and with that she must be content.

The next evening found the Eagletons meeting Robert Medland in the same drawing room, tempers cooled, yet all wary. Annie lurked in the hall, ready to serve as an impromptu chaperone.

"The idea is that Sibyl must be seen out and about, or otherwise people might wonder. If Lord Buckingham has prattled about the affair, it will serve to make the curious even more curious." Lord Eagleton had discussed this strange business with his brother-in-law, reaching the conclusion that it was best to go as Robert Medland had suggested. He far preferred Medland to Buckingham, anyway, so he was not averse to the change in partners in the least.

Odd that Sibyl had such high esteem for Medland, yet made no push to get leg-shackled to him. The chap possessed plenty of brass as well. He'd invested in the funds most wisely. The lack of a title made no difference.

Lady Lavinia merely nodded while watching Sibyl's departure with Robert Medland. That she remained unconvinced brought Sibyl a few trepidations.

"I wonder what she will do now?" Sibyl confided to Robert once safely in the carriage and on the way to Astley's Royal Amphitheatre of Arts in Lambeth.

"I gather you believe she favors Buckingham's suit?"

Not able to see precisely what expression Robert wore on his face, Sibyl hesitated to answer. She knew he could not be serious in his offer, yet she wondered a little. It was too tempting to read what she desired in his proposal. "It is possible," she said at last. "She is much taken with a title."

"And you are not." He sounded almost regretful.

The exterior of Astley's place of entertainment was not imposing in the least. It appeared to be constructed with ship's mast and spars, with a canvas stretched on fir poles and lashed together with ropes. However, the interior looked splendid.

"Rumor has it that George III gave Astley that chandelier." Robert looked up to the enormous fixture containing fifty patent lamps. "They also say that the timbers came from one of the vessels his brother, William, served on." The two took their seats in one of the boxes in the center of the house. Annie sat immediately behind them, where she could observe every little thing.

"The book I consulted avowed they came from one of Napoleon's man-of-wars. Either way, the place is impressive."

Sibyl gazed about with delight at the ring of sawdust separated by the orchestra pit from what she had heard was the largest stage in London. The proscenium arch rose up as high as the gallery above the three tiers of boxes. She wore the look of an entranced child as the show began.

"I think the clown quite jolly," Sibyl said, laughing when he had entered the ring to shout, "Here we are!"

Robert watched the nonsense between the scruffy clown and the ringmaster in his elegant military costume with a benign eye. When a dainty miss came prancing out on her pretty horse, Sibyl sighed, clutching at Robert's sleeve with an excited hand.

So absorbed was she, Sibyl remained unaware when Robert transferred that hand to his own warm clasp.

"I declare, I know this is for children, but I find it vastly amusing," she said most unnecessarily. It was evident from her shining eyes and delighted expression that she found Astley's all she had hoped. Accomplished riders, rope walkers, and acrobatic feats alternated with displays of horsemanship. "How daring they all are," she said when it came time to depart for home.

Annie took a few steps away at a look from her mistress.

Sibyl again placed a hand on Robert's arm, staying him. "I wanted to ask you something before we return to Grosvenor Square. Why did you offer for me? It was not necessary, you know. You had rescued me. That is all a knight is required to do. There is no longer any danger."

The look from Robert silenced her, for it was unfathomable. On the silent trip home, he failed to answer her question. Sibyl feared the worst.

8

SIBYL WANDERED ABOUT the morning room with a strained expression on her wan face. Long hours spent pondering her fate had not left her bright-eyed.

"It is most kind of Lady Wayford to invite us to her breakfast, is it not, dear?" From her usual position in a chair by the window Lady Lavinia studied her girl, a look of concern in her eyes. "I hope you are in better looks by this afternoon, however. You seem rather faded today."

"And so I should," Sibyl declared without spirit.

"Perhaps a walk in the park will restore some roses to your cheeks? Call Annie and take yourself off. I shall look for improvements when you return."

Sensing that the suggestion was more in line of an order, Sibyl agreed, then left for her room to don a muslin pelisse and a neat chip straw bonnet, and to locate her butterfly net.

The day proved to be quite pleasant, actually. Although there were few people out and about so early in the day, Sibyl felt a rise in spirits with the gentle breeze caressing her face, the sun warming her out of the doldrums.

At least she had no fear she might confront Lord Buckingham while hunting elusive little butterflies in the vast green of the Park. Besides, the Park hardly seemed the place he might be found at this time of day. Now, the fashionable hour when all of Society was on the strut might be different. Sibyl wondered how soon she would be replaced in his affections. Somehow, he would have to find one who was perfect.

Sibyl studied a couple walking toward her. The two struck a familiar chord in her memory. Mrs. Medland and the earl! Sibyl gasped with surprise at the sight. She had been so wrapped up in her troubles, she had paid scant attention to this development, if it was one.

If Robert were about to wed, it would be natural for Mrs. Medland to wish herself elsewhere. The thought did not console Sibyl at all. Although she admitted she far preferred to see the earl with the kind Mrs. Medland than the beautiful, but somehow off-putting, Lady Wayford. And Sibyl wished Lady Wayford a million miles away rather than at Robert's side.

"Let us go a different direction, Annie. I would rather not interrupt that couple approaching us." Not that they took the least notice of the few governesses and their charges strolling in the park. In a backward glance, Sibyl decided the rest of the world seemed not to matter to them. If Lady Wayford thought to snare the earl, disappointment awaited her.

Annie spotted the first of the catch. "Oh, see, miss, I believe there to be a butterfly yonder." Annie knew nothing of science, or of collecting for that matter. She seemed to understand her young mistress had found something to bring a sparkle to her eyes, and that was quite enough for her. She had wisely followed Sibyl through the long grasses and across the park with nary a complaint.

"Wonderful!" Sibyl darted forward until she could throw her gauze net over a little specimen of the Brimstone, its sulfur-yellow wings with tiny red dots a pretty sight. She followed the suggestions for preservation found in the book Robert had given her.

"Collecting is more than merely netting the butterflies, Annie," Sibyl informed the maid. "One must properly mount and preserve them. How fortunate I am that it is unlikely anyone will think ill of me for my diversion. There once lived a Lady Glanville who was thought mad for chasing butterflies. She had an enormous collection, but no one understood her passion for the creatures, and the question of her sanity was defended at a trial."

"You could always turn to collecting seashells," a familiar voice said. "I'm told a great many ladies do that. One lady I met goes so far as to make arrangements with sea captains, for the shells can be very dear when bought in London."

"Captain Ransom," Sibyl said, looking up at the man who approached, trying to conceal her disappointment that he was not another gentleman. She placed the Brimstone specimen in her moderate-sized collecting box, then rose from where she knelt in the grass. "I shall consider that when I have examples of all our English butterflies." She was conscious she must look a sight, rumpled from her exertions, a lock of hair escaping to tickle her cheek. Romping in the grass did not lend itself to propriety. At the moment she did not care in the least.

"Ought you be here in the park unprotected?" Loosely holding the reins of his horse in one hand, the captain walked closer to where she stood. He gave her collecting box a curious look. In the distance, his fellow officers could be seen heading back to their barracks from their morning ride. Captain Ransom glanced from the box to Sibyl, his admiration bringing roses to her cheeks.

She opened the lid, showing him her very first acquisition. "Is this not a pretty little thing?" Then glancing about her at the nearly deserted area, she added, "Annie, here, is all the protection I should need in Hyde Park in the morning, sir." She had a feeling he did not agree, for he also looked about them, his frown telling her he thought a villain might pop up from anywhere.

"Allow me to escort you to your home, Miss Eagleton. I cannot rest easy without seeing you are safe."

Sibyl was not pleased to be taken from her pleasant morning diversion, but she said nothing. The three of them, not counting the horse, made their way to the house on Grosvenor Square where the gallant captain bowed over Sibyl's hand with a courtliness to rival Buckingham's. His eyes as well as his words revealed his keen interest in the general's pretty daughter.

Sibyl blushed at his kind compliments. "Such flummery, sir."

"I shall see you again, fair lady." He saluted her, displaying excellent manners, then mounted to ride off in the direction from which they had just come.

"Ah, there's a real gent, if you asks me," Annie breathed in admiration at the tall, handsome officer.

"He appears to be all that is gallant, does he not?" Without a backward look, Sibyl hurried inside the house, seeking her mother with a happier heart. Perhaps tomorrow she would venture forth again to see what might be found in the London parks. The book Robert had given her contained a great many illustrations with notations for each. She rather considered the earl's suggestion that she collect butterflies might prove to be a delightful diversion.

Several hours later, when Lady Lavinia and Sibyl presented themselves at Lady Wayford's neat town house, Sibyl wondered if Mrs. Medland might be attending. However, no sign of her could be seen in the tastefully decorated drawing room. A good many people were clustered here and there, chatting with what seemed to be enthusiasm. She suspected she was touched with cynicism when she guessed that gossip formed a large part of their conversation.

Lady Wayford apparently embraced what many called the Regency style, adapted by Holland from the Directoire period. The simple, chaste lines of the furniture offered a pleasing harmony, which Lady Wayford had complimented with soft colors and rich fabrics. The uncluttered room, with its rosewood tables and chairs and an elegant sofa covered in deep rose silk, presented a distinct contrast to the lady herself.

A hint of vulgarity reared its ugly head only when it came to the lady. Her gown's neckline dipped too low for daytime, surely. And ought not that elaborate jewelry be worn in the evening? Sibyl wondered what she might do to save Robert from such a fate as Lady Wayford. Even if Sibyl had rejected his noble offer, it did not mean she cared the less for him.

"What a charming room, Lady Wayford," Lady Lavinia said with true delight as she gazed about her.

"How kind of you to say so. My late husband selected the furniture shortly before he died. It seemed to be folly to consign it all to the heap when it had just been purchased." Lady Wayford's glance as well as her tone was dismissing.

Blinking her eyes at what she had heard, Sibyl wondered if Lady Wayford realized she had just insulted Lady Lavinia.

It seemed she did not, for she ushered Sibyl and her stepmama across the room to introduce them to two young ladies in attendance at the widow's late afternoon party, which she termed a breakfast. Sibyl was surprised at the large number of people in the room; she had expected only a few to be here.

While Lady Lavinia exclaimed over meeting another of her

friends from her come-out days, Sibyl attempted to make conversation with the girls she met.

Mary Ransom possibly was related to the wealthy banker, but there was nothing of the world of commerce about her. A quiet dumpling of a girl with soft brown hair and plain blue eyes, she possessed a gentle, inviting spirit and a soft, melodious voice. She beamed delightedly from her rather ordinary face. Inquiry brought the interesting information that Mary liked to paint, and hoped Sibyl would join her on an excursion to the Summer Exhibition, or at least a visit to the Royal Academy when possible.

"Would you by any chance have a brother, or relative, who is a captain in the Guards? My papa introduced me to Captain Ransom. In fact, I saw him just this morning." Sibyl turned an interesting shade of pink as she recalled the compliments heaped on her head by the gallant captain.

"That's my brother, Charlie. We don't look the least alike," Mary declared cheerfully. "However, money appears to be great compensation for my deficiencies, if you know what I mean. He did tell me that he had met you. I had hoped to see you today, as well."

The other of the pair of girls Sibyl had been left with was Miss Belinda Valler. She studied Sibyl with her cool gray eyes, as though trying to decide whether or not she wished to become better acquainted.

Sibyl returned to the topic of the Royal Academy, not wishing Miss Valler to be left out of the conversation.

"Well," Belinda declared, "if you want to crane your head off your neck, that is the place to go. I vow, I thought my head would drop off after we had been there for a short while."

"Unfortunately, that is all too true," agreed Mary. She settled complacently on her chair, then continued, "However, one who is truly interested in art would not let such a trifle get in her way."

Not wanting to encourage the argument she could see developing between the two, Sibyl inserted, "I daresay that one can go any number of times, if one wishes to spread the viewing out to acceptable lengths."

"Do say you'll come with me. Mama has had her fill and

I cannot go alone." That a maid would tag along was accepted by the girls. Even in a place like the Academy, one did not venture without protection.

"I should like that," Sibyl replied, realizing as she spoke that it was true. Lord Buckingham must be relegated to the past and Robert put out of her mind. Young as she was, there was much to do and plenty of time in which to do it.

The sight of Robert chatting with his hostess did not particularly cheer Sibyl. Had she known he was to attend, she might have stayed away. She shifted in her chair so that she might be spared the sight of those two. The silence that had hung over the carriage last night bothered her more than she could say. How she longed to restore the old friendship with Robert, were it possible. Yet she dared not pursue it, or him. To dream beyond friendship was utterly foolhardy.

The visit with the girls proceeded nicely. Sibyl almost forgot Robert was present. Before she left, arrangements had been made to go with Mary Ransom to the Royal Academy the following day.

Belinda Valler paused by the door, then said in her cool manner, "I hope you will both attend my ball two weeks hence."

Chattering broke forth as each girl declared the date of her ball, issuing invitations without consulting their parents, while sauntering along the street to their respective carriages. It was known a girl might wish a great number of gentlemen to be present, but acceptable young ladies were utterly necessary. Upon such a network did the Marriage Mart function.

Just as Sibyl was about to enter their carriage, she heard her name called. Upon turning around, she was surprised to discover Robert striding along the walk until he reached her side.

"I did not have the opportunity to speak with you inside." His handsome face revealed his curiosity about her appearance at the party.

"Lady Wayford kindly invited us so that I could meet two young ladies she felt might be congenial. Thoughtful of her, was it not? I am to visit the Royal Academy with one of them tomorrow. They both have balls coming up, as do I." Sibyl knew she chattered, yet she couldn't seem to hold her tongue.

She studied his eyes, knowing so much could be seen in them if she only knew how to interpret what she found. Would he attend her ball? Daring to plunge ahead, she hesitantly said, "I hope you will be coming to mine; I know your mother will."

"I should like that, if possible. There are problems." He stopped abruptly, leaving the sentence hanging in midair. "You go to the Royal Academy tomorrow afternoon?"

Sibyl couldn't imagine why he might be interested, but she nodded.

"Lady Lavinia mentioned that she plans to have your portrait done in oils by Sir Thomas Lawrence. Is that true?"

Why Robert looked so annoyed was more than Sibyl could imagine. *He* was not going to be required to pose for hours.

At this remark Lady Lavinia leaned forward in the carriage to interrupt. "Now, do you not go on about what a dangerous gentleman he is, for I know every woman is forever fancying herself to be in love with him. Sibyl is far too sensible for such nonsense. Besides, there will be her maid in attendance."

Robert looked at Lady Lavinia, then Sibyl. Sibyl thought his expression dubious at best. He bid them good day and returned to Lady Wayford's. Sibyl wished she had thought of a way to lure him from there without being too obvious. Alas, nothing had occurred to her.

The Eagleton carriage wound its way through the press of traffic until they reached the relative quiet of Grosvenor Square. The earl greeted them as they entered the house. It was evident he had come in shortly before.

"We did not see you at Lady Wayford's breakfast."

"No, was she having one today? I daresay I missed seeing the invitation."

Lavinia bestowed an amused look on her brother. "I have never known you to miss anything you wished to attend. Are you becoming forgetful? 'Tis a sign of old age, I fear."

Rather than laugh off her teasing, he paused to stare at her in a peculiar way. "Do you think I am become so old, then?"

"You? Nonsense," Lavinia declared stoutly, sensing her brother's unease. "If half the lads of today had your intelligence and wit, not to mention fine figure, Society would be a far more charming place to be."

He half-grinned at this bit of flummery. "Nicely said. And you look lovely today as well. You were used to wear white all the time. I believe the colors well become you."

"It was Madame Récamier, you know," Lavinia confided. "She always wore white and my spinster heart thought it quite romantic. I have no further need for such. Henry likes me to wear pink, rose, and greens. Like Sibyl, here. White ill becomes her and I shan't insist on her wearing white to her ball. It is to be next week, you know."

Cranswick nodded politely, sure his sister would handle everything, allowing him to pay a portion of the bills as the baron would never permit him to pay for the whole. But after all Lavinia had done for him, the earl felt it encumberant upon him to return his esteem in some small way. He turned to his niece. "You enjoyed the afternoon, Sibyl?"

She flushed under his benign gaze. The earl always made her feel as though he could see to her heart. After the night before last, she was not certain she wished that. What she felt toward Robert Medland was too private to be shared.

"Yes, sir. I met two charming young ladies I liked quite well. I have missed the company of other girls since I left school." She compressed her lips, thinking how well she liked the company of someone else.

With that remark, Sibyl excused herself, leaving the earl and his sister to chat a bit longer while she hurried to her room.

That evening they were to attend a production at the Drury Lane. Sibyl did not expect to see Robert there, although the possibility existed that Lord Buckingham might appear, as the work was vastly popular. He liked to be seen among the *ton*.

As it turned out, both gentlemen were present and Sibyl spent the evening trying not to look at Robert with Lady Wayford or Buckingham with a delicate blonde gowned in cream in a box nearby. Sibyl welcomed several of the gallant young officers who claimed to know her father, not caring whether they did indeed or not.

When Sibyl met Mary Ransom at the entrance to the Royal Academy at Somerset House the next day the hour had just turned two of the clock. The paintings were located on the second floor of the north wing and the girls eagerly made their way up the stairs with their maids trailing after them.

For the occasion Sibyl wore a flower print trimmed in the lace she admired so much. One never knew who might appear. Perhaps Captain Charlie, as Mary called him, might come. In her heart, Sibyl knew she wished to see Robert. But fate being what she was, that was unlikely—even if Sibyl had told him of her intended visit.

When they entered the Great Exhibition Room, Sibyl stopped in her tracks, staring up at the walls with a mixture of horror and amazement.

"Miss Valler had the right of it. One could indeed strain one's neck in a very short order," she commented to Mary. Every inch of the walls boasted a painting, some enormous, some more moderate in size.

A huge Saint George and the Dragon vied for the eye with a small, exquisite Madonna and Child. Large allegorical works hung cheek by jowl with moderate sized landscapes of great beauty. And then there were portraits of all sizes. Only the ceiling was exempt.

"I wonder how one is supposed to see the paintings at the top? Who decides which goes where?" Sibyl demanded in her confusion.

"Ah, fair lady, there you have the crux of it." A nattily dressed gentleman Sibyl judged to be on the shady side of forty stood at their side. He was balding, with a fringe of dark hair, and had remarkable dark eyes that appeared to absorb a great deal in his searching glances. He possessed an appeal one could sense immediately. "The best thing to do is to paint, and let them hang them where they will."

"Are you a painter?" Mary inquired avidly.

The gentleman bowed, his eyes twinkling with delightful charm. "Sir Thomas Lawrence at your service. And you are Miss Eagleton," he said, turning to Sibyl. "I am to do your portrait, I believe. Someone," he waved his hand vaguely in the air, "was kind enough to tell me who you are. You possess a delicate roseate beauty I shall enjoy putting to canvas."

Sibyl was so curious, she forgot to blush at his extravagant praise. "I should like to introduce Miss Ransom, who is vastly interested in painting. I assume you have a studio elsewhere, sir. Why are you here today? Is one of your new portraits to be placed on view?''

Sir Thomas sobered. ''No, I had to settle a dispute with Benjamin West regarding the hanging of a painting. His vanity grows with age, I fear. And I also met with a gentleman who desires me to paint his portrait. It seems he is to inherit an earldom shortly, and his mother implores him to be preserved for posterity. Fortunately for me,'' he added with a nice twinkle in his eyes.

''I much admire your style,'' Mary inserted shyly. ''I wish I might study here at the school. What a pity women are not allowed.''

Sir Thomas chuckled. ''I fear you would blush to your toes as they are Life Classes, hardly suitable for a young maiden.''

Mary bloomed a horrid pink at that bit of gentle teasing. Taking pity on her, Sibyl asked Sir Thomas his opinion of a painting she admired, and he spent several minutes pointing out works of art he felt of particular value.

After he had gone on his way, Sibyl turned to Mary, motioning her to a bench covered with green cloth. ''You do not think it overly bold of us to visit with him, do you? He seemed like such a nice man, hardly the sort for mothers to worry about.''

''Worry? Who would worry about an old gentleman like him?'' wondered Mary.

''Someone was concerned because I am to have him paint my portrait. Mama said he does not require many sittings, for he paints rapidly. How odd that anyone should object to him.'' Sibyl wondered what Robert might find improper about having one's portrait done by Sir Thomas. She also wondered who the new earl might be. This conjecture fled her mind when she heard Robert's voice.

''Miss Eagleton and Miss Ransom. How nice to see you.'' Mr. Medland, dressed in a fine brown coat, biscuit pantaloons that fit to a nicety, and shining Hessians, materialized at their sides.

''Mr. Medland, what a surprise.'' Sibyl decided it wise to match his formality. That delightful friendship they had known had been lost, it seemed. She mourned it, even as she wondered how she might retrieve it, or more. "You said nothing about being here today. Tell me, what do you think of that landscape over there? It is a scene of great tranquility."

"The Constable? Very nice." Robert studied Sibyl, speculating about her reaction to anything he might say. If only he could confide in her, tell her his true thoughts. He dared not, for she had made her own views too clear. He had to think, plan, work out something for his future.

"I wonder if *he* gives lessons," Mary said, with a wistful little sigh following. "I would dearly love to paint in oils, although my mother forbids it as being unladylike. As if an artist cared for that!" She chuckled in her endearing way, then continued, "I am confined to Watercolors. Perhaps if the Society of Painters in Watercolors would allow women to become members I might enjoy that. I am determined to succeed."

For a moment, when Sibyl met Robert's gaze, sharing amusement at Mary's words, it was as though the scene with Buckingham had not occurred, nor the silence following the delightful evening at Astley's when she had asked him why he had offered for her and he had said nothing in reply.

Sibyl still suspected Robert had merely offered for her hand out of a sense of duty, for she knew him to be an honorable man. His silence seemed to confirm it for her—although she could not help but wonder if he had deliberately sought out her company this afternoon.

Putting sad thoughts from her mind, Sibyl turned to Mary, coaxing her to forget her desires for the moment. "Come, let us leave here, for I vow my neck aches with looking, not to mention my head."

"Mary, so there you are." Captain Ransom marched up to where the three stood before the Constable painting, a vexed look on his face. "I have been hunting you this age." Then he recalled himself, bowing with admirable precision and grace to Sibyl, nodding civilly to Robert.

Robert found himself maneuvered aside as the dashing captain began to shepherd Sibyl from the room. He glanced down at little Miss Ranson, offering her his arm. "I believe we had best hurry if we intend to keep up with them."

"Charlie is always impatient, sir," Mary said with the tolerant air of a sister well acquainted with the nature of her older brother.

The four strolled down the steps and out of the building. Sibyl watched where she stepped, mindful of the dirty paths and her delicate leather slippers.

Captain Charlie was amusing, if a bit forward. Yet she felt drawn to Robert. His gray eyes had once looked upon her with such warmth and kindness. Today, those eyes seemed terribly impersonal, like a polite stranger's. Except they had flashed with what seemed to be irritation when Captain Charlie appeared on the scene.

What color eyes did the captain have? She couldn't recall. Buckingham's were an icy pale blue; she could hardly forget that look of contempt when he stared down his aristocratic nose at the sight of her held so tightly in Robert's strong arms. Had he gossiped about her to his friends? Her stepmother had doubted he would say a word, for it would reflect upon himself. Sibyl devoutly hoped so. Yet she had been an item with Buckingham. It did not take long for the *ton* to take note of a pair, or to cast speculation when that pair went separate ways.

"Allow us to escort you, fair ladies," said the gallant captain, ignoring his sister's sniff of disbelief. With a glance at Robert, the captain ventured, "Perhaps a visit to Gunter's shop would be in order?" It was clear to all he was reluctant to leave Miss Eagleton's side.

"I should like that very much," declared little Mary Ransom quite firmly.

Sibyl darted a glance at Robert, catching his gaze upon her. She nodded her agreement. Within minutes they were seated in Mr. Medland's fine carriage, the maids sent home in a hackney. Since Miss Ransom's brother was deemed an appropriate chaperone, and Mr. Medland was a friend of the family, Sibyl thought there to be no impropriety in such an excursion.

Robert studied the piquant little face across from him. It occurred to him that he hadn't sought the peace and quiet of his study for some days. He hadn't even thought about doing so. Something would soon have to change.

9

MISS MARY RANSOM decided to take advantage of having an escort other than her brother to request, ever so politely, that they perhaps might visit the Egyptian Hall. Gunter's was a treat; she wished to prolong her enjoyment of the day.

"Have you been there, Miss Eagleton?"

Sibyl turned her gaze to where Robert sat. He had consumed his ice and now appeared polished and at ease. She ate the last of her pineapple ice, then said, "No, I have not, and I believe it would be an interesting sight." She suspected Mary was more interested in seeing the fascinating delights at the hall than in Mr. Medland. Nevertheless, Sibyl envied Mary her escort.

When they arrived at the Egyptian Hall on the south side of Piccadilly almost opposite Bond Street, Sibyl found the exterior quite impressive viewed up close.

"You approve, Miss Eagleton?" Robert inquired as he assisted Sibyl from the carriage, the gallant captain seeing to the entrance fees for them.

"I did happen to notice the hieroglyphics carved into the wall while on my way to Hatchards. 'Tis difficult not to be impressed." She ruefully noted the tall, thinly draped statues over twice the height of a person, and avoided comment on them. That would be highly improper. She dropped her gaze from the frontage of the building to meet his. What did he feel? What thoughts were concealed behind that bland visage? For only a moment his eyes softened, gleaming with something of his past humor, then he returned to the polite mask he had assumed.

"You enjoyed the paintings today?" He tucked her arm next to his, sauntering toward the entrance of the museum with no hurry, in spite of the impatient look on the captain's face.

"I confess my favorite was the Constable view of the Stour

Valley and Dedham Village. One could almost feel the soft, harvest-scented breeze, the gentle late-summer sun. "I think it prodigiously kind of a lady's future husband to arrange such a gift, to remind her of her happy girlhood."

"You think it so unusual for a husband to be kind to his wife?" He assisted her up the steps, most unnecessarily, she felt, yet she did not shrink from his side. They walked past the elaborately carved pillars at which she barely cast a glance.

"My father is, I believe, but I suspect he is not at all common." She removed her hand from Robert's arm to enter the building, aware the captain was giving them a speculative look.

"You have been considering what is required in a marriage, then?" His voice was low, barely audible.

"It has been on my mind, yes." Giving him an amused glance, she continued, "I daresay every unmarried woman does now and again."

The captain decided to wrest control of the situation from the quiet Mr. Medland. Really, for such an unassuming chap, he had a way of taking command. Before one knew it, he was running the show. Quite how he managed to do this without seeming the least obtrusive, Charlie wasn't sure. But he sensed a strong opponent in the gentleman.

"It says here that the museum contains curiosities from Africa and North and South America. My, how interesting! I cannot wait to enter the cavern." Mary shivered when she spoke the last words, apparently with anticipation.

Sibyl dutifully looked at all the stuffed amphibious animals, the fishes, shells, and pretty samples of minerals displayed. At the last cluster, she commented, "That sulfur sample reminds me of the butterfly I found yesterday, Captain Ransom."

It was Robert who answered her. "A Brimstone? Sulfur is sometimes called brimstone, you know."

Somehow, Sibyl found herself at his side again, listening to his softly spoken words with intent interest.

"Perhaps you would like me to arrange with the trustees of the British Museum a private viewing of their butterfly collection for purposes of study?" Again he spoke softly so that Mary and her brother might not overhear his words. They were for

Sibyl alone. He had no intention of allowing others to intrude upon what he intended to be a special time.

Before she could stop herself, Sibyl flashed him a delighted smile. "That would be lovely. I find myself becoming more and more fascinated with the delicate creatures."

"To reward such a smile, I shall do my utmost." He bowed, then turned his attention to Miss Ransom with a proper politeness that made Sibyl grit her teeth in vexation, although she knew he behaved with utmost propriety to the young lady he escorted.

"Ohhhh," squealed Mary, as the four made their way through a basaltic cavern. The dim light offered the captain a chance to draw Miss Eagleton closer to his side, which Sibyl found not truly objectionable, although she could not feel anything stronger for him than a mild interest.

From this dark, rather eerie passage they entered an Indian hut, and from there stepped into a tropical forest that had Sibyl gasping with wonder. Animals peered from behind trunks of trees and from under the leaves of plants found in torrid climates. She tried to assimilate all this exotic flora and fauna while walking along the room.

"I never imagined it might look like this," exclaimed Mary with great delight, clasping her escort's arm with just a hint of trepidation. While the beauty of nature in all its tropical splendor was interesting, it was also a little overpowering to one accustomed to the tranquil scenes of England.

Mary dawdled at each animal, every turn of the path, until her brother at last nudged her ahead and out of the building. "Really, Mary, must you examine every leaf?"

"Miss Ransom is a lover of nature and the countryside," observed Mr. Medland with gallantry.

"She is excellently suited for the country, where nobody has brains," snapped her sorely tired brother. He had hoped to impress Miss Eagleton with his charms, and it was deucedly difficult if every time he turned his head that other chap took advantage.

Sibyl drew back in affront, thinking of all the people she knew who resided in the countryside and possessed a great deal of sense. The captain was indeed hasty with his comments, if this was a sample. She said nothing, but looked to where Mr. Medland waited with perfect courtesy to assist the ladies into the carriage. He had revealed not a trace of irritation with the awed Mary. Rather, he seemed pleased to allow her to view to her heart's content, pointing out various features to be seen.

Sibyl rather thought the proposed expedition to the British Museum would be most instructive if this was a sample of Robert's patience. It would also give her the chance to spend some time with him, perhaps to discover if something other than her intelligent refusal of his generous offer of marriage prompted the chasm that now yawned between them.

The captain was shortly deposited at the Guards, then Miss Ransom brought to her doorway by means of a cleverly devious route. She seemed not to mind in the least, beaming her farewell with great cheerfulness.

From the neat Ransom town house the carriage made its way through the press of traffic to Grosvenor Square. Robert assisted Sibyl from his carriage with nice ceremony, then escorted her into the entry hall, lingering a moment to feast his eyes on her charming face.

"I want to thank you again for the book. It is proving quite helpful." She wondered why he had entered the house with her. In the background, she could see Bentley watching—discreetly, of course. He wore his usually bland expression, but his eyes seemed to twinkle with approval.

"Why do we not go over to the park? Perhaps we may find more butterflies to add to your collection?" Robert had an ulterior motive, and he hoped she might agree. Once he ascertained her true feelings on a certain matter, he could know how to proceed with his plans.

Desiring to do just this, and also take the opportunity to explore a possible mending of their relationship, Sibyl hastily agreed. "I will inform my mama." Turning to Bentley, she inquired where her relative might be found.

The two wary, would-be butterfly collectors walked up the stairs to where Lady Lavinia was cozily ensconced in a chair by her sitting room window. Delia Medland sat opposite her. Both cast guilty looks at the young couple who entered the room, then turned to exchange wordless communication.

Sibyl wondered what the topic of conversation had been prior to her entry. Feeling it was perhaps better not to know this intriguing item, she merely smiled affectionately, then made her request.

"By all means, go off on your foray into the wilds of Hyde Park," Lady Lavinia responded with a perplexed air. "This sudden interest in butterflies is quite amazing, but I trust it is worthwhile. You can have Annie carry your box, or whatever it is you take along. And do not forget your parasol, my dear." Her gentle reminder that Sibyl best not allow the sun access to her skin, thus promoting the possibility of freckles, was scarcely needed.

"Thank you, Mama." Sibyl curtsied, then hurried to her room to refresh herself and fetch the things required for the expedition to the park. If Robert remained at her side very much longer, he would be required to remain for dinner, she reflected. Brightening at this thought, she hastened to the sitting room on winged feet.

Annie dutifully followed them to the park, and from the expression on her face she was clearly wondering if all the gentry had daft notions of how to spend their time. Evidently, chasing after wee butterflies was a pastime to be shunned as far as she was concerned.

Sibyl strolled along the path, wondering what to say. She longed to ask him point blank what had happened. Direct, straightforward. Nothing hidden. Ought she have accepted his dutiful proposal? Surely he could not want such a thing! How might any man of worth desire to be compelled to wed where he did not wish?

Lady Wayford also entered Sibyl's thoughts. Would Robert consider marrying the widow? Society might watch and wait, but Sibyl had heard of no entries in the betting books regarding the possible marriage of Mr. Medland to the marchioness. She imagined that was a simple method to know which way the wind blew.

"May I, Miss Eagleton?" Robert took the dainty net from her hand to swoop down upon a tiny blue butterfly. "Here, uncover the killing jar. We do not want to spoil the wings."

Watching while this was deftly accomplished, Sibyl replaced

the jar in the box, then continued to walk along at his side, ostensibly searching the long grasses and bushes for signs of butterflies. Actually, she was trying to think of a way to open a discussion such as she hoped to achieve.

"I believe I see Lord Buckingham in the distance," Robert said in a thoughtful voice.

"Oh, dear," Sibyl whispered.

"You have not confronted him since that fateful evening, then?"

"No," she said abruptly. Here was her chance to bring up what she wished to discuss. But did she have the nerve? "I did see him at the theater one evening. He was with a pretty young blonde. You were escorting Lady Wayford, I believe." She glanced at him to see what response the mention of the widow brought forth.

He darted an oblique look at her, then blandly replied, "Ah, yes. And as I recall, you were surrounded by a covey of gallant Guardsmen. Did you ever hear anything of the play that evening?"

Did he actually believe she had welcomed their boisterous attentions? Well . . . perhaps he could be forgiven for the assumption. She hadn't precisely ordered them to be silent, had she? Besides, she had found it extremely difficult to concentrate on the unfolding drama with the distraction of Robert seated at the widow's side directly opposite her box.

A reluctant laugh escaped. "Not much. They border on being a group of sad fribbles, do they not? Except for Captain Ransom," she added with honesty. "He seems nice." Mary's brother dislayed more propriety than the others.

"Do your tastes lean to the military, then? I had not considered that your father's background might influence you in that direction.

Her eyes grew wide with surprise as she heard his words. "Really, sir, I had not thought so at all."

"You said you would not wish to marry a gentleman of the peerage," he commented, while taking the net to swat through some grasses. His face was turned from her, yet his words were clear. "Is that still true?"

Not understanding in the least why he was pursuing this train of questioning, Sibyl answered impatiently, thinking only of Buckingham and his self-centered attitude, "I believe I should not care for that at all. At least, not from what I have seen to date," her natural honesty compelled her to add.

People were filtering into the park in greater numbers as the fashionable hour for being seen in that locale approached. Sibyl watched as a carriage she seemed to recognize drew to a halt not far from where they now stood.

"Lady Wayford," Mr. Medland said with what appeared to be warm welcome.

"Communing with nature, Robert?"

The coy twirl of her parasol was more appropriate to a girl, Sibyl thought. But then, the lady dressed in a youthful style, with delicate colors to enhance her blond coloring. Sibyl wondered if that blond hair could truly be natural, then caught herself up in horror. What was she becoming, to be so spiteful.

Help came from an unexpected source.

"Miss Eagleton, how lovely to see you."

Upon turning around, Sibyl discovered Belinda Valler approaching with Lord Buckingham escorting her. Lord Buckingham made a distant bow, his eyes frosty with disdain.

Belinda, however, knew nothing of the event that had split the former pair apart. She introduced all, smiling with great deference at Lady Wayford like she was an antique. Her little comments were innocent, dealing mostly with the weather and the throng of people. If she thought it curious the others had so little to say for themselves, she gave no indication of it.

Lady Wayford was the first to respond. "I vow, the crush of carriages is too much! I'd best leave you now." She bestowed a grim look on the two couples before regally driving off.

The silence was awkward in the extreme. Sibyl gave Buckingham a wary glance, then turned to Robert, saying, "I fear we had best get all those butterflies home," just as though she had a hundred to mount.

"What? Oh, by all means. Miss Valler, Buckingham. Have a pleasant afternoon." With this innocuous remark, he made to guide Sibyl off in the opposite direction.

"It was lovely to see you again Miss Valler," added Sibyl as Robert firmly turned her from that pair.

"I feel guilty, Robert," Sibyl confided. "Poor Belinda must wonder what that was all about. She does not strike me as being in the least stupid."

He patted her shoulder in that nice, but somewhat annoying, brotherly way he assumed at times. "Don't worry. I expect Buckingham will fill her head of other things in short order."

Undoubtedly he would, Sibyl considered. There would be paeans of praise to the young lady that somehow reflected glory on himself for being so clever to select her.

At the front steps of Cranswick House, Sibyl handed the butterfly equipment to Annie, requesting her to take it to her room. With this small measure of privacy assured, she turned to Robert. "Ever since our visit to Astley's I have wanted to ask you what has come up between us to cause restraint. I have felt it most keenly, you know. I wish we might at least be friends again." She placed one timid hand upon his arm, beseeching him with those large blue eyes he found so appealing.

Robert looked down at the dainty hand that rested so trustingly upon his arm. He could feel the warmth from it radiating through the fine wool of his coat. Glancing back out across the square, he wished he could be alone with her. How he would like to explain everything, convince her that her ideas of the nobility were wrong. Not all peers were like Buckingham. Her uncle was a charming fellow, but of course he was also older.

It depressed him to consider the uphill battle he had to fight. All he could do was try. "We are friends, Sibyl. Never fear on that score. I'll admit it somewhat wounded my pride to have you refuse me."

She shook her head in dismay. "But, it was all my fault. Why should you pay for my foolishness? Except, it would never have happened if Buckingham hadn't been such a nodcock as to declare he intended to ask Papa for my hand. I realized I could never marry him. I must love and respect the man I wed."

"And you neither love nor respect me?" he inquired with a whimsical expression on his handsome face. "Nay, do not answer that, for I suspect my pride will take a further battering."

"I do respect you, you must know that," she said urgently, her hand pressing his arm in her concern. She dared not reveal that she loved him. He appeared to care for her, but how? Most likely as a sister, judging from his behavior. That was certainly not the way for a man in love to act!

He smiled, a trifle grimly, she thought, and longed to smooth it from his mouth. She remembered the touch of those firm, warm lips all too well. That kiss had haunted her sleep every night. She had twisted and tossed in her lonely bed, wondering over and over why she had been such an utter peagoose as to think she might escsape unscathed from that mess with Buckingham. Her punishment had been to discover that she loved Robert Medland, and he was most likely to take her in disgust, or at the very least ignore her. Lady Wayford would never have done such a gauche thing.

"Regarding our trip to the museum, I shall pick you up at ten of the clock the day after tomorrow. I need to contact one of the trustees to make the arrangements for us."

"I shall be looking forward to the day . . . Robert."

"Sibyl." He bowed over her hand, lingering as long as he dared. It was highly improper to conduct a conversation on the front steps of a house as prominent as Cranswick. He, too, had yearned for privacy, yet knew it unlikely to be granted.

She paused a moment to watch him take leave in his carriage, then went up to her room. How pleasing to be closer to their old relationship. There was still a constraint, though she could not imagine what caused it.

On the landing of the first floor, she heard voices coming from the drawing room. Curious, she walked to the door, where she saw the earl and Mrs. Medland in earnest conversation. Before they could take note of her, she backed away on silent slippers, continuing her way upstairs with a speculative look on her face.

Her family, for she considered the earl an uncle, even if it was only by marriage, seemed to be greatly involved with the Medlands. Would those two marry? Mrs. Medland had been heard to make rather strong comments on the frivolous life the earl had led these past years. Could that prevent her from an alliance with him, even if she cared for him? Surely marriage to the earl would be preferable to sharing a house with Lady Wayford, should Robert wed the widow, which Sibyl devoutly hoped would not be the case.

Closing her bedroom door behind her, Sibyl wandered to the window, dropping her pelisse and bonnet on the bench at the foot of the bed as she passed it. There were a prodigious number of "shoulds" and "woulds" in her thoughts.

Robert did not attend the assembly at the Brentwood's that evening. Neither did Lady Wayford. Why Sibyl should have made a connection between the two, she did not know, but she did. The notion that those two were together did not make for happy thoughts.

Belinda Valler glided toward Sibyl, greeting her with evident pleasure. "How lovely it is to have friends at these affairs." She led Sibyl to a secluded arrangement of chairs by a corner window. "You left rather abruptly this afternoon. I trust there was nothing untoward that was said? Lord Buckingham tends to be a trifle off-putting at times. He does love to discourse about himself, as perhaps you discovered?"

"Then you know we were somewhat of an *on-dit* not too long ago?" Sibyl breathed a sigh of relief. That particular bit of information would no longer have to be hidden from Belinda.

"I was so informed by Lady Wayford. Whatever did you do to the lady to set her hackles up, my dear?" Belinda leaned forward, resting her arms upon the chair as she contemplated the young woman at her side. Her cool gray eyes were full of speculation.

"I would not be so ungracious as to malign the lady," denied Sibyl, an understanding glint in her eyes.

"Perhaps she seeks to perform that task for you? While her words were spoken with honey'd sweetness, they were acid sharp, nonetheless. 'Tis curious how a lady who possesses so much in the way of wealth and beauty should go out of her way to make spiteful remarks about you."

"I do not see her here this evening."

"No, there are quite a few people missing. Lord Buckingham is not present, either. Come, we had best return to the fray. I suspect there is some gentleman who is just perishing to dance with me."

Sibyl laughed and gave no thought to Lord Buckingham, Lady Wayford, or Robert for the rest of the evening. She was caught up in the whirl of the party, loving the dancing and attention she had never reaped before in her life.

How glad she was that Lady Lavinia had persuaded her, by fair means or foul, to come to London.

The following day Sibyl slept very late, then chose to walk in Green Park, hoping to find a butterfly not seen before. Her collection was not growing very fast.

She had just captured an excellent example of what her book told her was a Tortoiseshell butterfly when she chanced to glance up. Kneeling in the grass next to a beech tree, it was likely she was not observed by those in the carriage that passed on the not too distant road. But she saw them clearly. Robert and Lady Wayford.

He drove his curricle, tooling his team of matched grays while bestowing particular attention on the lady at his side. Since his face was turned from her, Sibyl couldn't be sure of his expression, but Lady Wayford had the pleased look of a cat that has just settled among a flock of canaries. Sibyl recognized that "I shall catch my prey" smugness on her face.

The butterfly was dropped in the killing jar, then placed in the box. "I believe we shall return home, Annie."

"I see another one, miss. It be bigger, I think."

Shading her eyes with one hand, Sibyl thought she did too. Sighing, for she would dearly liked to have stomped home in disgust, she nodded and proceeded across the gently sloping contours of the park.

The elegant Peacock butterfly hovering over a yellow flower that grew at the edge of the reservoir proved to be elusive. Sibyl ran after it, holding her net in the air, dashing about hither and yon, trying valiantly to snare the pretty thing. From time to time she glanced about, hoping against hope that no one she knew would see her in the heart of the park, running like a hoyden.

"Ah, if it isn't Miss Eagleton."

The nasty tone in which those words were spoken was quite familiar to Sibyl. She stopped, slowly turned about, accepting the loss of the Peacock butterfly with resignation. "Lord Buckingham. What a surprise to find you in the park at this time of day."

"Obviously, you did not think to see anyone. In fact, I rather suspect you did not think at all," he said in a most censorious manner.

"You are passing through on your way to your club, perhaps?" she said with hope. He walked in the direction of St. James's Street, where most of the various prominent men's clubs were located.

"I am." He bowed slightly in recognition of her correct assessment. "Are you about to return home?" he said with a chilly gaze slanted down that nose he so proudly tilted in the air. "I shall hail a hackney for you." Those words were spoken as though he might be required to summon something horridly distasteful, as indeed it might seem to him. Peers rarely, if ever, seemed to drive in anything but a proper carriage.

It was not one of her better days, she decided. Motioning Annie to follow her, Sibyl gracefully curtsied, then began to move away. "No. I must catch a Peacock. Good day." If that didn't convince him she was unworthy of his name, she didn't know what else would.

With Annie's help she did indeed nab the elusive Peacock butterfly, then decided to return to the house before she was caught by anyone else.

When Robert gathered her up the following day at precisely ten of the clock, Sibyl longed to question him about Lady Wayford. One didn't do that, of course.

They drove off in his curricle, permission to omit the maid leaving Sibyl to feel that her mama considered Robert in the light of a son rather than a suitor. The depressing notion was nudged away, and she pasted a smile on her lips.

His tiger took care of the carriage and horses while they approached the museum.

They walked through the lower rooms, then up the staircase to the first floor. At the top of the steps stood two enormous giraffes, like guards, on the landing.

"Imposing fellows, are they not?" he said in that light whimsical way he had at times.

"They look rather odd in contrast to the frescoes." Bacchus and friends frolicking across walls and ceilings was not what one expected in a decorous museum. Upon reflection that this had once been the home of the notorious Montagu family, Sibyl decided it was not too surprising. Those gentlemen had pursued wealth and position with single-minded intensity, enjoying the pleasures to be found along the way, of course. ''Another fine example of the peerage.'' She ignored Robert's stare at her non sequitur.

''We shall concentrate on the department of greatest interest to you—where the butterflies are found.''

Sibyl found it fascinating to study all the various kinds. She had a long way to go before she could come anywhere near this collection. But she was able to actually see how the insects had been mounted, the proper way of displaying them, and peruse books that explained their habits, which certainly would help to find them. There was little point in hunting where none were likely to be found.

When Robert brought her home, she expressed her appreciation to him.

''It was excessively kind of you to do this for me.''

''If I had a sister, I would likely assist her as well.''

The words were polilte but hardly encouraging. ''My ball is tomorrow evening. I do hope I shall have the pleasure of saving a dance for you.''

He bowed over her hand, giving the impression of agreement. Yet later in her room, she realized that he had not replied to her hint. Would she see him on the morrow? Could he be so cruel as to not attend her come-out ball?

10

SIBYL FOUND IT impossible to sleep. She knew she ought to remain snuggled beneath the mound of covers for several more hours, but how could she? Today was her ball!

Slipping from her bed, she pulled on her dressing gown, then walked across to peer out the window. The trees in the square rustled with a gentle wind. Tradesmen went about their business with hearty voices and seeming good will, intent upon making deliveries as quickly as they might.

The pretty blue and silver gown she was to wear this evening hung on the outside of her wardrobe to avoid being crushed. It shimmered in the slanting morning sun, seeming to glow with a life of its own.

When Annie peeked in the door to see if Sibyl was awake, she opened her eyes wide with astonishment that Sibyl was up and actually dressing for the day. The blue habit skirt had already been pulled on, and the habit shirt fastened at the neck, the ruff touching her chin as she struggled with her jacket.

"Bring my chocolate and a few buns, please. I would go out for a breath of fresh air. I vow, I cannot remain in the house. Mama will declare me to be underfoot, and scold. Please send word to the groom I wish my horse to be brought around directly."

Once the chocolate and buns had been consumed Sibyl dashed down to the entry and out to her waiting mare as though the house might claim her, prevent her from leaving. Even now the servants were stirring, putting a final polish on the ballroom.

Consequently, the groom found himself trailing behind Sibyl down South Audley Street. Why she chose to ride along this direction when she might have cut over to the park on Grosvenor Street, Sibyl preferred not to consider.

At the corner of Mount Street and South Audley, Sibyl

paused, looking toward the house belonging to the Medland family. Did Robert sit in the breakfast room even now? Was he coming this evening? How she wished she knew. But a young lady, a proper young lady, did not visit the home belonging to a gentleman or his family by herself. Even if invited, her mama would accompany her. She remained a few minutes, her thoughts almost melancholy, before turning away.

The small shops that dotted South Audley were open for business, but it was basically a quiet street. Sibyl ignored these signs of commerce, turning at Mount Street to amble toward the park.

The ruff of her neck tickled her, and she rubbed at it with a gloved hand, while contemplating the blue of her habit. How pleasing it was to know oneself modishly dressed, fine as five-pence, as her papa would say.

Once in the park she found the early morning dew lying heavily on the ground. Although a damp morning, the sun would soon burn off the moisture, and it looked to be a fine day. Cantering along the Row, she wondered if she might espy Robert indulging in a similar pastime.

Before long she thought she saw familiar figures ahead. It seemed to be none other than Lord Buckingham riding with Lady Wayford! That drift of white gauze from the neck of her smart black habit was distinctive, unmistakable. Especially when combined with her familiar black horse riding next to the one Sibyl recognized as belonging to the viscount. What an unlikely pair for anything, let alone a morning ride. Sibyl reined in her mare. "Daisy," she confided to the gentle horse, "I do believe we shall turn around. I have no desire to be seen by them."

It was but a matter of minutes before Grosvenor Square again came into view. Sibyl slid from her mare, handing the reins to the groom. She fondly patted Daisy, offering her a piece of sugar as a farewell treat.

Inside the house the usual morning calm had evaporated, replaced by scurrying maids, rushing footmen, and an unusually harried Bentley.

"Ah, Miss Eagleton, your mother is looking for you." His expression warned Sibyl to hurry.

"Naughty girl. How could you take off on this morning of

all days? Delia has promised to help with the flowers. Do assist her." Lady Lavinia held up a length of delicate white cambric to her nose in a romantic gesture while consulting a long list.

Figuring it was hopeless to expect any normal sort of breakfast today, Sibyl helped herself to a piece of fruit, then ran up to her room to change from her habit. In short order she was suitably dressed in a plain muslin morning gown and entering the ballroom to seek Mrs. Medland.

It was a magnificent, high-ceilinged room done in cream and gold with rich blue draperies hanging at tall windows. Sibyl found Mrs. Medland in the far corner of the room surrounded by buckets of white flowers of every description.

"Already arranging flowers at this hour?" Sibyl cast a glance over the long table covered with urns, vases, and assorted baskets. She hadn't seen such an assortment of containers since Lord Buckingham fancied himself in love with her. She swallowed the last bite of the small apple, then drew near the table.

"There are such vast amounts and the day will speed by in a hurry." Mrs. Medland seemed ill at ease, darting guarded looks at Sibyl before returning her concentration to the flowers at hand. Her designs were exquisite, far lovelier than any Sibyl had seen to date at the various balls. Clearly, Mrs. Medland was a creative genius when it came to flowers.

Sibyl studied the arrangements completed, then began to duplicate them in like vases. With deceptive casualness she inquired, "Was Robert up and about when you left your house?"

"I fear he had gone out when I came downstairs." The lady kept her eyes on the flowers. There was nothing amiss in that, except she usually looked at people when speaking to them.

Sibyl paused, giving Mrs. Medland a puzzled stare. Something in her tone of voice alerted Sibyl to a problem.

"Gone? I do hope to see him at the ball this evening. It would not seem right if he were not there." She carefully watched the lady at her side for signs of anything amiss. Sibyl could feel her nerves suddenly tensing, a sense of danger charging through her. A panicky feeling threatened to swell up inside. Robert not be there? Unthinkable! She depended upon him, far

more than he dreamed, she was sure. He had been her stay
through so many trials.

"Don't worry, please, my dear. I feel sure Robert will not
be absent."

Yet Sibyl wondered if something hung unspoken in the air—
the words, "if possible."

"He did not leave any message, other than that business
required his presence. I trust he shall return before long." Delia
continued to poke lilies into her vase.

Sibyl thrust the stem of white stock into the arrangement she
worked on, uneasy, the pleasure in her day dimmed.

By late afternoon the threat of impending doom had been quite
dispelled. A nosegay from Robert had arrived, dainty white
rosebuds clustered in a silver holder with cascades of blue ribbon
flowing from it.

Mrs. Medland had long since departed for her home. The
ballroom was now a fairyland in white flowers with swathes
of blue fabric draped over narrow tables to accentuate the
blooms.

Above, long white tapers awaited the touch of the match. The
chandeliers would be lowered, then the candles lit by several
footmen working as fast as possible. Once raised again,
hundreds of candles would bring light to the glittering scene
below.

Sibyl dutifully inspected the various rooms before going up
for a much-needed rest. She doubted if she actually would shut
her eyes to sleep.

"I do not want you to look hag-ridden, my girl," declared
her stepmama. "Try to sleep. When your friends arrive, you
want to be fresh to greet them. This will be a night you will
never forget as long as you live."

Giving Sibyl a long hug, Lady Lavinia saw her to her room,
tucking a soft throw about her before leaving for her own room
and a similar rest.

Lady Lavinia was not as sanguine about this evening as she
indicated to her girl. She had seen disquieting signs in her tea
leaves this morning. In the area that foretold family affairs she
had discovered a sword. Quarrels and separation, loss, even
a possible death loomed around her. But who was to be so

afflicted? At the bottom of her cup had been a snake, the symbol of hatred and enmity. Lavinia did not think the events were necessarily portends for herself, for she had been thinking of the day and night ahead of them. Now she feared, for there had been no encouraging sign in her cup, nothing to cheer her or mitigate the rest.

"Henry, I do hope all will go well." Her worry was clearly written on her face and her husband sought to comfort and reassure her.

"Nonsense, my love. Sibyl will take as well tonight as she has every other time she has been out since the night of the Medland musicale."

"But if something happens? That snake." She shook her head. "Hatred and enmity are not to be found within this house, it must come from without. There could be so many who envy her, fear her, or merely wish her harm. One never knows what lies in the heart of another."

Together, they settled on the sofa in their sitting room, lost in thought for some time. Lavinia nestled in the arms of her husband, wishing Sibyl might know such comfort.

Sibyl finally rose from her rest, unable to be still with her head spinning from all the wild thoughts tumbling around in it. Would he find her pleasing this evening? She had come such a long way from the shy creature just down from the country. Had Lord Buckingham not taken a fancy to her, who knows what might have happened. Perhaps Robert might have declared for her hand and really meant it?

But of course there was Lady Wayford to consider. She was witty, elegant, and possessed of a considerable fortune, left by her departed husband and not yet spent. Her blond beauty had not faded with age, nor had her charm ceased to exert its attraction.

What a blessing Lord Buckingham had not revealed what had happened that night he had entered the drawing room to find Sibyl in Robert's arms. Since no one, not even Buckingham, knew Robert had done the proper thing by asking her to marry him, a scandal of disastrous proportions would have followed. As each day had passed and no sign occurred of anyone's being the wiser, Sibyl had relaxed. Indeed, she didn't know what had brought it to mind this evening, unless it was merely reflection of her past with Robert.

"What do you think, Mama?" Sibyl pirouetted about before her looking glass as her stepmother entered the bedroom.

"Lovely, my dear," Lady Lavinia declared absently, but with genuine fondness. Then she continued with what was on her mind. "The Duke of Devonshire will be here. I wonder that he should tear himself away from his collecting of books long enough to attend," Lavinia said with asperity. Every lady in London schemed in vain to snare the duke for her daughter or ward. He seemed impervious.

"I am impressed," bubbled an irrepressible Sibyl, not caring in the least that the bachelor duke was to grace her party. He would stay a short while, then take himself off to his club. He seemed far more inclined to spend time by himself than in the middle of a ball.

Dinner was declared sumptuous, an epicurean delight. Mrs. Medland graciously beamed her approval at the earl.

Lady Lavinia thought there was a line of tension to Delia's jaw, a hint of worry about her eyes, but marked her observations up to her own apprehensions.

Sibyl glanced at the empty chair where Robert was to have sat. Mrs. Medland had made vague apologies, something about his carriage undoubtedly having trouble. It had spoiled Sibyl's dinner, however. She had eaten automatically, bites of this and that, whatever happened to be on her plate.

The gentlemen escorted the ladies from the table, for once ignoring the usual form of good port and conversation after dinner.

In the ballroom the orchestra played softly in the background. Candlelight brought out a luminescent glow to everyone below. Gowns shimmered, eyes sparkled, the scent of the white flowers wafted through the air along with the delicate lily of the valley perfume that Sibyl wore.

She stood beside her parents to welcome the guests. They came in droves. The first ball at Cranswick House in ages was not to be missed by anyone so fortunate as to receive an invitation. Rumor floated about that even the Prince Regent might drop by.

Lady Lavinia smiled serenely as though the sword and the snake had not been seen in her teacup this morning.

Sibyl danced first with her papa as was customary. Then she drifted into the arms of Lord Cranswick. From there, she was claimed by the handsome Captain Ransom.

"You look very beautiful this evening, Miss Eagleton. Mary is beside herself that she could be here just to see you shine. She has become very fond of you, but then, many of us are, you know." He tilted his head to study Sibyl's face.

There was little to do but smile at this kind remark. "Mary is a dear. I do hope she is having a lovely time."

"Your stepmother has a sharp eye. She has seen to it that Mary will not sit out one dance, and I appreciate that more than I can say."

The country dance ended at that point and Sibyl floated into the arms of the handsome and charming Duke of Devonshire. She could see where Princess Charlotte might have fancied herself to be in love with the man. Not only was he utterly delightful, but he had that magnificent annual income reputed around 70,000 pounds per year. How anyone might spend such an amount was totally beyond her, but she wondered if it might not be possible, given the chance.

A hush fell over the assembled group as the Prince Regent was announced. Sibyl went forward to drop a royal curtsy, then face her future king with what she hoped to be a calm demeanor. She endured the surveillance as best she could.

"Taking little thing, Eagleton. Cranswick, nice to see you entertaining again. Devonshire, you here? We are delighted to see you. Cards?" The two unlikely cronies set off toward the room set aside for cards, the Prince nodding agreeably to various people he was looking upon with favor at the moment.

As Sibyl breathed a sigh of relief, her stepmother patted her on the shoulder. "Well done, Sibyl." The threat of a sword and a snake seemed to recede.

It was some time after the Prince had left that Sibyl noticed the newcomer. "Mama, I was not aware that we had invited Lord Buckingham."

"La, child, I thought it necessary. He is everywhere received, and I was sure he would not come. He is very late, is he not?" Lavinia felt a chill, as though a door had been left open. She glanced about to see if one of the footmen had been busy. The rooms were not overheated, in spite of the number of people.

"Odd he does not seek us out," murmured Sibyl, curious at this peculiar development.

Lady Lavinia fixed her gaze on the gentleman, then caught sight of his companion. "Even more odd is the lady at his side. I had no idea he was close to Lady Wayford."

"I saw them riding in the park this morning. I did not wish to confront them, so I turned around to come home. You invited her as well?"

"We owed her an invitation, child. Mr. Medland has been paying her particular attentions as of late. I thought her to be an agreeable partner for him." Lavinia glanced at the tall doorway through which everyone must pass to enter the ballroom. "However, he has not come."

Sibyl realized that her mama knew nothing of her attachment to Robert, nor how she had depended on his coming this evening.

"Has he not?" she replied with credible surprise. "But then, there are so many here, how could I know if one were missing?" She welcomed Captain Ransom for his second dance, a lancers, and went off on his arm with every appearance of happiness.

Before long, Sibyl sensed something was very wrong. The manner of looks she was now getting were not the sort fondly bestowed on the belle of the evening.

Any number of people left, purposefully strolling through the door and from the house as though driven.

Bewildered, she sought out Mary. Sibyl was hurt to see her friend was about to leave as well.

Mary's dear face was calm, but her eyes were anguished. "Sibyl, 'tis most unfortunate. A terrible rumor is floating about the room. 'Tis said you were found alone in the drawing room with Robert Medland, and that he was kissing you. It is the sort of thing people love to believe is true. While he has paid you attention, it is noted that he is absent tonight. Lady Wayford allowed to Mama as it might be that he felt pressured to wed a green girl who had set out to trap him, although she denies knowledge of such. Oh, how I long to slap that smug face of hers. Such feigned innocence! To think I thought she was our friend.''

An icy calm fell over Sibyl as she turned to survey the remaining people in the room. With so many gone, it was easy to see the lady, smiling, flirting. ''How can she do such a thing while a guest in our house? 'Tis most ungracious of her.'' All the lady would have needed to do is to plant the seed. The rest would be accomplished by the gossip passing from one to another.

''How could she say such a thing? Lord Buckingham was escorting you for some time.''

''And they say that hell hath no fury like a woman scorned.'' At Mary's questioning look, Sibyl added, ''I ought not tattle, but the gentleman was going to ask my papa for my hand after the ball this evening had things not drastically altered. I turned him away in what I thought was such a clever means.'' She gave a bitter smile, then continued. ''I foolishly believed that because he was a gentleman he would not say anything. Obviously, he merely bided his time for the best moment to seek revenge upon me.''

''You mean there is a truth to the rumor?'' whispered Mary, her face revealing her sympathy for her friend.

''I shall tell you more tomorrow. I cannot bring myself to discuss it tonight. You understand?''

A warm touch of her hand was all Mary was permitted before being propelled toward the doorway. Here, she stopped. Captain Ransom engaged his mother in earnest conversation for a few minutes, then they turned about. Mary hurried to rejoin Sibyl.

''My brother impressed Mother that it is improper to listen to foolish gossip. I did not tell what I knew, for I suspect there is quite a story involved. I confess I am surprised, however.''

Belinda had been enjoying a great success all evening. Now she joined Mary and Sibyl, glancing at Lady Wayford with hostile gray eyes. ''Busy little bee, is she not? I have heard wisps of talk. I traced it back to her. What a nasty thing to do, to try to spoil a girl's come-out ball.''

''I fear the damage has been done.'' Sibyl turned her back

on the sight of Lady Wayford moving into the arms of a gentleman for a waltz.

Mary added, "Can you accept we thought her a friend? Mother always wondered why she had been invited to that breakfast when we did not socialize. I suspect we have been used."

"Clever lady," murmured Belinda, studying the woman under discussion. "I do hope that all she deserves befalls her." From the tone of her voice, one might think Belinda wished Lady Wayford well. Only the cool gray eyes revealed otherwise.

The earl presented himself to Sibyl, begging the waltz.

"Quite a few people have left, sir."

"I am aware of the rumor. I have carefully noted those who believe such a scurrilous tale." At her questioning look, he nodded slowly. "We must do nothing to reveal what we know. It is his word against ours, for you must realize Buckingham has spoken of this to another. If only Medland had come. Delia said he intended to be here. I wonder what happened? There might be a death in the family that came sooner than expected. Delia mentioned something about a cousin of her husband's that had taken ill. Medland has gone up there twice to visit the old chap."

"I hope that is the case—not that I wish anyone dead, but it would be nice to feel there is a reason other than that he detests me."

The earl gazed into her sad eyes, approving the firm control the chit had on her nerves. A good many young gals would have a severe attack of the vapors by now, at the very least.

"We cannot deny what happened, for that would merely add fuel to their fire. We suspect why Buckingham has done this, but Lady Wayford?"

"She seemed interested in you at one time, sir," Sibyl dared to say.

The earl laughed. "Perhaps. I thought to draw her away from Robert, thinking you two might be a fine match. But when you turned him down, I looked elsewhere."

"Maybe she desires revenge as well?"

"I doubt it. I had not seen that much of her, and besides, why wreak her vengeance on you? No, I believe her motive stems from another direction. She has interest in Medland, I think." He gave Sibyl a speculative look.

Sibyl gave a dry chuckle at the notion that she might deflect the interest of Robert Medland from the beautiful blond widow. "You assume too much, sir. He has been kind to me, nothing more." More's the pity, she added to herself.

It eventually came to an end: the tension, the pretense, the everlasting smiling and nodding as though a nasty little rumor was not circulating the room behind fans and in wickedly amused asides.

That most of these people were supposed to be friends mattered not at all. Friendship went sailing out to sea when it came to impropriety. If a girl behaved in an unseemly manner, so as to create gossip of the worst sort, it could haunt her to her dying day, her family as well. If Sibyl had been alone with a man, was found kissing him, and they had not been betrothed immediately, she was ruined.

"Tomorrow will be better," comforted Lady Lavinia to anyone who might listen to her. She must think. Between her and Henry, not to mention her clever brother, William, some means of extricating themselves from this horrible dilemma would be found.

Robert entered the library that was now his still scarcely able to believe all that had happened since yesterday. He stopped before the fireplace, inhaling the rich aroma of old leather-bound books, the scent of tobacco, and the very feeling of age and wealth.

Pale spring sunlight filtered through the many tall windows to cast patches of light on the Persian carpets scattered about like so many fallen leaves. He left the comfort of the fire to wander down the long room, pausing by the globe mounted in a fine oak stand. Spinning the old world around, he wondered how he was going to tell Sibyl about all this.

There were hundreds of books on the shelves set into the walls of the room, yet not one of them could adequately help explain how sorry he was to have missed her ball last night. Nor was there a book to inform him the best way to tell her what had happened.

It was all so fantastic. A distant cousin, one he had barely known, had declared him his heir. All the closer relatives had produced naught but girls. A careful search had proved Robert to be next in line.

"I wonder how the ball went?" he murmured to the painting above the far end of the room, hung between two windows that overlooked a fine expanse of parkland. The gentleman in the painting looked down with amused eyes, as though secretly laughing at Robert's dilemma.

"I'm a fool to want her when she has made it plain she desires nothing of me." The man in the painting, an ancestor, Robert supposed, didn't alter his expression. "I thought to win her with gallantry, but still she spurns me. I would that she changed her mind. If word seeped out of that farce in the drawing room, Society would destroy her."

Turning aside from the painting, Robert strolled back to the fireplace. When he returned to London his life would alter drastically. There was a residence, he'd been told, in the older part of Town, not Mayfair. Most likely he would sell it, or perhaps lease it out. Income from property was always desirable.

And then the problems would begin, the ones he disliked, for they were so full of hypocrisy. Women. With what he now possessed, he would be more sought-after than ever. He had watched the maneuvering of so many of Society's darlings as they attempted to snare the man of the moment, the one with wealth or more. And now he would be near the top of the list. Highly eligible.

There was no getting away from it, however. Unless . . . Unless he could persuade Sibyl to marry him first. Her fervent defense of him had encouraged him, leading him to believe she might accept him. At least he knew she cared about him. He need not speculate about the sincerity of her feelings. Perhaps it might turn to love some day?

"The solicitor has arrived. Would you care to see him in here, or elsewhere?" The elderly butler bowed, most likely having a difficult time with the change in authority.

"In here will be fine." Robert crossed to greet the respectable gentleman who approached.

"Milord, I have all the papers in order for you to sign. When we are finished with this work, you will be the Sixth Earl of Stafford in truth." The solicitor spread the papers out on the desk for Robert to study and ultimately sign.

Robert looked down at them and all he could see was Sibyl's dear little face as she had earnestly declared that she had no use for a peer of the realm.

What was he to do? The sixth earl sat down at the desk and began to go through the papers one at a time, signing where required, studying all he had just inherited. There were great responsibilities—a village, a church with its living, several farms, vast acreage. He would need a wife, children.

What was he to do?

11

THE LOW MOAN of the wind as it lashed at Cranswick House, tearing at the stone, tugging at the roof tiles, woke Sibyl from her uneasy slumber. Reluctant to open her eyes, she listened to the sound—mournful, melancholy. How appropriate of the weather to echo her feelings this morning.

Annie edged open the door, peeped inside, then entered with a tray of hot chocolate and fresh scones. "Oh, miss, such a storm out you never did see. Blew in 'round about an hour ago and gettin' worse by the minute, it is."

From her bed Sibyl could see low, threatening—almost black—clouds scudding across the sky. Annie lit a candle by the bed, then poured out the chocolate when Sibyl had made no move to do so. " 'Twas a grand ball last night. Lady Lavinia told us all we could sleep an hour later this morn. A kind lady she be, for sure. Cook was up betimes to bake scones, for she was certain you would welcome them on such a gray day."

"Thank you, Annie," Sibyl said faintly. "Please give Cook my thanks. They smell delicious." While Annie chattered away, the thoughts that had nagged at Sibyl most of the night could be held at bay.

Even as she sipped her chocolate, rain began to pelt against the window. Annie left the room, intent upon her duties for the day. By the time the earl and guests came downstairs, the house would look, for the most part, as though no ball had taken place the night before.

How welcome it would be not to be faced with reminders of the disaster of last evening. The only memento she had kept was the nosegay Robert had sent to her. Why she kept that, she wasn't sure. The dratted man hadn't come!

Although the prince and the Duke of Devonshire had attended the ball, the gossip most likely would have done its work by the end of this day. How the *ton* adored a good scandal.

"Dreadful out, is it not?" said Lady Lavinia from the door where she paused to inspect Sibyl. Seeing no sign of tears or tantrums, she came into the room, crossing to stare out the window at the wind-tossed trees in the square.

"The worst I can imagine. I wonder if Robert has returned? His mother was quite worried last night," Sibyl said by way of explanation for her concern. "It would be impossible to travel in this wind. I daresay the carriage would be blown right off the road."

"I have no idea. And I suspsect that if this is one of those wretched rains that batter the city for days, it will be some time before we do know."

"Will there be much damage, do you think?"

"That I could not say. I do know it will curtail the spread of the tittle-tattle a certain lady was so rude as to hint at last evening. I confess I do not know how to proceed."

"She did more than hint, I believe. Belinda said she traced the rumor back to the source, for she was so angry at such an insinuation. Lord Buckingham was at Lady Wayford's side, ma'am. How else might she have learned what happened?"

Lady Lavinia darted a vexed look at Sibyl. "Do not say those words, miss." Forgetting that at the time she had entertained other plans for Sibyl, she continued, "And when Robert offered for you, *you* refused him."

"I would rather remain a spinster than accept a husband out of mere duty on his part. Remember, he has been quite attentive to Lady Wayford until now." Sibyl drained the last of the chocolate from her cup, amazed at how hungry she had been. Didn't those ladies in travail succumb to vapors? Certainly they did not indulge a healthy appetite. She ought to be going into a green melancholy.

Lady Lavinia nodded. "It remains to be seen how he reacts to this latest development."

Sibyl set aside her tray, then slipped from her bed. She walked to her stepmama's side, placing an urgent hand on her arm. "Do not demand that Robert wed me. Remember, as your brother said to me last night, it is our word against Lord Buckingham's. People might wonder if he is being spiteful after a rejection. Could we not imply such? Surely there is something else that might be done besides forcing poor Robert to marry me against his will.''

As Lady Lavinia had not been paying attention to Robert Medland when he was around Sibyl, she could not know the state of his affection in that direction. As far as she knew, his courtesy to Sibyl might stem from other reasons. Perhaps he wished to further the earl's suit with his mother. ''You can still defend him after his failure to support you last night by being here, at your ball?''

Refusing to admit she had been thinking similar thoughts, Sibyl shook her head. ''We know not what occurred to prevent his attendance.'' A sudden notion struck her, and she gasped, ''Ma'am, you do not think he has been injured, or worse? Perhaps he is hurt, lying even now in some humble inn. I will not believe he might be dead.''

''Oh, I doubt that,'' replied her ladyship, who nevertheless began to look worried.

''Look!'' Sibyl pointed out the window, where a coach had overturned in the street, the horses in dire straits. Even as they watched, the driver and grooms fought to free the animals. ''It appears the coach was empty. What a blessing. But you see, it would not be safe to travel about in this wind. If Robert waited to return until today, he must stay where he is for the nonce.''

Lady Lavinia shivered, turning from the dreadful sight out in the square. ''Mayhap you have the right of it. Dress, and we will gather in the morning room to discuss this situation.''

Sibyl stood by the window a few moments, horrified as the coach seemed to disintegrate before her eyes. If the storm was this bad within the city, what might it be on rural roads and the river? Ships at sea could be dashed to pieces. Poorly built houses tumbled to the ground. Other carriages smashed to bits and pieces!

Reminding herself she could do nothing about the weather, she quickly dressed. Once garbed in a cheerful raspberry kerseymere, she ran a brush through her hair. She then neatly tied a cambric morning cap over her soft brown curls and went to face her relatives.

At the threshold of the morning room, she tightened the shawl she had wrapped about herself, then entered. The earl was seated by a window, her papa close by. Lady Lavinia fluttered about, waving a wisp of cambric in the air as she voiced her thoughts, which were much the same as Sibyl had heard earlier.

"What can we do? I declare we must attack this in some manner!" the lady concluded. "I refuse to acknowledge defeat."

Sibyl slipped onto a chair set a small distance from the others. She studied each face in turn, wondering what her fate was to be.

"Any thoughts about this, puss?" Lord Eagleton inquired of his subdued daughter.

"I say, face it out. Why not? If we retreat, they will believe the worst about me. If we act as though as we are in the right and Lord Buckingham a rejected suitor who is intent on causing mischief, we might succeed."

The gentlemen exchanged looks, pursing their lips as they considered Sibyl's words.

When their combined gazes fell upon her, Sibyl faced them quite bravely, hoping she could muddle through this awful mess in fair order.

"It might work," the earl said slowly. "It is possible we could even get the culprit to atone for his actions."

"Aha!" Lady Lavinia declared with eagerness. "I saw it in the tea leaves just now. There was a net in my cup again." At her brother's puzzled expression, she added, "A net means a safe ending to a period of anxiety. I do not know of anything more anxious than this."

"Amen," whispered Sibyl, mostly to herself.

Before anyone could comment on this, a footman appeared in the door. "Forgive me, milord, a man from over to the Medlands' came with a message. He said Mr. Medland did not return last night. Mrs. Medland is that worried and begs the earl's assistance."

"You cannot go out in the dreadful weather, William," Lady Lavinia asserted.

"Nonsense, Lavinia. I have a good coat. And I trust I am not the sort to melt in a bit of wet."

Biting her lower lip lest she vex her brother, Lavinia watched as he requested his greatcoat be brought, then donned the many-caped garment.

When he had left the house, she turned to her husband. "William is overly concerned for a mere friend."

"I believe he is no longer 'a mere friend,' Livvy."

Sibyl stole from the room to permit her parents a private discussion. In truth, she wanted to be alone. So, Robert had not come home last night.

She walked through the hall to the staircase, then up to her room. There she sat by the window. The wreckage of the coach had been scattered across the square. Little remained to indicate an accident occurred. Had this happened to Robert this morning when he set out to return? Where had he been? What did these mysterious trips involve? A dying relative? She wondered and worried not a little for her dear Robert. She loved him, no matter what.

The funeral must be delayed, what with the nasty rain and horrendous wind that had blasted the area for the past hours. There was no sign as to when it might let up.

Fortunately, the former earl was to be buried in the family vault in the small parish church close by. There would be no problem of waterlogged soil and grave diggers to consider.

Robert turned from one of the library windows to face the fireplace again. This was by far his favorite room in the vast house he had inherited. It wasn't merely the warmth and welcome of the leather-bound books lining the walls. Nor was it the bright colors of the rugs scattered about the room on the polished oak plank floor, like so many colorful flowers from a fanciful garden. He sensed his distant relatives had spent much time in this room. The leather-covered chair behind the desk was sadly worn. Evidence of the desk proved it had been much used for writing. Within these walls he seemed to sense a communication through the years with those in the past, unlikely as it might be.

He missed Sibyl. Oddly enough, she was the only one he wished were here, sharing in his discoveries. Her bright, inquisitive face would light up the sight of the exquisite staircase that wound up from the ground floor, spreading out like a butterfly's wings, scrolled as delicately as any of those creatures.

He wanted to show her the master suite, with the handsome

carved bed and the massive wardrobes one might get lost in quite easily. How she would chuckle over that.

And there was a plunge bath. It was located not far from the master suite. He raised a brow in speculation as he contemplated the sight of her delicate form swimming about in the warm water.

Sighing, he returned to reality and the knowledge that there was little likelihood of her ever seeing the house, let alone the plunge bath, if he couldn't persuade her to accept him in his new role. Of all the females in the world that he had to fall in love with, why did it have to be one who cared not a penny whistle for the peerage?

Sibyl paced about her room, then, tired of her own company, she ran lightly down the stairs to the morning room. Here she found her parents alone by a cozy fire, reading and embroidering. Lady Lavinia had a work candle lit, in spite of its being the middle of the afternoon. The sky remained dark with the rain lashing the house in unceasing torrents.

"How long can this continue?" Sibyl asked, wandering about the room like a lost kitten.

"Possible it may go on for a day or two, puss. You may as well settle down with a good book. Surely there is one around here that you have not read as yet?" Lord Eagleton placed his history of the Greeks on his lap while watching his only child.

"Have you read that last book of Miss Austen's, *Mansfield Park*?" inquired Lady Lavinia.

"I shall reread *Pride and Prejudice,* ma'am. I think I liked it the better." Knowing she would severely try the patience of her parents were she to continue these ambulations about the room, Sibyl found a copy of the book and settled down by the window to read.

When the earl entered later, just before dinner, he found three pairs of eyes immediately fastened upon him.

"Well?" Lavinia said, speaking for them all.

"No word from him today. I feel sure the weather is responsible and pray to God he is safe. The only thing we know for sure is that he set out for his relative's estate before dawn yesterday. I have it on authority that all roads are impassable, so even were he to send a message, there is no way it might reach his mother.''

Sibyl listened to all this, making no remark. What they must do would have to be done without the benefit of Robert's help. In a way, it was as well. If he wasn't here he could hardly be pressured into marrying her.

The thought did not entirely cheer. But then, she was the one who had insisted upon this nobility of action. She had no one to blame but herself.

When the storm at last abated the following day, the city proved to be in a sad state. Along the Thames, boats had been tossed about like matchsticks. Houses had lost roofs, rain and wind had done incredible damage all over the city. Piles of damaged carriages awaited repair. It would be difficult to get about for some days.

'' 'Tis a blessing in disguise for us, girl,'' Lady Lavinia said emphatically. ''Those tattlemongers have been kept to their hearth these past days. It is to be hoped they will find the shocking damage to the city of greater import than a supposed kiss in a drawing room.''

''Unattended.'' Sibyl smiled at her stepmother. ''Do not forget that minor detail.''

''You must go for your sitting. Sir Thomas has been made to wait upon you for too long. Fortunately, our carriage was protected in the mews and suffered no damage.''

''I hope it will not be too boring.''

''Remember, you are to look enchanted with the world. Nothing of your troubles must show on your face. If people learn you sit for Lawrence, perhaps they will think the rumor all a hum.''

Sibyl was not convinced, but went up to prepare herself for the outing. Truth to tell, even had she to sit still for hours, it would be a relief to get out of the house and away from her dear family. As much as she loved them, the continual speculation about the scandal was excessively wearing on the nerves.

With all the admonitions still ringing in her ears, Sibyl set off in the carriage with Annie happily at her side. Damage suffered from the storm could be seen all along their route. Windows were broken, trees snapped off, even an urn had been toppled from its column.

She found Sir Thomas in his studio.

"Ah, the delightful Miss Eagleton. Come, let me show you what I have in mind. Your father spoke with me last week as to what he would like to see. I quite concur."

She studied the rough sketch, amazed at the likeness when she had not even sat for the artist. "I like it very much. Papa told you about the butterflies." In the painting she would hold her net, and a butterfly would perch on one finger. It seemed unusual, not the customary painting of a young girl.

"Ah, so. We begin." That was the last coherent speech for some time. She found herself positioned, quite comfortably, against a pillar. A net was propped in her hand, lest she tire and drop it, and she tilted her head in what he claimed was a charming way. At least she thought that was what he said. It seemed that artists when deep in the process of creating were not to be understood clearly.

Just when she thought she might drop from sheer boredom, she was told, "Enough for today." He then suggested a color for her gown.

Curious about what had been done, she was disappointed to discover the painting covered with a cloth.

Sir Thomas set a time for the next sitting, then escorted her to the door. If there was any gentleman alive less flirtatious, Sibyl couldn't imagine what he was like. So much for Robert's fears.

"I am looking forward to my next subject very much. He is the new Earl of Stafford. Quite a surprise, his inheriting. It will set the *ton* on its collective ears, for certain," Sir Thomas remarked with pleasure.

Sibyl flashed him a polite smile, not caring a fig for information of a new peer. Annie opened the door and they went to leave. A gentleman stepped forward to the door.

"Good afternoon, Sibyl."

"Robert!" Sibyl breathed with delight.

"Lord Stafford!" Sir Thomas said at the same time with proper deference.

Darting a confused look at the artist, then back at Robert, Sibyl frowned, then said, "*You* are the new Earl of Stafford?"

"I am," he said with due modesty. "I have been in the country for the funeral, and to make arrangements regarding the estate. I didn't know the gentleman well, for he was a distant cousin. Due to a crop of girls, I am the one to inherit."

"I see. I wish you well, sir." She dropped a polite curtsy, then made to move on.

He reached out to stay her. "Sibyl, I am sorry to have missed your ball."

"It could not be helped, sir. Felicitations on your inheritance." Again she made to pass him, aware the artist was a fascinated listener to this stilted conversation.

"Something is wrong, else you would not treat me like this. Allow me to visit this evening? Tomorrow. When?"

"We are to attend a party at the Ransoms' home this evening. Perhaps I shall see you there?" She tried to instill a modicum of frostiness in her voice. She would not let this man close to her again—for his own protection, if nothing else.

Robert firmed his lips. Captain Ransom's family. He most certainly would make every effort to find out what was afoot in this direction.

"Good day, Lord Stafford," Sibyl said, emphasizing his title.

Robert stood where he was, watching her march down the final steps to the street, then enter the waiting carriage.

"Frustrating creatures, aren't they?" Sir Thomas said with sympathy. "Come, my lord, I wish to show you what I propose."

There was nothing to do but follow the artist inside his studio and study the blasted drawing for the painting his mother insisted be done.

The door slammed with a most satisfying thud when Sibyl let herself into the house, much to Annie's horror, for she had a strict sense of what was proper.

After handing her pelisse to the maid along with the modish bonnet that had pleased her several hours ago, Sibyl stalked to the morning room where she expected to find her stepmother.

"Well? How did the sitting go, love? Tedious, I expect."

Lady Lavinia looked up from the copy of a fashion journal she perused.

"I saw Robert, Mama."

"Robert? I declare, so he returned at long last. Delia will be so relieved. She has been worried to death."

"There was a death, actually." Sibyl smiled grimly at her stepmother's look of shock. "Our Robert is now the Earl of Stafford. What think you of that piece of news!"

"Dear me," Lady Lavinia replied faintly.

"I agree completely. Now what do we do? You can scarcely importune the new earl to wed your little scamp of a step-daughter, can you?" Sibyl's voice revealed her wonder and hurt, the fears she felt that she would be cut from Society and, especially, Robert.

"Sibyl, that is no way to speak."

"I fear that pretty shyness I possessed when we were in Mablethorpe has disappeared. I wish we had never come to the city. Although I would not have married Albert Norton. Ever!" Sibyl declared in a ringing voice.

"We did not intend such, love," my lady confessed ruefully.

"Oh!" wailed the now exasperated young woman. Sibyl gave Lady Lavinia an anguished look, then fled the room. In moments she reached the sanctuary of her bedroom where she crossed to the window. Not far from here Robert sat in the same studio, having his portrait done by the same artist. Would anyone make something of that as well?

How she hated those gossiping tongues. Oh, she knew a great deal of the trouble was her own fault. As Papa had said, she ought to have consulted him when she sought to discourage Lord Buckingham. Why hadn't Robert said something then? He couldn't possibly have wanted the inevitable results were they discovered. Could he?

With that intriguing idea spinning about in her brain, Sibyl changed her clothes, then went down to dinner in a better frame of mind.

"Very pretty, puss," Lord Eagleton declared with an approving eye on his daughter as they waited for the others.

"Thank you, Papa. I felt a cheerful color would be the thing after all this nasty weather we have had." She smoothed out the cherry-pink sarcenet gown with a gloved hand.

"You are off to the Ransoms' this evening?" queried the earl, with a watchful eye on Sibyl as he spoke.

"Yes, we are. Mama has come to like Mary's mama very well. She stayed to lend support on the night of the ball, as well," Sibyl reminded him.

"Captain Ransom seems a fine young man," Lord Eagleton said. "I have spoken with several men at the War Office, and they indicate he has an excellent future. Due for a promotion to the rank of major any day now." He studied her suddenly rosy face with shrewd eyes. "That mean anything to you?"

"He is naught but a friend, Papa. A very kind friend."

"You said the same thing about Robert Medland, as I recall. I imagine you have changed your views about that young man, even if he has inherited a title. As I recall, you were never one to be impressed by that sort of thing."

"Oh, no, that is not true at all," Sibyl declared earnestly. "He is an honorable man, genuine and kind, indeed. I meant it when I said you could find no one who is more straight-arrow, Papa. I may have come to a sad end as far as he is concerned, but that does not lessen my respect for him in any way."

"And his title?"

What Sibyl's opinion was of Lord Stafford's new title was not to be known, for just outside in the entry hall Lady Lavinia could be heard crying with delight.

"Robert, you naughty boy. Why didn't you warn us? I vow, 'tis the outside of enough to learn of your elevation to the peerage in such a shocking manner. Now, do you stay with us to dinner that we may hear all about it."

"I should be most pleased. With my mother here, our house is sadly empty."

"I imagine it will not remain that way for long."

Sibyl winced at the arch tone of her ladyship's voice. She could well imagine how Robert would enjoy that particular teasing. She only hoped that Robert had not overheard the conversation between her and her papa. They had made no attempt to keep their voices down. Mrs. Medland had arrived earlier, rushing up the stairs to confer with Lady Lavinia. Sibyl had felt safe in speaking out as she had, with no thought of a listener in mind.

"Good evening, sir, Miss Eagleton."

"Lord Stafford," murmured Sibyl as she curtsied, trying to study his face. He did not look to have heard. She doubted if he had.

Dinner proceeded most agreeably. Lord Cranswick and Mrs. Medland, Lord Eagleton and Lady Lavinia, and the new earl chatted with great enthusiasm over his change in fortune.

Sibyl listened, for the most part. It was amazing how fascinating boiled cod and potatoes, potted hare, and fricassee of veal could be. The surreptitious looks she darted at Robert seemed to reveal a subtle alteration in him. Had he become taller of a sudden? There was a new air of authority about him she could not help but admire. Indeed, he commanded the eye.

Just wait until the young ladies of the *ton* found out about his elevation. All those who had scorned a mere mister would eagerly seek out an earl. How sad for Robert. He deserved far better than that. Would he be able to find happiness? Or true love? Of course Lady Wayford had been in his pocket for some time. She would be pleased. An earl ranked higher than a viscount.

"Sibyl?" Lady Lavinia's voice intruded on the mental wanderings. "Do finish, love. We must be on our way."

Sibyl placed her crumpled napkin by her plate, and rose from the table. "I am sorry, Mama. Woolgathering is ever a besetting sin for me."

The ladies left the table, allowing the gentlemen to enjoy a visit over their port. Sibyl had a good notion that her papa and uncle would be quizzing Robert about his new estate and the prospects ahead of him. How she wished she might listen to that conversation.

Lady Lavinia had other ideas. "Sibyl, do play for us while we wait upon the men. Really," she exclaimed in an aside to Delia, "I do not know why the men persist in that annoying habit of after-dinner port."

"I suspect they enjoy the respite from our genteel conversation, my dear," Delia replied, laughing at the disdainful sniff from her friend.

When the men at last joined the ladies, Sibyl was conscious of a charged atmosphere among them. What had happened during that talk? They acted like little boys with a secret they were bursting to tell, but wouldn't, just to tease one.

"Robert is coming with us, my dear. We shall all go together," said Lord Cranswick to his sister.

"And I have a request to make," Robert added. "If you don't mind, I would rather hold back the news regarding my title, if you please."

"Doesn't take much to fathom your reason for that, my boy," Lord Eagleton said jovially. "Out to circumvent the mamas, eh?"

Robert gave him a rueful grin, nodding his agreement.

Sibyl said nothing to this, but wondered how long Robert thought to conceal his new position in Society. Sir Thomas knew about it. Most likely he would be only too delighted to puff off his new client to others of the *ton,* thus allowing the news to spread. The evening would tell.

They settled in the coach, with Robert regaling them with news of the damage the storm had wreaked upon the countryside between his new estate south of Cambridge and London.

"Terrible, terrible," Lord Eagleton murmured, his distress amplified by worry about his home in Mablethorpe. What would conditions be there?

At the Ransoms' they were greeted by the family with warm regard, Robert welcomed nicely as well. Mrs. Ransom well recalled that Robert had escorted her little Mary about town that one day.

"Well, well," offered young Captain Ransom with a hearty manner, "good to see you, Medland. Have an interesting trip?"

Omitting the most interesting detail of his journey, Robert enthralled a growing cluster of listeners about the horrors of the storm.

Lord Eagleton watched for a moment, then pulled Sibyl aside, whispering, "Robert had offered again, puss."

12

SURE THAT IF she looked at Robert her face would reveal every emotion flitting through her mind, Sibyl studied her gloved hands as though they were the most fascinating things in the room. "But, why, Papa?"

"What sort of a question is that, puss? He is a man of honor. His mother has told him of the rumors started at the ball. He seeks to do the right thing." Lord Eagleton glanced at Mrs. Medland, then continued, "She also informed him of the role played by the elegant widow."

"Never say she gossiped about Lady Wayford!" Sibyl raised her head to cast a surprised look at Mrs. Medland. What purpose did her tattling serve, unless it was to make Robert come to the widow's defense? There was nothing like an accusation to bring a man around to supporting that very person.

"Well," Lord Eagleton hedged, "he needed to know the truth. Now, behave yourself." With that admonition he took himself off to the card table.

Sibyl turned to watch her friends.

"How lovely it is now that the storm has passed and the weather is nice once again," Mary declared in happy tones. "I think we ought to celebrate."

Belinda clasped her hands with enthusiasm. Turning to the young man at her side, she chuckled, adding, "What about it, Mr. Hadgley? Should we contemplate a party of some sort? What form do you think it ought to take?"

Looking startled, as though no one ever consulted him, on anything, Terence Hadgley puffed out his chest a bit, then pronounced, "A picnic, by Jove. Venture into the verdure of Richmond Park." When the others laughed, he preened, aware that he had made a small sally, and pleased with Miss Belinda Valler for making it possible.

Sibyl rather liked Mr. Hadgley, for he was a slim, unpretentious man of means. Nicely tall, having kind blue eyes and light brown hair with elegant side whiskers, he was modish without being extreme. But she could have throttled him for proposing a picnic for the group. She could see at a glance that all who were gathered in that small discussion were to be involved. Perhaps it did not include her, as she still stood apart?

Robert disabused her of that nonsense immediately. "And Miss Eagleton can add a few more butterflies to her collection. I expect it hasn't grown in the least while the weather has been so nasty. We must remedy that situation at once." He stepped to her side, drawing her into the circle of young people with an adroitness worthy of an ambassador. Sibyl found her arm tucked next to his side like she had suddeny become attached to him.

There was nothing to do but accede with grace. "I think it would be lovely."

"I have begun collecting wildflowers to press," Belinda said to Mr. Hadgley, obviously enjoying the delight of that young man at being the center of everyone's attention. "They make far better pictures than my poor watercolors ever did."

Charlie had switched interest from Miss Eagleton to Miss Valler with the fickleness of a town beau. Looking annoyed that such an unassuming person should capture the challenging Miss Valler, Captain Ransom eased into the threesome to inquire, "What? You do not paint, Miss Valler? Most young ladies attempted such."

"Actually, I do not, but Mary does." The glance she gave him was unusually flirtatious for Belinda. "Although I confess I adore a trip to the country to collect wildflowers, I find it awkward to manage by myself."

Casting a triumphant look at Terence Hadgley, Charlie smiled at Miss Valler. "I shall deem it a pleasure to help you. Think of me as your personal assistant, Miss Valler?"

Her wry smile and the amused gleam in her cool gray eyes revealed she was aware of his little ploy. "Captain?"

"Perhaps we should plan in greater detail?" He offered her his arm, which Belinda appeared to accept with quiet pleasure.

The two strolled off deep in discussion of whether a press

was absolutely necessary, and what sort of paper she used for mounting, and what she intended to bring along.

Mr. Hadgley accepted the departure of Miss Valler philosophically, for truth to tell, he found extremely clever girls intimidating. Now, Miss Mary Ransom was quite a different matter. A cozy, comfortable girl with a handsome dowry, she made a chap feel masterful and top-of-the-trees.

"Miss Ransom, what does a young lady require in the way of supplies and comforts while painting? A special pillow perhaps?" He drew her to a chair, where she proceeded to enchant him with a brief list, then flatter him by listening avidly to every word he had to say.

"Neatly done, Lord Stafford," Sibyl murmured. "Although for what purpose. I cannot imagine."

"Fie on you, Sibyl. Can you not accept that it would be enjoyable for a group of people to join together for a picnic in the country? A perfectly innocent diversion?"

"Actually, I have not been to Richmond. Is it really as pretty as they say it is? And shall I find different butterflies there?" She decided she was not the person to judge how innocent a picnic might be.

"There are rolling green hills for Miss Ransom to paint and sufficient wildflowers to satisfy Miss Valler, not to mention provide attractions for numerous butterflies. I believe you shall all find it immensely pleasing."

Sibyl, in fact, found the entire notion disquieting. Never before had Mr. Medland manipulated people and events so adroitly. Was this a new side of him? Or had becoming an earl brought latent characteristics to the fore? She gave him a puzzled look. How frustrating to have it returned by a slightly sleepy and highly amused smile from him.

"We shall see, Mr. Medland." She had stressed his name only a little, but enough to let him think twice about teasing her any more this evening.

Lord Cranswick looked up from his game of whist to watch the young people for a few moments. His gaze then wandered to meet that of his brother-in-law. Their wordless communication intrigued the ladies, but no amount of nudging could satisfy their curiosity.

The picnic was set for two days hence, provided the weather continued to hold. Belinda and Mary each offered to contribute tasty treats, but the new (and secret) earl insisted this was to be his surprise.

Sibyl found the remainder of the evening to be vastly confusing. Her papa had whispered that Robert had again offered for her hand, but now Robert acted as though nary a word had been said. And his character had changed, she was sure of it. The mild-mannered, polite man still existed, but new, disturbing traits had appeared. The air of command might be subtle, but she suspected even the others felt it. Otherwise, why would they fall in with every one of his suggestions and plans without so much as a quibble?

He treated her with exquisite politeness that she could not fault. Yet, here too she found a faint difference. There now was a sureness of manner, a strong confidence she might admire, but sensed somehow intimidating. Robert had changed.

"The country will be a lovely change for you, my dear. How thoughtful of Robert to remember you have been cooped up in Town all these weeks with little opportunity to hunt for your butterflies." Lady Lavinia wrinkled her brow at those last words. She still found it difficult to understand why Sibyl had taken to butterfly collecting.

Sibyl studied her reflection in her looking glass, not satisfied with what she saw, yet not knowing what to alter. "Do I look acceptable, Mama?"

"Cornflower blue muslin is quite nice with your eyes, and those pretty ruffles around your neck are vastly becoming. I adore those loose sleeves, so very graceful, love." Lady Lavinia walked around to study her stepdaughter with a shrewd eye. "That dark blue spencer is just the touch. You had best take a shawl along, just in case the wind turns chilly. Do you have a parasol?"

"Yes, Mama." Sibyl gathered a soft white *cashmere de laine* shawl from a drawer, picked up a white parasol, then inspected her neat blue kid walking boots before leaving her room to walk down the stairs. Lady Lavinia trailed behind her, offering suggestions as they went.

"Do not forget your net and collecting box. And please do not even think of running after those creatures. What if someone should see you?" Lady Lavinia made her horror of her step-daughter's behaving in such an unseemly manner quite clear.

"They seldom sit still to wait for one to catch them, you know," Sibyl replied with a deal of amusement.

Lord Stafford was waiting in the morning room, Bentley informed her ladyship and Sibyl as they reached the ground floor.

"Ah, good morning ladies. You are prompt, Sibyl. I like that in women, although most of them seem to believe men prefer otherwise. We had best be on our way. Captain Ransom, Hadgley, and I discussed the arrangements, and we decided the best thing for all was to take three carriages. With the paraphernalia each lady requires, and having our grooms along to manage things, it seems the most practical." He tucked Sibyl's hand next to him in that odiously protective way he had, then turned to Lady Lavinia. "We shall have a lovely day, I'm sure. I will bring Sibyl back to you at a decent hour."

Lavinia fluttered along behind the two young people, her white draperies floating around her, and the lappets on her morning cap flapping in the breeze she created as she walked. "I am sure, dear boy. Watch out for cutthroats and footpads."

The door closed behind them and her further admonitions were cut off in midstream. "She is a dear lady, if a bit of a worrier," Sibyl said in apology.

"And you are especially precious to her as you are a responsibility given to her by her dear husband." He paid attention to his matched grays as the curricle set off along the street. Traffic was especially heavy this morning, what with carts bringing supplies to the city for the reconstruction of the damaged buildings.

Sibyl hadn't thought of her stepmother in that light and she mused over his words for a few minutes. "Perhaps you have the right of it. I could wish she would forget all this business about finding me a husband."

His startled glance gave her amusement. Not for one minute was she going to let him think that she had been told of his offer, or was encouraging it. "You have no wish to be wed? Forgive me, but I was under the impression that was the reason for your coming to London.'' His smile toook away any sting his words might have.

"That was my parents' reason. I wanted to remain at home. I would have, too, had not a perfectly horrid neighbor boy declared his intention of marrying me. He fancies himself irresistible, you see.''

"I do see.'' Robert chuckled in that endearing way he had.

Sibyl tried to dislike him and found it impossible. "So, I came under duress.''

"And it has been so very difficult for you?'' He flicked a glance at her before returning his concentration to the road ahead.

She remembered her ball and the nasty rumor circulated by Lady Wayford. The only source for the story was Lord Buckingham, even though he had apparently not prated it about. He had been at Lady Wayford's side, and that was quite enough. How fortunate the storm had provided a drastic change of topic. However, she was not confident that she was out of the woods yet. It remained to be seen how the coming week went, whether invitations continued to arrive at Cranswick House.

"There have been moments. Had you been at my ball you might understand better,'' she said before recalling that his mother supposedly had told him all.

"Ah, yes, your ball,'' he said slowly. "I was sorry not to be there. As you now know, I had obligations.''

"What is your new home like? North and east of here, I recollect you saying.''

"It sits on a hill, rather like a small castle. There is no moat, but you can see a slight depression. My favorite room is the library, for it is full of atmosphere—old books, aged leather and tobacco scent, colorful rugs. The kind of a place to appeal to a man.''

Sibyl could not help but wonder why such a cozy place was to be confined to a man, but made no comment on that. "And?''

"There is a plunge bath not far from the master suite. Apparently the earl who added it on liked to swim about in privacy at any time of the year. Also, he seemed to believe that a husband and wife should share a bed all the time, for there are dressing rooms to either side. His and hers, so to speak.''

He bent his head to see what reaction Sibyl had to these words, wondering if she understood the implications.

"On a hill? And like a small castle?" she repeated. Really, it was too much that Robert was not only true-blue, but now owned a castle on a hill. Without realizing she spoke, Sibyl softly said, "I have always dreamed of living in a castle on a hill. I expect there are masses of daffodils in the spring as well."

Wisely, Robert made no reply to this musing, tucking the information in the back of his mind.

The others had arrived at the chosen site just before Robert drew up his carriage. They stood chatting with evident pleasure in the day.

Around them the park spread out in green splendor, majestic trees dotting the landscape with artistic arrangement. Sibyl wondered if someone like the esteemed Capability Brown had come to Richmond to design the landscape, but decided not to inquire, lest she be thought silly.

"They seem in good cheer," Robert commented as he handed the reins to his groom, then prepared to assist Sibyl from the carriage.

"Mary is all that is amiable. Belinda is nice, too, though a bit more difficult to know."

"People are not always what they seem, are they?"

"No," she concurred, thinking Robert topped her list of unfathomable people at the moment.

Belinda set out to look for wildflowers with Captain Ransom strolling at her side. He carried sheets of blotting paper in hand and a happy look spread across his face as he watched Miss Valler's delight at finding some particularly fine flowers.

Not far away, Mary tromped along until she found an admirable scene to paint, then settled down upon the stack of pillows Terence set out for her. He went out to fetch a jar of water, returning with a handful of pretty wildflowers stuck in the jar. Then he adjusted her parasol, an exceptionally large white one, so as to offer the best shade.

He waved to where Sibyl and Robert stood with the collecting box and net. "Off to nab some rare ones?" His chuckle was not malicious, but nevertheless Sibyl wished they might find something worthwhile.

"Just you wait. We shall endeavor to outdo you all." Robert

offered his arm, but Sibyl pretended not to see it. She was confused, uncertain with this new, more polished man. He wasn't the same, and she wasn't sure she liked all the changes. The closer she came to him, the more difficult it became to maintain rationality.

"I think I see one over there," Robert said, pointing to a flutter of yellow. "Come with me, and quickly."

Lady Lavinia invited Lord Buckingham to join her on the sofa, exclaiming how much she admired his waistcoat. "How I wish all young men might dress with your taste, dear sir."

The viscount preened in the knowledge that he was without peer in his discernment. "How may I serve you, my lady?"

Lady Lavinia chatted all around the subject she wished to discuss, pouring the butter boat over Buckingham's head with effective results. He was given to think he had been the victim of a manipulating woman (Lady Wayford), and owed poor Sibyl his attentions once again, if for no other reason than to atone for the gossip that might have resulted in the scandalous cat-lap the lady had spread.

"You, dear sir, have been a victim, as has my poor little Sibyl. She is helpless unless you come to her aid. Gallant knight that you are, I know that you can spare a bit of your valuable time to righting this wrong. After all, she is highly worthy of someone of your understanding. What a pity if she should turn to someone inferior."

His look of pure horror was almost comical, she decided. Really, the man was a cockscomb, so vain and uppish. No wonder Sibyl opposed marriage to the man. Yet, he ought to redeem himself and that Wayford chit.

"What do you propose, ma'am? I fail to see what I can do at this point. She disgraced herself, you know." Buckingham looked down his aristocratic nose, while seeming to accept the idea that he must resign himself to atoning for his actions. Why he must atone and not Medland it had apparently not occurred to him to wonder.

"I believe she was merely testing you. She wanted to be rescued from his clutches, don't you see?"

"Frankly, the notion had not suggested itself to me at all," he said with a frostiness in his voice.

"It helps to know how a young gel's mind works. Will you do it?" Then, dumping on the last of the butter, she added, "Think on how grateful such a pretty little thing will be when she again may know the bliss of your company. Not many men have what you possess, my lord." Lady Lavinia gave him a knowing look, then waited for him to consider her suggestion.

She didn't make the mistake of thinking him stupid. He might be slow, but never dull-witted. However, she had found a hammer in her teacup this morning. It meant there was work, perhaps unpleasant business, to be done, but Lavinia would need to be ruthless to achieve her aim. She had sent round a note to Buckingham shortly after.

If ruthlessness was demanded to get her girl a proper husband, the one Sibyl clearly desired whether she knew it or not, Lavinia had to take the reins in her hands. Life was becoming a deal too complicated. Delia was little or no help. She had fallen helplessly in love with William and that matter would have to be resolved just as soon as Sibyl was fired off. Lady Lavinia fanned herself, wondering how these dear, but indecisive, women would manage without her aid.

"What would be the best way to achieve this, dear ma'am?" The look Buckingham bestowed on Lady Lavinia made her wonder if he had cottoned to her plan. He appeared too canny by far. Then, it was possible he merely looked his normal devious self.

"Of course you know best how to appeal to a woman of taste, but I should think that taking an interest in her little diversion might do the trick," Lavinia said in an innocent manner. "The trouble is, she has hunted the local area for butterflies. Such noble, beautiful creatures. They are so exquisite, like rare gems. If only she might be able to journey to the coast, I am sure there must be varieties there not to be found in the city. Of course, I do not pretend to have the brains of a man, but I suspect Mr. Medland might take exception to anyone's removing Sibyl by carriage. What a pity there is not another way. Boat, for example. Something different to appeal to her curiosity, don't you know?"

"Boat?" This word was followed by a long silence.

Lady Lavinia waited patiently, knowing some things took

longer than others. She could only hope he didn't see the holes in her plan.

"There is a steam packet boat now sailing from London to Gravesend. I believe it stops somewhere along the way. We need not travel the entire distance, surely there would be butterflies in Greenwich, say?"

"Admirable, my lord. How wonderful is the working of a first-class mind," Lady Lavinia exclaimed with surprise. She had not thought Buckingham to be so inventive. "I suggest you proceed with your arrangements and let me know how it goes. I shall do my part, you may be sure." What her part was to be, precisely, was not explained.

He left not long after that. Lady Lavinia suspected he did not quite understand why he was involved in all of this. It might be that he felt Sibyl would do him credit. Perhaps his conscience nagged at him a little. No matter what it was, Lavinia was pleased. At least, she hoped her scheme would go well. It all depended on how each person reacted. People were so apt to do unpredictable things when faced with a crisis. She would need to keep her wits about her.

"Take care," Robert cautioned as Sibyl, net in hand, went running after a large pretty blue butterfly. She was extremely graceful. Her blue muslin gown was the same color as the butterfly, making a pretty picture, indeed. How nice it would be to capture her like this, carefree and happy in the early summer sunshine. He was no artist, but he hoped that Lawrence fellow could manage to put some of this same spirit into that painting.

He quite definitely intended that painting to hang at Stafford Hall. He rather thought the drawing room would be the most likely spot for it. The high dome allowed light to flood the interior, making it a cheerful place in which to gather. Yes, he could see Sibyl there. She would enjoy the gardens at Stafford as well. Bound to be untold butterflies. Perhaps she might take up another diversion, one involving children.

Just then, Sibyl gave a little scream as she lost her balance and went sliding on the grass to the bottom of the little hill where she had chased the butterfly. It had eluded her. She now had grass stains totally covering her, er, backside, but no butterfly.

Hard-pressed not to give in to whoops of laughter at the sight of that chagrined face staring up from beneath her bonnet, just daring him to be amused at her plight, Robert donned a suitably sympathetic mien as he hurried down the hill to her side. "Poor love, what a tumble you took. Any broken bones? Torn flounces?"

"If you so much as snicker at me I shall do you great violence, Robert Medland. Earl or no earl!"

He smiled. "Oh? What is my punishment to be, my love?"

"I am not your love, you great rudesby," she snapped while trying to get up in spite of her foot's being caught in the hem of her dress.

"Ah, I rather believe you are, more's the pity. You are not very cooperative. Now if Lady Wayford were here, she would invite me to assist her."

Taking a deep breath, Sibyl counted to ten, then sweetly replied. "Assist me. Please?"

Robert glanced over to where Terence sat at the side of Mary Ransom, taking no notice of anyone else. In the distance Belinda and the captain were involved in setting wildflowers in precise angles on the blotting paper prior to tightening the small clamps of her portable press.

"With pleasure, my little love."

"I do not understand you in the least. And they say that ladies are difficult to comrpehend," Sibyl complained.

Robert did not reply; he bent over to help her to her feet. He set her firmly on the ground, then dusted off the back of her skirt, observing that the grass stains were most likely permanent. "Pity about your gown; it was such a pretty thing."

She glanced behind her, but was unable to see what it was that caused his concern. "What is it?"

Now he had stepped closer. "Grass." He tilted her chin, and after a penetrating look in her soft blue eyes, took a leisurely kiss that would have scandalized anyone who had seen the two of them. The grooms were on the far side of the hill, so they didn't see. The other couples were too involved with their own interests to even care where Robert and Sibyl were. But Sibyl knew.

For one delicious minute she allowed that kiss to continue. A minute is a long time when you are experiencing every sensation possible to a loving heart. There were little tingles shooting up and down her spine, while a strange desire to plaster herself against that sturdy masculine form so nicely close to her grew and grew. Her arms slid about him, thoroughly relishing the feel of him.

"Robert!" She gasped, then blushed a lovely pink with the enormity of her feelings. She did love him, yet he mentioned that odious Lady Wayford to her. What was a girl to do? Sibyl gave him an anguished look, then marched off to find the picnic hampers, feeling torn this way and that.

"Now what?" Robert wondered aloud. "Blast and damnation, what is going on in that peculiar little mind?"

Sibyl fumed silently to herself. He said she was his little love, but he did not say a word about loving her. In her viewpoint there was a vast difference between the two. So he had caught her out, knew she fancied him. Stupid of her to be so open, revealing. He didn't let on a thing. Only his eyes occasionally told her what was in his mind. And she hadn't been looking at his eyes just now.

"Shall we enjoy this marvelous repast everyone?" Sibyl caroled across the grassy parkland.

"Oh, I say, I'm dashed hungry." Terence carried a watercolor painting carefully in both hands, while Mary walked at his side, her face wreathed in smiles at this beautiful, beautiful day.

Charlie assisted Belinda to the area where a cloth had been spread out. He gingerly placed the small portable flower press in their carriage, then returned to offer his lady a selection of food from the array Sibyl was placing on the cloth.

If anyone noticed the constraint between Sibyl and Robert, there was no indication of it. But then, Sibyl reflected, Mary flirted with that nice Terence Hadgley to the exclusion of an awareness of the time of day.

Even Belinda Valler seemed caught in the charm exuded by the dashing Captain Ransom. Oddly enough, he appeared to be as taken with her as Terence was with the comfortable Mary.

Yet they all seemed aware of Robert Medland. Sibyl suspected that they sensed the change in him. He had always been self-confident, well-mannered, and considerate, while yet modest. Now there was something additional, his air of self-control, a certain toughness bordering on a core of steel. Somehow she had the feeling that were he to take a notion to walk off with her, he would, and no apology, either.

That was a bit frightening. Yet she absolutely refused to permit him to know she was intimidated by this new power he radiated. Once, she might have fled. Now, she was going to fight. Somehow. Only how did one fight the man one loved to distraction? How might she contrive to get him to declare not only for her hand but for her heart?

For she would settle for no less than his love.

"What a wonderful day this has been. I say three cheers for Mr. Medland." Mary raised a glass of lemonade in the air in a salute.

"Three cheers," they agreed, followed by happy shouts.

Unassuming as always, Robert bowed slightly, then grinned, totally destroying any aloofness he might have had.

Sibyl wondered if he would tell them of his newly aquired title now, and waited. She caught his gaze, and gave him a quizzical look. Mr. Lawrence wouldn't keep the news forever.

Robert shook his head ever so slightly in reply. He knew what she asked with those pretty blue eyes of hers. The time was not yet quite right. When he had convinced Sibyl that it was as necessary to marry him as to breathe, then he would tell the world. Not until then. At least, he amended, not unless it was absolutely necessary.

Sibyl shivered at the look Robert gave her. Whatever was going on in his mind, that he should have such a . . . a predatory expression?

13

WHEN SIBYL JOINED her stepmother in the morning room, it was with a great deal of trepidation. Could the lady possibly detect the lingering effects of that kiss in the meadow? Neither Mary nor Belinda had said a word, or for that matter, even looked askance when Robert tended to Sibyl with polite courtesy.

Of course, he *had* behaved with an odiously distant manner. How off-putting! And he had that nasty little chuckle when Mary had exclaimed in horror over the grass stains on Sibyl's blue muslin. Sibyl had been hard-put to explain that small matter. Once home, that blue muslin had been hastily removed, chucked in the corner of her wardrobe, and another blue gown whisked over her head.

"Did you have a nice afternoon, ma'am? The picnic went prodigiously well. I found several new butterflies. Lord Stafford provided an excellent repast."

"What happened to your blue muslin?"

Sibyl blessed Lady Lavinia's excellent memory. "I slipped on some long grass. The gown is horridly stained—beyond redemption, I fear." Hurrying over that bit of information, Sibyl rushed on. "Mary painted a lovely watercolor of the park view. She really is most talented. Belinda found a great number of wildflowers, enough to make several of her exquisite flower pictures. Her taste is so nice, the results are far above the average."

"As long as you have not placed yourself beyond redemption with hoydenish behavior. Nothing so turns away a gentleman's attention as improper conduct."

"What makes you imagine that Lord Stafford, once our Robert, cares the least for my conduct or want of same?" Sibyl strolled close to the window, catching up the knotted fringe of the drapery to fiddle with it, thus avoiding her stepmother's intent gaze.

"Nothing is impossible. Come, have a cup of tea with me. I would read your fortune today."

With obvious reluctance, for she was not certain she wished to have her fortune read, Sibyl sank down upon the nearest chair, then watched as her stepmama poured out a steaming cup of tea from the pot. It had been sitting beneath the tea cozy Lady Lavinia had knitted to insure proper warmth. When Sibyl peered into her cup, she noted a quantity of leaves shifting about on the bottom. How disgusting.

Catching sight of her stepmother's expectant face, Sibyl obediently drank up her tea, taking care to keep those dratted leaves from her mouth, then handed the cup over to her.

After following the proper ritual, Lavinia studied the dregs of tea in the cup. In a few moments, she looked up at Sibyl, her face a reflection of her distress.

Alarmed, Sibyl reached out one hand, exclaiming, "What is it, dear, ma'am? Something terrible, I'll warrant. Tell me at once! No need to wrap it in clean linen."

Dropping her gaze to the cup, Lavinia hemmed and hawed a few moments, then shrugged. "To be forewarned is to be forearmed, they say. I fear you have a false love. It is quite clear; there is no mistake. However, a true love is in the distance, if you will but have patience."

"A false love?" Sibyl echoed, her voice a thread of sound. The image of Robert as he bent to pull her to her feet, draw her into his arms, and that dear face as it descended toward hers, all returned with startling clarity. As did the kiss. She was shaken to her innermost self. Robert false? How utterly, utterly dreadful!

"I am sorry, my dear. I expect you had hopes?"

Collecting her wits, Sibyl strove to present a calm demeanor. "Of course, ma'am, what young lady does not? It is not pleasant to contemplate falseness in anyone, particularly someone you love."

Lavinia bent her head to study the cup again before refilling it with tea. She handed the hot beverage to Sibyl. "I suspect you need a bit more of this to restore your nerves. Drink, you will feel better soon."

A grateful Sibyl accepted the cup and drained the contents, then rose from the chair where she had perched like a bird about to take flight. "I had best put away my things. The butterflies must be mounted properly," she explained in a dull voice.

"Oh, I had a visitor this afternoon. Lord Buckingham came to call. He was sorry to have missed you. He wishes to apologize for what happened the night of the ball. It seems Lady Wayford extracted the information about his break with you by rather unscrupulous means. I would not be surprised in the least did she coerce him. At any rate, I trust you will give him an opportunity to atone. He seemed most anxious to see you." Lady Lavinia sat very still while she viewed her stepdaughter with curious eyes.

Now, Sibyl would have rejected any sight of Lord Buckingham out of hand had she not just heard of false love. That had shaken her so badly that all the memories of the evening of her ball, the horrid way Lord Buckingham tended to self-interest, all faded from her mind.

"How . . . how nice." Sibyl stared out of the window with dull eyes, seeing again the face of, not Lord Buckingham, but Robert, her love—her false love, if the tea leaves were correct. And they always had been in the past.

Well, Robert could just keep that wicked chuckle and those twinkling eyes to himself. Or perhaps share them with Lady Wayford. It seemed the two deserved each other.

"I shall be pleased to see Lord Buckingham in the event he calls." That her voice had as much enthusiasm as one presented with a dead frog did not seem to matter to her listener.

"Excellent, my dear. I am sure this will all work out for the best. Just trust me."

"Most assuredly, ma'am. Now if you will excuse me?"

"Go." Lady Lavinia made shooing motions with her hands, and shortly she was alone in the morning room. The reflective expression on her face was not that of a dissembler or a liar, as it well could have been, given the cunning way she had managed the reading. Rather, it was a fond, wistful look of caring and hope.

Upstairs in her room, Sibyl set her collecting box on a small table near the window, then sat down to place her new butterflies in the display box. Robert had bought this for her, she reflected. And the book. And the killing bottle, as well. He had encouraged her, laughed with her, and kissed her. What had it accomplished but heartache? When she had really needed him, he had not been there. Oh, she was aware he had an excellent excuse. Between death and the weather, there could be no better. But he had been gone, and how she had missed him.

Why had Papa said that Robert had offered for her hand again? That truly puzzled her. Outside of that wicked kiss, he certainly had not displayed the least intent of wedding her. Not a word. And that hurt. Kisses meant precious little unless they were accompanied by the right words. She would like to hear words of love. It was an admission wrung from her honest heart with reluctance. Those words from Robert would mean far more than any declaration from anyone else.

Although it was enough to bring on a fit of the dismals, she was no peagoose. Best to get on with her life. Tomorrow she would again visit Sir Thomas for another sitting, then perhaps do a bit of shopping for a new gown. Not blue muslin with flounces, she decided. Perhaps lilac, for a lost love.

The following afternoon found Sibyl patiently sitting for Sir Thomas, trying valiantly to capture the expression of joy and happiness he seemed determined to fix on canvas. She wore a cream and rose silk sarcenet gown—and an excessively wistful expression.

"Think of the one you love most, Miss Eagleton. Surely there is someone?" he teased.

That only produced a woeful face bordering on tears. The artist tried a different approach. "Think of a place where you are happy, or perhaps a dream you hold dear?"

That request brought to mind the castle, a precious castle with a hint of a moat, that perched upon a not-too-high hill somewhere north and east of London.

"Miss Eagleton," the artist coaxed, "there must be something which gives you joy."

She thought of her dear family, her closest friends, and with that Sir Thomas had to be satisfied.

When it came time to depart, she went behind a screen where

Annie waited to help her into the plain gown she had worn to the studio. She heard a door open, footsteps, and she froze. But it was only a messenger.

"Hmm. Miss Eagleton, please forgive me, this note requires an immediate reply. When you are restored, you may leave by that door close to you. That way you avoid seeing my next client. So often, that is what people wish."

Sir Thomas had not forgotten that initial meeting when the very air seemed to vibrate between Miss Eagleton and Lord Stafford. He wanted to avoid any unpleasantness.

"Th-thank you, sir." She made haste, for she suspected that Robert was due for his sitting. Why, oh, why must they be scheduled on the same day?

She had finished changing her gown when the door opened again, footsteps entered the room. Sibyl was about to leave the safety of the screen to request Sir Thomas arrange a separation of sitting times when she heard Robert's voice. To whom did he speak? Sir Thomas had not returned.

"You had best go, my dear. I fear the sitting will be far too tedious for one so gay as you." Robert's voice carried quite clearly to the figure behind the screen.

"La, I expect you have the right of it. Until this evening, *cheri*. You will not forget Lady Jolliffe's masquerade? What is your costume to be? I do not wish to miss you, for your handsome face will be concealed behind a mask. Do not tell me you will wear a tiresome domino!"

"Of course not," Robert soothed. "I will be a cavalier in a suit of plum velvet with an inordinate amount of lace. What extravagant fellows they were. My hat is black with an enormous plum-colored feather on it. I doubt you will miss me, one way or the other."

"Robert, you naughty man. As if there were anyone to compare to you. *Adieu.*" Rapid steps to the door, a slam, then silence.

Sibyl grabbed her cape, motioned Annie to get out the door, then hurried after her. Dashing down the steps, Sibyl arrived at the street just as Lady Wayford made to enter her carriage. Sibyl caught her breath, her hand clutching her throat as the implications began to sink in.

So, the suspicions Sibyl harbored were correct. Robert spoke from both sides of his mouth. On one side he made sounds as though he wished to wed Sibyl. But from the other, he spoke soothing words of affection to the evil Lady Wayford.

How could he? Knowing what Lady Wayford had tried to do to Sibyl the night of the ball, how could he court her, make assignations with her? And after that wicked kiss bestowed upon Sibyl! What a stupid, naive little goosecap she was to have trusted him so utterly. Wretched man!

"Come, Annie, I must be off to the modiste's to select a particularly pretty gown, a lilac one, I believe." She had refused to take the family carriage, not wishing the driver to be kept waiting for such a long period. Now she hailed a hackney, wrinkling up her nose in distaste at the various smells that assailed her as she entered. Since it was but a short distance, it could be tolerated. And it certainly kept her from dwelling upon the perfidy of men. Robert, in particular.

While they jogged along in the hackney, Sibyl mulled over what she had heard. Lady Jolliffe was giving a masquerade this evening? Yes, an invitation had come, for she recalled her stepmama discussing the event with Lord Cranswick. Neither intended to go. Cranswick planned to take Mrs. Medland to the theater, and the Eagletons were to go as well.

Sibyl had begged off, not wishing to play gooseberry. How she would like to catch Robert with Lady Wayford. The wretch. Blackguard! An idea began to take form. It would require daring. It was probably foolish beyond permission, not to mention dangerous. She would.

At the Madame Clotilde's, Sibyl first selected a lovely sheer lilac silk with a deeper lilac underskirt. She found a cluster of lilac silk flowers to attach to her cottage bonnet and thought the ensemble would be very chic.

"Madame, I have another request, a very special one."

The modiste leaned forward so as to hear the softly spoken words. "A secret. *Oui.*" An affair of the heart, no doubt. Romantic as any Frenchwoman, the modiste drew Sibyl to a chair, then begged her proceed.

"I find I wish to go to Lady Jolliffe's masquerade this evening after all. The gentleman is going to wear an elaborate dress, that of a cavalier gentleman, all plum velvet and lace. I wish to contrast with him with something daring, something he'll not suspect. Can you help me?''

''Daring? You wish to conceal your identity?''

''He once called me *mon ange*. I do not desire to be that this evening.''

''The opposite of the angel is a devil. Perhaps . . . you might attend as a lady pirate. Foaming lace at the throat, black pantaloons, those boots that fold at the tops, a large hat to cover your pretty hair. *Voila!*''

''Oh dear.'' Sibyl gulped. To be seen wearing tight pantaloons, high boots, a loose shirt, and a dashing hat. Horrors! ''I shall do it,'' she declared in a somewhat wavering voice. ''Can you tell me how to proceed?''

Swiftly, the modiste sketched the outfit she had in mind, then thought for a moment. ''Wait here, my dear. I believe I have some of the necessary things, the rest we can obtain in short order.''

Sibyl watched her leave with a few trepidations. But her resolution had firmed. There would be no turning back.

When Madame Clotilde returned, she wore a broad smile. ''I shall deliver all the things to you by seven of the clock. Now, let me measure your dainty foot.''

Lord Cranswick and the Eagletons were to dine at the Medlands' first before going on to the theater. Sibyl had demurely offered them her good wishes, then watched them depart with a sigh of relief. Once they were gone, she hurried to the library where she found the discarded invitation. Clutching it to her bosom, she headed to her room.

''Bentley, a package is to come any moment. Send it up to me at once.'' She began to march up the stairs when a footman came with a parcel that had been delivered at the back entry. It was a large box and bore Madame Clotilde's imprint.

''I shall take it now, if you please,'' Sibyl commanded in a polite way.

In her room, she divested herself of her demure white muslin, flinging it across the bed with unusual abandon. Her petticoat followed. From the box she pulled a white satin shirt, foaming, as Madame had said, with heavy lace at neck and wrist. It served to disguise her neck and hands very well. Next came black pantaloons of sleek knit fabric. They probably had been made for a youth, but they fit Sibyl charmingly. She fastened the buttons at the waist, then picked up the fancy boots.

"La, how shall I walk in these things?" However, they were a surprise, for they were but featherweights, in soft leather that felt amazingly good on her feet. Next, she found a red sash for her waist.

Then from her drawer she took a tiny, but deadly, pistol to tuck along the band. Sibyl checked to see the gun was properly loaded. The subject of danger had arisen. The modiste had wished Sibyl to be prepared for anything. Since Sibyl's general papa had taught her to handle firearms, she was ready with the pistol he had given her some time ago.

At last she donned the large black satin mask and the enormous hat with a red feather that curled wickedly about the brim. She tossed the black cape across her shoulders.

Standing before her looking glass, she stared at her reflection with wary concern. Could anyone detect her identity? Would there be anyone who expected her to attend? Deciding that the answers were negative, she waited until she felt it safe to leave her room. By now, Bentley and the others would either be in the kitchen or in the housekeeper's room, having the last of their meal.

The hall was silent. No one was about as Sibyl slipped down the stairs and out the door. What a blessing that the Jolliffe house was but two streets away. While all others would arrive in carriages, Sibyl could sneak over there on foot with none being the wiser, then return the same way.

Carriages were drawn up in a line; gorgeously dressed ladies and fancifully garbed gentlemen entered the Jolliffe house in clusters of twos and fours. Sibyl waited until the latest group had entered, then she approached the door, her invitation held in a black-gloved hand.

The butler glanced at the elegantly printed paper, then at the wisp of a fellow, and nodded him inside.

His thoughts seemed plain to Sibyl. She smiled grimly as she considered his expression. He might have as well said, "Go on in, you young sprout.'' She placed her cape where she could reach it in a hurry, then went up the stairs.

Lingering in the hall upstairs, she listened with great care to the voices around her. Detecting one she thought familiar, she drifted in the direction of a lady dressed as a woman of the court of Charles I. The neckline of her scarlet taffeta gown skimmed the fullness of her breasts, quite scandalously to Sibyl's young eyes. The bodice fit snugly, the scarlet skirt opened in the front to reveal an elaborate petticoat. The falling ruff on her sleeves revealed dainty gloved hands that languidly fanned a face where small round patches were placed with abandon. The veil draped over her head did little to conceal the blond hair dressed in soft ringlets, with a fringe over her forehead. The wicked Lady Wayford, without one doubt.

Sibyl circulated around the lady, noting the gentlemen who paid her court. There was no cavalier dressed in plum velvet and a fancy hat.

''I vow that's no lad in those pantaloons. Come here, my lass. Join me in a dance.''

Sibyl whirled about to confront a tall man dressed as another pirate, a husky, masculine pirate with a bold, roving gaze that prowled her person most intimately.

''No, I'd really rather not,'' she stammered, then caught sight of Lady Wayford's interested eyes. She was not to notice her. So Sibyl reluctantly nodded. ''Very well.''

''That's the spirit. This is a party, y'know. Deuced fine thing if nobody wanted to dance.''

Fortunately the dance of the moment was one that did not require close contact with one's partner.

Since few of the social customs of the day prevailed at masquerades, and no young unmarried woman would dare to attend unchaperoned—if then—Sibyl found the pirate demanding her company for one dance after another.

Breathless, she begged off the fifth dance with him, declaring, '' 'Tis thirsty work, sir. I need a cooling drink.''

''Ale?'' His eyes held a wicked glint.

She gave a vigorous shake of her head. ''No need for you to bother. I shall get my own.'' She didn't trust the man, for his looks had been a shade too bold, his hands a mite too willing to hold. She slipped from his side before he had a chance to object.

Weaving her way to the table where beverages were to be found, Sibyl had just poured a glass of lemonade, first asking if it indeed was such, when she heard Lady Wayford give a cry of delight. Slowly Sibyl turned about, edging into the shadows. Robert Medland had at last arrived.

"La, sir, what a fine cavalier you make."

He did look most elegant. Red-heeled boots gave him added height, the lace-edged collar emphasized his broad shoulders, and the breeches gave evidence of a fine figure.

"That's a fancy doublet you wear, my love," cooed the lady in question (or was it questionable lady?) as she ran her hand over his chest in a most suggestive manner. Sibyl gritted her teeth lest she make a noise of disgust.

Beneath one arm he held his hat, its cocked brim concealing the beginning of a magnificent plume that curled about the hat in an elaborate sweep. Sibyl would have liked to filch that ostrich plume, and wondered if she dared do so. It would be a souvenir of her wicked evening with the somewhat depraved of Society.

Not that they were actually so wicked. The laxity of masquerades was well known. If you did not approve of such, you simply did not attend.

She bided her time and watched. When she planned this venture Sibyl hadn't realized how difficult it would be to stand silently by and watch the man she loved as he paid court to her enemy. Never had she felt such pain, not even when as a child she had fallen and badly injured her shoulder. This pain centered in her heart and the ache seemed to spread all through her body.

"So there you are, lass. Pretending a bit of shyness, are ye? Well, we'll soon see to that."

Fortunately, Sibyl had finished her tall glass of lemonade, for he jerked it from her hand, plunking the glass on a nearby table with a clumsy thud.

"Now, by Jove, you'll honor me with a waltz."

"No, I think not."

The pirate paid no heed to her softly spoken denial. Unwilling to draw attention to them, she subsided, reluctantly stepping into his hold, aware of a number of curious eyes upon them.

As long as none belonged to the new Lord Stafford, she might be safe.

But would Robert penetrate her disguise? If he was entranced with Lady Wayford, it was unlikely he would bother to notice a slim pirate lad.

The bold pirate swung her about in some rather fancy steps, different from the more elegant version Robert had taught her. Robert. That dratted man popped up everywhere in her memory. If only she might banish him to his odious castle on a hill, there to molder into dust.

She was picked up and swung about in a shocking whirl. Had she skirts on, her petticoat would have been visible to everyone. As it was, she caught sight of many amused faces, Robert's among them.

"Put me down, you fool," she hissed.

"Aye, when I feel like it. This is the most fun I've had since coming to Town." She was swung once again, then mercifully the dance ended, and she backed away from him with wary steps. And bumped directly into someone else.

She turned to apologize and her breath got lost somewhere between her lungs and throat. Robert stood before her, smiling down into her eyes in that lazy, sensual way he had. "Sorry," she croaked in a voice as unlike her own as she might muster.

"That's all right, my little pirate." His voice was like rich velvet, softly stroking her senses.

Sibyl gulped, gazing up at him with fear creeping into her eyes. If she stayed here one minute longer he might guess. Then she would indeed be in a pickle.

"Afraid of him? Not to worry, I'll take the next dance. Perhaps he will find someone else."

"My toes are just fine," she hastily assured Robert. "He is graceful, just so full of energy." But that big pirate frightened her half to death, she added silently.

Robert reached out to tuck a small brown curl beneath the brim of her hat, his gaze thoughtful as he studied her eyes. "I believe I know you."

"Oh, no," Sibyl declared softly, "for I am sure I do not know you." And in a way that was the truth, for the Robert she knew was high-principled, honorable, and genuine. This Robert was a cad, a breaker of hearts, and a liar.

His look, what she could see of it, was skeptical. Sibyl wondered frantically how she might get away from there.

"Come." There was nothing to do but join him in the minuet that now commenced. It was a stately dance, allowing her to catch her breath after that romp of a waltz. Yet, she found something sensuous in the way he advanced, then retreated, holding her hand so lightly, yet firm and in control.

She dared not meet his gaze. Blue eyes were common, but yet she suspected she might reveal her knowledge of him. She felt foolish playing the role of a pirate, her slim legs exposed while dancing the part of a lady in the minuet. Tiny, precise steps seemed ludicrous when performed in her boots, no matter they were soft and light. She glided to the right, then left, forward and backward, did a quarter turn, then approached him again. Hand in hand they walked side by side, then face to face. It seemed to her that in a way the dance was patterned on court-ship—if one had a true courtier, that is.

When he at last escorted her to the side of the room, she vowed to escape as quickly as possible. She had seen enough and done far more than enough for one night. Robert stood revealed in his true character. She might not have believed it had she not witnessed his betrayal for herself.

Lord Buckingham might be wrapped up in himself, but at least he would not be absorbed in another woman.

"You seem flushed, my dear lady. Permit me to fetch you a drink of something cool."

She grasped at the chance to leave. "Yes, how thoughtful of you. I fear 'tis the far side of the room. It would be prodigiously kind of you, my lord."

As soon as he was somewhat lost in the throng of people, she darted from the heated room to the hall. She stayed close to the wall, trying to make her way silently to the front door without being seen or heard.

"I say, love, wait up. We'll find a more congenial place to spend the rest of the night." The large pirate lurched through the open door, staggering toward the stairs with far too accurate steps. He might be somewhat castaway, but he was not yet three sheets to the wind, and still could make trouble for her.

Sibyl ran. Abandoning any effort at skulking her way from

the house, she dashed down the remaining steps and headed for the door, grabbing her cape as she went. She had about reached her goal when she slipped on the tile and fell. It was all the time the tall pirate needed.

"No need to play coy, love." He hiccuped, then roared a belch that must have been heard upstairs but for the noise of the music. His laugh was uninhibited. "Faith, and I'm a jolly lad this even. We'll be a fine pair, lass."

Sibyl picked herself up from the floor, wincing at a bruised backside. Behind her was the door. The butler had taken himself off, unfortunately. She was alone. This man was advancing on her like he meant business, and she very much feared just what that business might be.

"Taken to frightening young girls, Roger? Shame on you." At the head of the stairs stood a cavalier in plum velvet holding a glass of what appeared to be lemonade.

The large pirate paused in the act of reaching for Sibyl while Robert made a languid descent, one casual step at a time. While his eyes were turned elsewhere, Sibyl pulled the little gun from her waistband and trained it on the pirate. She backed up until she felt the knob of the door in her back, then groped for it with her free hand.

Robert attained the ground floor, placed the glass on a table, then took off his elegant hat, the ostrich plume waving grandly in the air as he held it toward Sibyl.

In a quandary, Sibyl let go of the knob to accept his hat. "It's all right. I can get out of here by myself. I suddenly felt the need to leave."

"I suspected as much when I found you had deserted me, my dear." There was a dangerous purr in that velvet voice that shook Sibyl more than the threat of the pirate.

As the bemused pirate fell to the floor with one neat punch, Sibyl tucked the gun back in her band, and, her cape swirling madly, dashed out the door, not bothering to leave the hat behind her. When she had run a block, she ducked into the shadows. Pulling out the plume, she tossed the hat aside, then, after checking to be sure that no one was about, she fled to Cranswick House. The front door was unlocked, praise be. Her parents and Cranswick were still out.

The entry hall was silent, especially when contrasted with the volume of sound at Lady Jolliffe's house. Sibyl tiptoed up the stairs to her room, reaching it just as she heard noises from below.

After locking her door she placed the cape into the box, then pulled off the boots, dropping them beside it. The pantaloons went next, followed by the sash and fancy shirt. On top of it all she placed the hat and mask. Only then did she take a deep breath.

The ostrich plume now curved across the back of her chair, boldly plum against the prim cream. She drew out the crimson feather from the hat she had worn and placed it with the plume on the chair. A crooked smile tilted her mouth at the sight. Then the smile faded, and she shut her eyes against the image it provoked. Going to her wardrobe, she found her nightrail, put it on, then crawled into bed. There she wept for lost love and a slightly shattered heart.

14

"SCANDALOUS," declared Lady Lavinia just as Sibyl entered the breakfast room the following morning. The clock in the hall struck ten times.

Sibyl winced, whether it was from the slight headache—due most likely to that bout of crying—or to her stepmama's voice, she was not sure. She darted surreptitious glances at her ladyship while selecting a sparse meal from the sideboard. "What is scandalous?" she ventured to ask at last, unable to stand the suspense any longer. Had Mama discovered last evening's expedition to the Jolliffe masquerade?

"A stagecoach proceeded without the driver, the horses taking it upon themselves to merely gallop off, and the vehicle overturned. Three people were killed! And several were badly wounded." Lady Lavinia placed the newspaper on the table, pushing it away from her plate. "I do not think I shall read any more. I have quite lost my appetite. Nothing good ever happens." Then, observing her stepdaughter's nearly empty plate, she added, "That is no reason for you to starve yourself, love. I feel certain something good must happen to you."

Sibyl felt her guilty conscience nagging at her, yet she dared not reveal the truth. How disappointed her stepmama would be in her behavior. That kiss had been bad enough, this daring escapade would be too much. Sibyl suspected it might be sufficient for her family to remove her from London to the quiet air of Mablethorpe.

"I am not hungry, Mama." By ducking her head, she managed to avoid close scrutiny. Her looking glass might not show the results of that round of tears, but Lady Lavinia had sharp eyes.

Fortunately, the lady had other things on her mind. "The play was quite good last night. Pity you did not go with us. We saw

Captain Ransom there with Miss Valler, and Mary Ransom had
that nice young Mr. Hadgley at her side. Mrs. Ransom is such
a delightful lady, and chaperoned them most properly. I was
surprised not to see either Robert or Lady Wayford.''

"Perhaps they were attending a party, ma'am."

"I wonder, would Robert actually go to such an affair as the
Jolliffe masquerade?'' Lady Lavinia rose from the table, walking
to the window.

Sibyl breathed a sigh of relief, for she had no doubt her cheeks
flamed with knowledge. She was not sorry when her stepmama
drifted from the room, a vague explanation floating behind her.

Abandoning her attempts to eat, Sibyl also left the table,
wandering out into the entry hall just as Bentley opened the front
door.

Sibyl backed away, wishing she might make a dash for the
stairs. Robert entered the house, and he carred an enormous
black hat in his left hand. There was no plume curled wickedly
about the brim today. He looked as though he might breathe
fire at any moment.

There was no possible way he might connect her with last
night. She had worn a mask, her hair had been covered, as had
most of her body, albeit rather snugly.

Robert slowly advanced upon her. "Good morning."

Sibyl retreated down the hall, backing as he neared. His words
were innocent; his face was not.

"G-good morning. A bit of a wind out, but the sun is nice,
is it not? I think it lovely to have the nasty smells blown from
the city. I plan to hunt for butterflies later, if it warms up a
little. Did you wish to see someone? The earl? Lady Lavinia,
perhaps?'' Her words tumbled out in wild profusion. She
continued to back away from him, not trusting that expression
one whit.

The door to the morning room was ajar and it suddenly
punched Sibyl in the back, halting her retreat. "Oh!"

"Where were you last night?"

That deceptively cool voice didn't fool her. Fiery sparks
snapped from those usually serene gray eyes. "Home. Mama
asked me to the theater with them, but I wished not to play
gooseberry, so I stayed home,'' she fabricated.

"I see. I attended Lady Jolliffe's masquerade last evening. Delightful party. There was a young girl there who had a spot of trouble, though. Roger Bainbridge got a trifle foxed and swept her off her feet. Put on a bit of a show, what with dancing a rather scandalous waltz. I danced with her as well. She had blue eyes, was of medium height, and a soft brown curl escaped from under the brim of her hat. Something like yours, my dear." He reached out to touch a curl that had managed to be missed when she put on her morning cap.

"Blue eyes and brown hair are not uncommon, my lord."

"Odd, she called me that, too. Yet most people call me mister, or perhaps, sir." He pushed Sibyl into the morning room, glancing around to note it was quite empty of people.

"Slip of the tongue, forgive me." Sibyl tried to escape from the hand that now held her chin, but found it impossible. "What do you want from me?"

He shook his head. "Ah, that is difficult to say."

He let her chin go, and Sibyl backed away from him, retreating behind a small table as though it offered real protection. "Why?"

"I felt sorry for that young girl last night," he continued as though she hadn't spoken. "She obviously was frightened of Bainbridge." Robert paused, then added, "He's a monstrously big fellow, and usually amiable enough when not castaway as he was last night."

Robert began pacing about the room, glancing out the window, then about at the pleasant arrangement of furniture. Sibyl wanted to scream at him to get on with it, accuse her, do whatever he had come to do. Only not this silence, this awful waiting for an ax to fall. He carried that huge black hat in one hand, tapping it against his thigh in a steady, monotonous manner that set her nerves further on edge.

"So?" she asked in a commendably serene voice.

"So I went to her aid. She had slipped away while I fetched her a glass of lemonade, you see. When I found she had left, I decided to check, as Bainbridge was also missing. The fellow was about to grab her, and the girl had fallen so she was ill prepared to defend herself—except for a pistol she probably did not know how to fire. I knocked my friend to the floor. While

I performed this deed, the little pirate—did I mention she was dressed in skin-tight pantaloons and a clinging satin shirt that revealed far more than she thought it concealed?—escaped from the house.''

He paused again to rake Sibyl with that fiery gaze, then continued, ''I ran outside, thinking there might have been a carriage. But, no, she went on foot. All I found was my hat, and that not until this morning when I was on my way over here. Interesting, what?'' His question was rhetorical, his voice was deadly.

''Very,'' she replied in a suddenly faint voice.

''What did you hope to see? Or do? By heaven, Sibyl, you could have been in serious trouble with the bird-witted prank.'' He did not raise his voice, but that whisper was far more dreadful than shouting.

''How did you know it was me?'' She did not waste time denying she had been the pirate. He knew too much, that was obvious.

''I'll wager any sum that a certain purple plume is right at this minute in your bedroom.'' He tossed the hat on a chair, then took a step closer. ''And a gun. Do you really know how to use that thing?'' He shook his head while reaching out to grab her shoulders, giving her a slight shake.

''My papa taught me to handle firearms early on, as he was required to be gone so much.'' She tried to squirm from his hold, but merely succeeded in having his hands tighten their control of her.

''Do you realize the scandal that might have erupted had your identity become known? As it was, I was forced to convince several people you were someone quite different.''

''Thank you.'' A tear shimmered on her lashes, quickly followed by another. They gently rolled down her petal-soft cheeks, one after the other. ''I am sorry.'' Her gentle blue eyes gazed up at him, filled with genuine remorse.

He shook his head, groaning as he pulled her against him, wrapping his arms about her in a crushing embrace.

Sibyl felt somewhat smothered, yet it was as though a blanket of warm security had fallen about her. If only he loved her. He must be ready to throttle her. She could hardly blame him, with what having to knock his friend senseless, his hat taken, then defending a hey-go-mad scamp of a girl to skeptical friends.

"Why? Just tell me why?" The words were muffled, spoken against her morning cap, now slightly askew.

Sibyl ran her tongue over her lips in apprehension. What could she possibly say to him to deflect the truth, that she had gone there to spy on him? "Curiosity?"

He drew his head back to look down at her, his doubt causing his brows to draw together most fearsomely. At her tremble of fear, he again shook his head, ever so slightly, then claimed her lips in a sweet kiss.

It was brief but ever so potent, Sibyl decided as she stared up into his face moments later.

"You ought not have done that. Do you not recall the trouble you got into the first time you kissed me? I said nothing of the second, but this third one, well . . ." She turned away from him, missing the softening of his eyes, the tender smile that crept over his face. "You need not insist we must marry. No one knows about those other kisses, although we ought not to be alone in this room." She left the circle of his arms to take refuge by the windows.

"You are not very careful, my lord," she continued. "A less scrupulous girl could trick you into marriage. And I suspect you have other plans."

Addressing the back of her head was not very satisfactory, but Robert tried. "I admit I have certain plans that I do not care to have anyone interfere with."

Sibyl stiffened her spine. Had she not seen him with Lady Wayford last evening? There had been a sense of intimacy between them. She did not understand it, but suspected it had to do with a very private relationship of which she knew nothing. And wanted to know nothing. What he did with his life meant nothing to her anymore.

She sniffed. "I rather suspected such." Turning to face him once again, she tilted her head with a courageous hint of defiance. "If you would excuse me, Lord Stafford, I also have plans. I thought to go to the park. Butterflies, you know." Her look mocked him. "By the bye, if you wish that plume, it *is* in my room, along with a certain red one."

He looked aside, sighing with frustration. Placing his hands at his back, lest he succumb to an urge to shake her very, very hard, Robert gritted his teeth, then said, "By all means, Miss Pirate. Only know that I intend to hold this over your head from now on. One step out of line and I shall inform your unsuspecting parents they have a hoyden of unparalleled proportions in their house."

She smiled sweetly, noting her headache had quite disappeared during this fracas. "Actually, 'tis the earl's house—Cranswick, that is. However, I shall bear your warning in mind, my lord. Next time I decide to exercise my curiosity, I shall make certain you are elsewhere."

"Sibyl, do not try me further. My patience has its limits." He flexed his hands at his sides, making it clear, he thought, what he had in mind.

"Really?" Her smile broadened. "For some reason I no longer fear you, my lord. For you see, if you tell on me, I shall tell on you." She dipped a deep curtsy, then waltzed from the room.

"She taunted me," he fumed aloud. "Walked right beneath my nose, with that cat-that-has-swallowed-the-cream-and-sausage look on her face. What can I do?" He decided to stroll along on her outing in the park, lest she fall into more serious trouble, although what could be worse than last night, he couldn't imagine.

Then he smiled in remembrance. How wonderful she had looked in those black pantaloons plastered against fine legs, that satin shirt outlining the swell of her breasts. She was quite a woman. He sighed. If he could manage to nudge her in the right direction, he might soon have her in his castle. His thoughts turned to the plunge bath and the smile on his face widened.

Sibyl grinned with great glee as she entered her room to dance lightly over to the chair by the window. Oh, she had fixed him, she had. She picked up the plum and red plumes, drawing them through her hands, enjoying the delicate tickle of the feathers against her fingers.

She was like a miser, one who stores up kisses, not money. What a temptation to realize she had but to tell her parents of

Lord Stafford's indiscreet behavior and Robert would most likely be compelled to marry with her.

Then her little balloon burst. He *had* offered for her. She had declined the honor. Was one allowed to reconsider? Not when the gentleman showed such obvious preferment for a lady of questionable virtue.

Reluctant to go ahead with her excursion in the park, somehow feeling butterflies were less important today, she nonetheless gathered up her net and collecting box, then put on a violet spencer over her morning dress sprigged with violet flowers. Deciding that her violet morocco slippers were adequate, she tossed aside her white muslin morning cap in favor of a neat little bonnet with the silk lilacs on the brim.

Thus it was a few minutes later that an impatient Robert enjoyed the view of Miss Eagleton, all violet and white, with her paraphernalia in her hands, walking toward the front door.

"Shall we? I trust your mother knows what you are about?" He caught sight of Annie scurrying to catch up with her mistress.

"Yes. But does she know what you are about, I wonder?"

Bentley held open the door for the three bound for the Park. "Any messages, miss?"

Surprised at his question, for she did not often have visitors, Sibyl shook her head. "If anyone asks, I am in the park."

They walked in silence for the most part. When they entered the park, Sibyl looked about her as though she fully expected to see an exotic butterfly come to greet her.

"What are you going to do now?"

"Hunt for butterflies."

"That is not what I meant, and I rather suspect you know it. What about your future?" He pursed his lips, then added, "If you select some man to wed that I believe to be all wrong for you, I shall be obliged to tell him of your scandalous past."

"You wouldn't." Sibyl walked a few steps, then turned to look at him. "You would. Why? What should it matter to you?"

"Your stepmother is a nice lady."

"Humbug. You, my lord, are nothing but a busybody." With that declaration, she flounced off through the long grasses, poking about with the end of her net in hopes of stirring a butterfly to flight.

"There be one," cried Annie, showing delight she had been the first to espy one of the creatures.

Sibyl shoved her collecting box at Robert, then lightly ran after the insect with orange-tipped white wings, net in hand. She had about captured it when two tiny field mice darted across her path, scurrying this way and that, causing her to abruptly stop and stare at the ground. Although she did not cry out, Annie was not so inhibited.

Annie screamed.

Sibyl dropped the net to the ground, then placed an arm about the maid. "Now, now, they are only a pair of wee mice. They can't bite you. Indeed, with that scream, they are probably halfway across the park by now."

Annie turned a brick-red, and looked to hide in her apron.

"Never mind, I feel sure another butterfly shall come this way."

At that moment a gentleman leaped from a nearby carriage and dashed to Sibyl's side. "I say, I trust all is well here?"

"Lord Buckingham? What a surprise, sir. I had not thought to see you again." Ever, she added silently. Glancing at Robert, she observed a tightening about his mouth, a narrowing of his eyes. He most definitely did not care for Lord Buckingham. Sibyl smiled rather wickedly, her eyes lighting delightfully with barely hidden mirth. Gracious, she was becoming a sad scamp.

Lord Buckingham glared at Robert. "I heard a scream. Are you troubling this lady?" Annie was not spared so much as a look.

"My maid saw some field mice. I fear it overset her nerves," Sibyl explained before Robert could defend himself.

"I am escorting Miss Eagleton on her search for butterflies," Robert said, sounding rather silly to Sibyl's acute ears.

Sibyl handed the net to Annie, then stepped forward to relieve Robert of her collecting box. "I would not burden you, sir."

"I shall be happy to assist you, Miss Eagleton," inserted Lord Buckingham. "You look quite charmingly this morning." His faint bow was all that was correct.

"If it is no trouble. I believe I see a Painted Lady over there. Mr. Medland already has one of those." She gave him a sly smile. "You will excuse me?"

Robert gave her a baffled look as he watched her skim across the park toward a flock of butterflies. Their brilliant orange, black, and white markings drew the eye quite as much as the young woman sneaking up on them.

"I imagine you have things to do, Medland?" Buckingham inquired with the utmost civility.

"More than you know, Buckingham." Giving Sibyl one last puzzled look, he turned to make his way across the park. Just as he reached the gate, it hit him. Damn and blast! She had seen him last night with Aurora, who admittedly had been painted, and was definitely not the lady of her title. But what had Sibyl observed?

Little by little, Robert went over his actions from the time he arrived at the Jolliffe house until Sibyl had backed into him and he had been sure of her identity. A man could remember the feel of a woman without seeing her face. That brown curl had helped, of course. But he had seen her figure, recognized it from the time he had seen her silhouetted against the bridge, gown all damp from the heavy mist, blown against her slender form with the strong breeze. When he had touched her, he had been certain.

But Aurora, confound her painted hide, had clung to him, exposing as much as she dared of her magnificent bosom. A man would have to be blind not to notice. He supposed he had smiled at her. Who would not? Robert wearily shook his head in dismay. It seemed nothing in this life was simple. Sibyl most assuredly was not. There were some complex convolutions going on through her brainbox that he would dearly have liked to know about.

Sibyl whirled about, slicing through the air with her net until one of the Painted Ladies was safely caught in the soft mesh. Giving a triumphant smile, she demurely walked back to where Lord Buckingham waited for her.

"Is this not a beauty? I shall handle it most carefully, to be sure." With growing skill, she transferred the pretty butterfly to the killing jar. Ignoring Lord Buckingham's moue of distaste, she placed the jar securely in the box, then turned to the gentleman at her side. Annie waited at a discreet distance.

"I am surprised, sir. I really had not thought to see you again." She plucked at the net in her hands while studying his aristocratic face.

"No, I suppose you hadn't. Got carried away, I expect. Dashed if I can see why he picked on you when he had Lady Wayford in his pocket. I mean, it isn't as though he wants to marry and settle down, is it?"

"One does not marry Lady Wayford?" Sibyl asked, brightening at this idea. The slap at her desirability, she ignored. One had to consider who spoke.

His pale blue eyes flashed with an unknown emotion as he stared at Sibyl, causing her to take a step backward in alarm. What had she said?

"The lady is a vulgar upstart. Beautiful, desirable, wealthy, and an excellent card player, but hardly marriageable." Lord Buckingham sniffed, then looked down his elegant nose at Sibyl for having the temerity to ask such an improper question.

"I see," Sibyl replied, though in truth she was not quite sure if what she suspected might be true.

He gestured toward the carriage, where his driver waited patiently. "A drive, Miss Eagleton?"

She nodded to Annie, signaling the maid to climb up with the driver. Sibyl offered her hand to Buckingham, then gracefully entered the open carriage. The net and collecting box were placed on the far side, then she settled next to Lord Buckingham with a sigh.

What on earth was she doing in this carriage, anyway?

Having told his driver to proceed, Lord Buckingham sat back to study the young lady at his side. He seemed to be as puzzled as Sibyl as to why she was here. "You are comfortable?"

"Yes, thank you. You know, I heard stories after my ball," she felt compelled to say.

"I cannot tell you how it grieved me to hear of them. A true lady would not repeat such tales."

"You must have mentioned the, er, scene you came upon to Lady Wayford, for she repeated it in great detail, or so I am told." Sibyl drew herself up, then fixed a severe gaze upon the bane of her existence. It was one thing to use him to tease Robert, another matter to consider the harm he had caused her.

The carraige silently proceeded through the park at a leisurely pace, the viscount apparently seeking the proper words and finding it a difficult task.

At last deciding, it seemed, to offer only the bare minimum of explanation, Lord Buckingham cleared his throat, then said, "I prefer not to discuss the means by which Lady Wayford happened upon the knowledge. Suffice it to say that it was rather, er, unorthodox."

Sibyl frowned, wondering what means Lady Wayford might use that could be unorthodox.

Her thoughts were interrupted when she thought she saw a familiar face in the carriage dashing past in the opposite direction. They had left the park and were near the intersection of Hyde Park Corner, where the turnpike road entered London.

"Is something wrong, Miss Eagleton?" Lord Buckingham was not accustomed to having young women pay attention to gentlemen in other carriages, no matter who they might be. Perhaps Miss Eagleton was not as worthy as he had believed?

"I thought I saw Lord Cranswick's son, Viscount Barringer, just go past us. His wife was not with him. I do hope Marianna is all right."

Lord Buckingham relaxed. Family was quite acceptable as a distraction, particularly married family. He spoke to his driver, and the carriage was directed toward Grosvenor Square.

"I am sure this is a lovely day for a drive, but I am all a-twitter to get home to discover what is going on. You do understand, do you not?" She gave him a curious look.

Unable to resist the gentle pleading in the soft blue eyes, Lord Buckingham unbent so far as to smile. "Of course I understand, Miss Eagleton. I shall have you there directly."

That he was not driving the carriage, indeed, he reclined in lordly splendor, did not seem to disturb him. When the carriage drew up before Cranswick House, he assisted Sibyl to the ground, then stared at the fine curricle that sat in front of them.

"Dashed fine equipage, that," he mused aloud. "I shall escort you to your mama, my dear," he said with that fine, patronizing manner he was wont to use.

Sibyl gritted her teeth as she smiled, then entered the house before him. Inside, she lightly ran up the stairs, her curiosity overcoming her good manners for once.

In the drawing room, she found the Earl of Cranswick, Lady

Lavinia, and her papa seated at the tea table. Viscount Barringer stood by the window, surveying the group. No tea had been poured. The four stared at each other with a mixture of emotions revealed.

Lady Lavinia looked upset. The baron seemed embarrassed. The earl looked fit to be tied. A red-faced George appeared about to pop.

"Hullo, Lord Barringer. How is Marianna? Well, I trust?" Sibyl advanced into the room, her hand politely extended. Viscount Buckingham seemed oblivious to the undercurrents flowing about the room. He lounged by a chair, studying the gentleman who had just arrived.

Lord Cranswick's son had chestnut hair that was a trifle windblown, but handsomely cut nonetheless. His eyes were a dashed odd color, like aged sherry. He was tall, well-framed, and bore a shrewd expression on his face at the moment, as if he had just challenged an opponent.

"Buckingham," George replied civilly in reply to the introduction.

"We were about to enjoy a cup of tea when we were surprised by a visit from George." Looking at Sibyl, Lavinia added, "I know you will be pleased to hear all is well with Marianna and their new little boy. They have named him William, you know, after his grandfather. However, she did not feel up to coming to London at this moment."

Sibyl glanced at George, wishing that Viscount Buckingham would take himself off immediately so she might find out what was going on around here.

Bentley brought another pot of tea and a jug of steaming water, and placed them on the table. Lavinia deftly poured out the tea, all the while making polite little chitchat.

George was his usual uncommunicative self, Sibyl noticed. Yet she felt the tenseness in him. Lord Cranswick fidgeted about in his chair until the tea had been consumed. Then he rose. "I believe you and I had best have our discussion in the library, George. You will excuse us, I trust? Business, you know, Buckingham."

"George had a dreadful trip down from Yorkshire," Lavinia explained to Sibyl. "One of his horses went lame, the carriage lost a wheel and it took days to get repaired. Poor boy thought he would never get here.'' To Buckingham she added, ''I am like a mama to him, I suppose, for I raised him from the time he was but a mere boy. He always was such a somber, serious little lad.''

''A fine man, Livvy. You did your brother proud with him,'' Henry said in a soothing way.

Sibyl gave her papa a grateful look, admiring the manner in which he offered a kind word to his wife.

Lord Buckingham at last seemed to feel he was *de trop* and rose from his chair, placing his teacup near where Lavinia sat. ''I must go. Can't keep the horses waiting forever, you know. I found Miss Eagleton in the park, somewhat in distress. I am happy to restore her to you.'' Ignoring questions, he took his leave.

''Sibyl?''

''Annie saw some mice and screamed. Robert was right there with us, but Lord Buckingham came on the run. Robert does not like him.''

''Can't say I am wild about the man myself,'' Lord Eagleton commented, ignoring the nudge from his wife's foot.

Lady Lavinia picked up the teacup Lord Buckingham had used to inspect the interior. She went through her little ritual, then studied it again. ''Hm, Lord Buckingham is in for a few surprises.''

Pushing aside that strange comment, Sibyl leaned forward in her chair. ''If someone does not tell me why George has come haring to London, I believe I shall burst.''

The Eagletons exchanged worried looks. Lady Lavinia spoke for them both. ''George has heard about the amount of attention his father is paying to Delia Medland. He is here to demand that his esteemed papa stop making a cake of himself. Can you believe such a thing?''

Sibyl stared at the door through which Lord Cranswick and his son had gone. It seemed the Medlands were considered to be trouble. Goodness knew that Robert was. But his mother? What on earth would Lord Cranswick do?

15

DELIA GLANCED UP in surprise when the earl was ushered into the charming drawing room of the house on Mount Street. "Why, William, what is the trouble? I can see you are greatly agitated." She placed her embroidery on a small table at her side, then rose to walk to him, her hands outstretched.

He stopped before her, his eyes searching her face with unusual intensity. "My son George, came to Town, arrived a short time ago." He touched one of her hands, then dropped it, standing before her, a frown on his face.

"Oh? I daresay you are pleased to see him?" Her manner was wary, for his voice revealed a certain strain. They had become close in these past weeks and she had begun to entertain hopes.

The earl began to pace about the room, his steps emphatic, his hands placed behind him as though he was restraining himself from using them. "The damned puppy had the effrontery to tell me he was concerned about my seeing a certain Mrs. Medland. Had heard rumors that you were an upstart and a money-hungry husband-seeker. You! A more graceful, sensitive, intelligent woman I have yet to meet." His lordship bestowed a loving look on the lady whose company he had come to enjoy so much. "How anyone might think such things, let alone say them!"

"But, he does not know me. He may be forgiven an opinion based, no doubt, on a letter. I trust he is but trying to protect you from a fortune hunter." Delia remained where she had paused, her face revealing her worry, and hurt, that someone disliked her so to write such things. Slowly she clasped her hands together, taking comfort from their warmth.

"I will not have it. No one tells me what I may or may not do, especially my son." Lord Cranswick drew himself up, giving Delia that look he used to effect when depressing the attentions of an unwanted person. "I shall do as I please."

"Now, William," Delia scolded gently. "He intends for the best, I am sure." She took a step toward where he now stood, wondering, hoping.

"It made me realize how much you have come to mean to me," he replied gruffly. "When I considered there were people who wished to separate us, I knew that was one event I wished never to have happen." He paused a moment, then continued. "Delia, I am aware we have not known each other for very long. At least, not well," he amended. "And you may have had some odd notions about the rackety way I have been living these past years. A bachelor does a lot of foolish nonsense when alone and lonely. You understand that is behind me?"

At her hesitant nod, he continued, "I suspect I ought to court you ardently, like all those young sprigs do. I am too old for such nonsense." Aware she was about to speak, he held up his hand. Then he cleared his throat. "Hear me out. I would like us—that is, would you condescend to marry with me, my dear? I can promise you that for the rest of our lives I will cosset and treasure you for the precious lady you are." For once, the elegant, polished earl looked unsure of himself, a boyish gleam of hope shining in his eyes that Delia found quite endearing.

"William!" the happy lady cried, walking swiftly to his side, a hand reaching out to clasp his. "You are sure? For I have come to love you dearly, and I would not easily let you go."

At which remarks, the dignified earl drew the lovely Mrs. Medland into his arms and concluded his proposal in a highly satisfactory manner. The kiss was not a short one, and neither were aware when they eventually acquired an audience.

"Ahem." Robert stood in the doorway, staring at the sight before him with amazed eyes. "I was unaware, sir, that you were paying your addresses to my mother in such a forward way. Explain yourself."

"Another one," muttered the earl in his beloved's hair as he reluctantly let her go. He wore the look of a man highly satisfied with himself and life in general, and his lovely lady in particular.

"William—that is, Lord Cranswick—has done me the honor

of requesting my hand in marriage, dear. I have accepted."
Delia floated across the room to confront her son, the earl
closely following her, as though to protect her from any possible
unpleasantness.

"And," inserted the earl with haste, "we intend to be married
as soon as it may be arranged, now that she is out of black gloves
for your distant cousin. I will not have any more busybodies
causing trouble. 'Tis bad enough for George to come haring
down from Yorkshire. Next I know, Samantha and her husband
will be on the doorstep, demanding I act my age, or some such
nonsense."

Robert entered the room with a smile and shook his future
stepfather's hand, all the while thinking furiously. "You mean
some tattlemonger wrote to your son, informing him of your
friendship with my mother? To what end, pray tell?"

William shrugged. "I really could not say. My marriage
would not seriously affect George—or Samanatha, for that
matter."

"Perhaps it was other than that, someone who has taken a
dislike of the Medlands for some reason? I have a few thoughts
regarding that. I believe I shall check on them immediately."
Robert's words floated back as he charged from the room, not
bothering to bid farewell. William and Delia frowned in puzzle-
ment, then turned their attention to more pressing matters, the
planning of a quiet wedding. This was nicely accomplished while
holding hands and gazing fondly into each other's dear faces.

Sibyl had tiptoed down to the ground floor in the hopes of
discovering what was going on when Bentley answered the door.
He ushered Robert in as though he was a relative, thought Sibyl
in a huff. She reluctantly approached him.

"I did not expect to see you again, certainly not today." She
did not quite know how to act. Had he recovered from the anger
over her daring and ill-considered visit to the masquerade? She
knew she had not reclaimed her usual tranquil state of nerves.
But then, when Robert was near her, she never did possess that
degree of calm.

"Your cousin has arrived." He knew, he was not asking.
"Stepcousin, if you will. Yes, George passed us as Lord

Buckingham and I were leaving the park. We followed him home, of course.''

"I know—your curiosity.'' Robert glanced about the entry with impatient eyes. "I would like to meet him.''

"How did you know he had arrived? He has not been here above an hour or so.'' She led Robert along the hall toward the library, where George had met with his father.

"Your uncle is at this moment at my house. It seems your cousin is not pleased about his father's seeing my mother, if you please. I have done all I could to protect her, to promote her happiness.'' Robert's anger was quite clear. Those gray eyes fairly snapped, his mouth firmed in a grim line.

"You are aware that Lord Cranswick has not paid court to any woman since his wife died many years ago? 'Tis not wonderful if George is upset. He does not know your mother,'' she added by way of apology that Robert's gentle mother might be rejected by anyone.

Robert raised an eyebrow. "Thank you for small mercies. She is a nice woman, not one to get in a pelter about.'' He stared down at the innocent-looking girl at his side as the idea that had occurred to him earlier grew, poisoning what he knew about her. "Someone wrote to him—or his wife—to spread a bit of tattle, no doubt putting a shady slant to the words.'' He paused, then continued, "You write to his wife, do you not?'' He paused outside the library door, facing her with the knowledge she might harm their future happiness with her reply.

"You cannot be accusing me of writing scurrilous tales to Marianna. That, I refuse to believe. Or are you? Did my foolish behavior of last night plant other notions in that skull of yours? Oh, it is a deal too bad of you to even contemplate such a thing.'' She stamped her foot, her voice ringing out in anger, while one dainty fist rose up in a half-threatening way. "I have said your mother is a fine person. I would never harm her. I am crushed that you could think so little of me.'' Whirling about, she made as though to race toward the stairs when Robert caught at her arm.

She glared at him, then looked pointedly to where his hand lingered. "Let me go.''

Robert shook his head, dropping his hand from her arm. "I thought . . . you *were* angry with me. Our friendship has been a stormy one. And we did have words this morning.''

''That is scarcely time enough to write a letter to Yorkshire, even if it were to fly there by means of a pigeon. It took George days to drive down. It had to be someone else.'' She placed her fists on her hips, glaring at him with anger seething inside her.

By the expression that now flooded his face, Sibyl could see he felt quite as foolish as he ought to. There must be another who could wish to create trouble for the Medlands. Sibyl had a suspicion or two.

She then wondered if he had made the association with the Painted Lady butterfly yet. Glancing at him, she ventured to say, ''I captured that Painted Lady this morning. It is a prime specimen. I have it mounted. It is so nice to pin them properly into place.''

His attention caught, Robert looked at Sibyl, wondering what she had meant by that particular remark. Then he recollected his earlier hunch. ''You wish to pin Painted Ladies into their proper place? All of them?''

''Just one would be sufficient,'' she replied with a demure expression now on her face. She placed her hands together before her in a parody of a shy clasp. However, her eyes betrayed her true feelings.

''Any particular painted lady?'' he inquired in an off-hand manner.

She gave him a fulminating look. ''I can think of one.''

They stood silently, her blue eyes confronting his suddenly amused gray gaze with a growing tension between them.

She could feel the air vibrate with her unspoken plea. Could she not please him, was she not as appealing as the widow? He must feel some attraction for her, else why his kisses? And had he not played the hero last night, coming to her rescue when needed? One thing for certain, he had her most confused. One moment she wished him to perdition, the next she wished to be in his arms.

He took a step toward her, his hand now outstretched. She swayed toward him, her face upturned, her eyes searching his face for she knew not what, precisely. She reached out one hand toward his.

''Sibyl,'' he whispered. ''I want—''

The library door opened. George stepped into the hall, stopping at once as he beheld the two in such a curious position. More sensitive than Lord Buckingham, George immediately was aware of the tension between his new cousin and this stranger.

"Ahem." When George cleared his throat, the two jumped apart as though stung.

"Oh! George. Ah, that is, Lord Barringer." In her flustered state it was a wonder she could remember her own name. "May I present the Earl of Stafford?" She placed a trembling hand on Robert's arm, drawing him forward. "Robert, this is Lord Cranswick's son. He is married to the most delightful lady." Turning to George, she added, "I am so pleased to know Marianna is doing well. She is a very special person."

"Stafford?" George glanced away from Sibyl, the smile on his face fading as he looked at the stranger.

"Mrs. Medland's son, George. His charming mother is Delia Medland." Sibyl glanced at his face, then at Robert's, hoping the two men would be civilized about this.

She took a step back—why, she really was not certain. But George had suddenly acquired a grim look on his face.

"Will you not join me in the library, sir? I believe we have a few things to discuss, not the least of which is our parents." He gestured to the room, then marched ahead in the direction of the windows, undoubtedly that he might see the other clearly.

Robert walked after George into the library, that room where so many events were accomplished—letters were written, rendez-vous arranged, and a gentleman might chat for hours with a young lady without fear of compromise, providing a book lay between them as a means of communication. Now two sons were to debate the attraction of their parents, for pity's sake.

Sibyl trailed along behind them, hoping that no one would shoo her away. She was tired of always missing the more interesting things. Slipping behind a tall chair in a shadowed corner of the room, she stayed silent.

The two men remained standing, each poised somewhat warily near the windows, glancing at each other as though sizing up the opposition.

Robert spoke first. "I believe I can appreciate your situation, Lord Barrington. You are apprehensive because, for the first time in years, your father is indicating an interest in a particular woman—my mother.'' He smiled hesitantly. ''I'll confess, I was a bit concerned, myself. However, it did not take long for the lady in question to disabuse me of the notion I ought to be an overprotective son. She knows her own mind, and will do as she feels best.''

''But . . . 'tis unseemly,'' sputtered George at this onslaught of words, none of which answered his concerns.

''She has a fine competence, one that she retains should she remarry, if that is of interest to you,'' offered Robert in a helpful manner. ''Since I inherited, I have made sure that she will be well taken care of regardless, since I plan to marry soon. Knowing her, I suspect she would not wish to reside with us, however much she likes my bride. Since she is about to marry with your father, that is no longer a problem.'' Robert gave George a man-to-man sort of smile.

''He has asked her, then?'' George inquired, beginning to sound more resigned to the idea.

''This morning, if my eyes and ears told me aright. It seems your trip precipitated the event. They both appeared like young lovers to my eyes. I trust you are not too disturbed?'' Robert seemed to reveal sympathy, as though he knew how the other was feeling just now.

Sibyl drew even further into the shadows. Her heart had nearly stopped at Robert's revelation of his future plans. The perfidious man, to dally with her while he planned to wed another. Stealing her kisses while he chased the widow? Shocking!

''It takes a bit of getting used to, I expect. Parents! And at their ages!'' George shook his head, while sharing an understanding look with Lord Stafford.

''Well, I also believe it foolish to waste time in a lengthy courtship. Once your mind is made up, it is best to proceed. Have I not the right of it?'' Robert now appeared to commiserate with George, seeking to align himself with his future stepbrother.

''I would have to agree,'' George admitted. ''I will confess, I was much the same. When you find the right woman, there is little point in dallying about.''

''Your father said something to the effect that you had not

consulted him regarding your wife. Our parents have the right to live as they please, I suspect.''

Looking about to refute this statement, George suddenly relaxed, his handsome face softening into a grin. "I suppose you are correct. Marianna warned me I was on a fool's errand. She said my interference would not be taken lightly.''

"Your Marianna seems a wise woman,'' Robert declared, smiling in relief.

"She told me to attend the wedding,'' George added, completing his confession with a rueful smile. "And you sir, am I to wish you happy?'' Both men had taken more relaxed stances, Robert going so far as to lean against one of the chairs.

He frowned. "To tell the truth, things have not been going the way I could wish there,'' he admitted. "But I intend to bring it to a conclusion soon. I want to get to my new estate before the summer is over, in the event my wife desires to make a few changes.''

Sibyl crouched lower behind the chair, devoutly wishing she had not followed the men into the library. It was bad enough to realize that Robert contemplated marriage, but to hear it discussed was beyond bearing.

"Why do we not walk over to my house?'' he invited. " 'Tis but a few blocks from here on Mount Street. You can meet my mother, soon to be your stepmother. I believe you will like her.''

"I am sure she is all that is fine,'' replied George in a jovial way, giving Robert a look that begged forgiveness. "My father has always been known for his excellent taste. I ought to have remembered that.''

"Good,'' Robert said, as he led the way from the room and down the hall. They began to discuss Robert's matched grays and shortly their voices faded away as the door closed behind them.

Sibyl rose from where she had hidden. How could they have so completely overlooked her presence? She might be a bit short, and she had slipped behind the high-backed chair, crouching toward the end of the conversation. But to totally ignore her as though she did not exist? It was the outside of enough! They obviously had forgotten she was alive. Although considering all that had been said, perhaps it was as well.

And Robert. Her heart grew heavy with sadness. Robert definitely was not to be hers. Could it be any plainer? How foolish her hopes had been. Any doubt that his attentions were directed elsewhere were now settled—the elegant, daring, beautiful, but slightly vulgar widow would be his.

Sibyl firmed her mouth, angry with Robert, herself, and the world in general. She left the library, walking along on unhappy feet.

"Dear, it is time for luncheon. Do you have any notion where those men might be?" Lady Lavinia inquired of her step-daughter.

It was a shock to realize that she now stood in the hall by the stairs. Looking up at her stepmama, Sibyl replied, "They went over to the Medlands. I suspect it will be the three of us for the meal. Best not to count on them." Inwardly, she added that was especially true for Robert. Best not to ever count on him again.

Lady Lavinia gave Sibyl a puzzled look. "What has happened?"

"Robert was here. Do you know your brother is going to marry Mrs. Medland?" As a ploy to divert attention from herself, nothing could have been more successful. She did not have to reveal that for an awful few moments Robert had accused her of trying to wreck his mother's happiness, or that George had been ready to plant a facer on Robert.

"I had hoped for such. Oh, my, a wedding!" She turned to greet her husband with a delighted smile on her face as he sauntered down the stairs. "Henry, William and Delia are to be married. I shall wager you a tidy sum that he will not be any more patient this time than the first."

"Not me, my love. I do not bet on a sure thing." He glanced at his daughter. "Are you feeling quite the thing, puss? You are uncommonly pale."

"Of course, Papa. 'Tis the city. I fear I like the sun and clear air of Mablethorpe better." Then, suspecting they wished to live in the manor house in coupled harmony, alone, she added, "I thought I might pay Marianna a visit. And after that, perhaps I might journey to see Samantha? They are such dear ladies."

Lady Lavinia considered her stepdaugther with a sober gaze,

quite obviously wondering what had taken possession of her now. "The Season is not yet over, my dear. How can you even think of leaving the delights the city has to offer a young girl?"

"I expect some enjoy it more than others, Mama. Shall we? I imagine our luncheon is waiting for us."

A light meal was brought in to the breakfast room, where Lady Lavinia preferred to have the early afternoon meal. It was a comparatively recent innovation. Prior to this, they had contented themselves with a roll and tea, a bit of fruit, perhaps. With the dinners so very late, according to city customs, Henry insisted upon sustenance. Truth be told, so did she. It seemed Sibyl did not share their hunger.

"You do not eat, Sibyl. Is something wrong?"

"What? No, no, nothing is the matter." She shrugged slightly, then offered a small smile. "I believe I shall go for a walk this afternoon, if you can spare me?"

"Of course. I suppose you want to hunt for more butterflies?"

"Yes. That is it. More butterflies."

"I daresay you have found nearly all the kinds there are in the city. What a pity you cannot go to the seashore. I fancy there might be different varieties to be found there."

"True," replied Sibyl with scant enthusiasm.

Lord Eagleton looked from the bland face of his wife to the polite one of his daughter, a perplexed frown touching his brow. "Do have a good time this afternoon. What is planned for this evening, my dear?"

"The Witherspoons are having an 'at home' and I expect we ought to show our faces. From there we are to attend a ball at the Darnleys'."

"It is sure to be a sad crush at the Witherspoons'. I imagine you plan to take a nap this afternoon? Both of you?" Lord Eagleton declared.

Hearing that particular note of authority in her father's voice that she did not care to cross, Sibyl answered at once, "Yes, sir."

"Fine. I'd not wish to see you hag-ridden at four in the morning, for it will likely be late before we return home."

Sibyl nodded, thinking that the rout, which was another way to refer to those invitations that merely stated that the people were to be "at home" on such and such an evening, was indeed likely to be a horrid squeeze. If she were fortunate, she might be stuck on the stairs, and make her way down before she got up.

But there would be no way she might escape the Darnley ball, so she put on a pleasant face, then said with as much cheer as she could muster, "I shall take a walk in the park air, enjoying the green before it fades with the heat of summer. Then, a good nap, and I shall be ready for anything."

Once in her room, Sibyl donned her blue spencer over her white muslin walking dress, set a pert jockey hat on her brown curls, then pulled on soft blue silk gloves. It took but minutes to locate her net and collecting box. In a short time she left the house, Annie trailing closely behind her holding the box.

It was early for the *ton* to be strolling in the park. They usually flooded in about four of the clock, leaving around six, more or less.

There were people about, however. She did not feel the least alone. She cut across the grass until she found a promising area. There were clusters of wildflowers that had been left to bloom in peace, untouched by an improving hand. Here, the dainty butterflies were most likely to be found.

She was closing in on the orange-tipped white butterfly that had eluded her before when she heard herself hailed. Glancing up, she saw Lord Buckingham striding toward her.

"Knew it had to be you," he declared with a patronizing air. "After all, you are the only one I know who chases after those dratted things."

"I do not precisely chase, Lord Buckingham," she sweetly replied, forgetting for the moment her race down a hill that ended in being swept in Robert's strong arms and quite thoroughly kissed.

"Of course." He smile was a touch benign.

She almost told him to go away, and then she recalled that Robert had announced this morning that he intended to marry soon. While he had not stated the name of the lady, it only stood to reason that had it been Sibyl, her name might have been mentioned. Would it not? She returned Lord Buckingham's smile. Even his attention was a balm to her wounded sensibilities.

"Finding anything worth your while?"

Annie handed her the net, with the little butterfly well and truly caught in it. Sibyl gave her a grateful look, then nodded. "Indeed, it seems I am running out of varieties." Recalling what her stepmother had said only that morning, she added, "I imagine were I to go to the seashore, I might find a different assortment. However, that is unlikely at present. Perhaps later."

She began to stroll along, noticing that a carriage was almost paralleling their progress, one containing a lady wearing pink and scarlet. She was blond, unless Sibyl's eyesight was amiss. Lady Wayford?

"That offers me an opportunity to do you a service, I perceive. Why not allow me to take you on one of the new steam packets? There is one that leaves the London Bridge Wharf tomorrow—the Old Shades Pier, I believe it is called."

Sibyl vividly recalled her visit to the river. "A trip to Gravesend, sir?" How appropriate.

"I feel sure that if you present the idea to Lady Lavinia, she would approve."

Since her stepmama had taken a dim view of the collecting, Sibyl wondered about that. Then she caught sight of Lady Wayford in her luscious pink and scarlet gown, waiting for them at a point where their path crossed the road. Only the dashing widow would dare to wear such a combination of colors. She looked sensational.

"Miss Eagleton. Montague." Lady Wayford nodded gracefully, the plumes on her bonnet fluttering about in the gentle breeze. "How lovely to see friends. I am all alone today, alas." She affected a rueful moue, then touched her perfect pink lips with the tips of her pink-gloved hands while peeping up at Lord Buckingham in a chiding manner.

Sibyl smiled back, albeit a trifle grimly.

"I forget, we all have our difficulties. How are you coming along, Miss Eagleton?" Aurora's voice oozed sympathy. Lady Wayford could afford to be gracious. She undoubtedly held the upper hand.

"Perhaps you have heard the news? Lord Cranswick and Mrs. Medland are to wed soon. My mama is all of a dither, with a wedding to help plan."

"Just one? I had thought perhaps you might have found a susceptible gentleman by now." Lady Wayford batted her lashes at dear Montague, her trill of laughter grating on Sibyl's nerves.

"One does what one can, Lady Wayford." Sibyl forced a small laugh past her lips.

Lord Buckingham at last seemed to perceive that the women were trading barbed comments and inserted himself into the conversation.

"We are contemplating a jaunt down the river to Gravesend in search of a few butterflies for Miss Eagleton's collection. Should be jolly fun, what?"

The two ladies fastened their respective gazes upon him, each looking grim for reasons of her own.

16

THE ROUT WAS precisely as Sibyl had feared—a smashing squeeze. If one more person had attempted to enter the house, the walls would most likely have burst.

She managed to avoid going up the stairs by pretending she had already been there and facing the way out. Her parents performed the honors for the family, for Lady Lavinia was that fond of Mrs. Witherspoon.

"Sibyl, I am so pleased to see you. Are you on your way to the Darnleys'?" Mary Ransom took both of Sibyl's hands in hers, her face beaming a smile to light up the room. Mr. Terence Hadgley stood on one side of her, Mary's fond mama on the other.

"Actually, I am waiting for my parents so we can go. We became separated."

"Terrible crush, is it not? We shall wait with you, for it would not do for you to be alone," Mrs. Ransom said decisively.

Sibyl gave her a startled glance. Anyone less likely to be alone in the entire environs of London she couldn't imagine. They stood chatting for some minutes before Mrs. Ransom cleared her throat. "I saw Delia Medland with your uncle this afternoon. They were driving along in his carriage, but they might as well have been on the moon for all they were aware. They certainly looked to be smelling of April and May."

"You have the right of it. They are to marry, and soon. Mama is in alt."

Sibyl exchanged a look with Mrs. Ransom, one that shared pleasure in the coming event.

At this point, the Eagletons joined them, Lady Lavinia fanning herself briskly. "I declare, why must people do this? I need air."

The group edged their way from the house to the street, where they soon sorted out their carriages. Mrs. Ransom went with the Eagletons, while Sibyl joined Mary and Terence in the Ransom carriage.

"I expect that Mama wants all the particulars," Mary said, knowing full well the ladies would be deep in details all the way over to the Darnleys.'

"I expect so," Sibyl replied politely.

"Are you all right? You do not seem yourself this evening." Mary looked at Terence, then at Sibyl. "Have you heard anything from the new Lord Stafford? Word is seeping out and about of his inheritance. You might know it would be a nine day's wonder."

"He was at the house this morning to visit with my stepcousin, George. It was nice they could get acquainted." Since Sibyl had fully expected them to come to blows, it was doubly nice they had left the house in one piece and most amiable.

"Did you hear about Lady Jolliffe's masquerade? Someone almost killed Roger Bainbridge. Knocked him senseless, and they had to call for a doctor." Mary shivered with delicious horror at the thought. "I wonder what happened? Terence thinks a thief came in and attempted to rob the house."

"Really," Sibyl said faintly, not aware the blow struck by Robert had been quite so deadly. "Well, it might have been worse."

"How?" demanded Mary, all agog.

"He could have been shot," Sibyl answered absently, thinking of the gun she kept in her drawer. She would have used it if necessary; she had been taught to defend herself.

"Heavens!" Mary declared.

Fortunately the carriage arrived at the Darnleys' house at that moment and the three joined the others before entering. Mrs. Ransom looked delighted at having obtained all the inside news from dear Lady Lavinia.

Once past the receiving line, Sibyl looked about her. Few houses could run to a ballroom; the Darnley drawing room had been combined with a sitting room to nicely take the place of one.

Sibyl smiled at Belinda Valler, who happened to be standing next to Captain Ransom. Although Sibyl doubted they would make anything of their slight attraction, she knew Belinda found it agreeable to have a willing partner she might depend upon. Captain Ransom no doubt wished to advance before settling down.

Beyond them, Lord Stafford chatted with George.

Her gaze lingered on Robert. Then she caught sight of Lady Wayford. The elegant widow was gowned in her favorite shade of pink and fluttering her lashes at none other than Lord Buckingham, of all people. How odd that a man who had nothing kind to say about her so often found himself in her company. However, they did seem to be arguing—politely—about something. Lady Wayford was one of those women who could look beautiful when angry, and she was breathtaking at the moment.

The ball was lovely, her friends charming, and the refreshments quite nice, actually. Sibyl could not wait to leave.

She was nibbling on a delicate pastry in the refuge of the morning room, now used for the food service, when a voice she knew all too well spoke.

"If I were a vain man, I might say you were trying to avoid me this ekvening." Lord Stafford's aggrieved tone was almost comical. She most likely would have laughed had her heart not felt weighed down at the moment.

"Since we both know you are not such, I expect you will have to think of another reason." Her eyes remained downcast; she would not look at the man she loved and who now belonged to another, it seemed.

"You have certainly stayed on the opposite side of the rooms ever since you arrived. How clever of you to manage that." That voice was searching, prrobing.

"Undoubtedly," she replied. She refused to give him the satisfaction of seeing how the news of his impending marriage affected her. Of course, neither he nor George seemed aware that she had been in the library. Such stupid men. "I understand they had to call a doctor for Mr. Bainbridge. I was sorry to learn that."

"Yes," he said a touch impatiently. "When you finish nibbling that pastry to death, will you dance with me?"

"My card . . ." she gestured helplessly, as though her card were full to overflowing. She hadn't counted on Robert's pulling the thing from her wrist to inspect it.

"Aha! As I suspected. You have kept a few open for me."

"I take it back. You are a vain man. And what makes believe I would save anything for you?"

"Because I know you."

"You do not know me, sir. Nothing at all about me. What you see is not me, it is a figure clothed in silks and muslins and placed on display by my stepmama in order to auction me off to the highest bidder."

"Rubbish. You told me they did not compel you to wed that boy back home. I warrant you will have your choosing here. Have you chosen as yet?" he said lightly. "Or are you cruelly debating the fate of some poor man? Are you as opposed to a peer as ever?" His gaze was intent, watching.

She gave him a disbelieving look, a wry twist to her mouth at those words. "Of course." The only eligible peer she knew was Lord Buckingham, and she'd not marry him.

"Come," he persisted, sounding somewhat annoyed.

There was nothing to do but to follow him. Others had found the refreshments and the room was becoming crowded.

Glancing at her hand upon the smooth sleeve of his coat, she made to remove it, then found it securely close to him. "Sir?"

"A waltz, Sibyl. Remember when I first taught you? You learned quickly." He led her into the throng of dancers, encircling her with an arm, clasping a hand lightly in his.

She could make no reply to that. Swinging gracefully into his arms, she found it impossible not to respond to the music. That was what it was, she knew, merely the music. Her heartbeat, the tingling she knew in her veins had nothing to do with this man.

"Lady Wayford told me that you plan to go farther afield in your hunt for butterflies. Is that so?" he asked.

At last she met his gaze. It was not fair that he look at her like that, with those gray eyes meltingly soft, that rich brown hair capturing sparks of gold from the candles. She dropped her gaze again to study the intricate folds of his immaculate neckcloth.

"I have plans, yes."

"Lord Buckingham is to assist you?" He swung her about in the confined space available to them, deftly, surely.

"I believe so."

"With the butterflies?" he persisted.

"Yes."

"You have to be the most exasperating female in the world. Do you have any idea how I would like to take you out and shake you?"

"You have become a man of violence, sir. First, Mr. Bainbridge, then me? Shall I call for a doctor in advance?"

She could see his chest swell as though he was about to burst, forced to hold his breath in, lest he do her harm. How pleasing it was to annoy him, she decided. He must be counting to ten. Delightful!

When the dance concluded, he made to lead her from the main rooms. Sibyl balked. "Fie, sir. I must seek my mama. You would not have me declared improper by those who judge such things? I bid you good evening." With those prodigiously polite remarks, she curtsied, then hurried to where she had caught a glimpse of her stepmother.

"You look tired, Mama. Do you have the headache as I do? I believe it is too hot in here, I feel almost faint."

Lady Lavinia became alarmed at the information that she looked tired. That would never do. Sibyl looked a bit peaked as well. "Yes, the heat is becoming unbearable. Find your papa and we shall leave."

Skillfully removing her father from the bookroom, where a number of men sat playing at cards and gossiping, she had her family out of the house in jig time.

Her parents exchanged a dismayed look, but said nothing. Tomorrow they would have to discuss the matter of a wedding with her, and this time there would be no winding about the finger by this young miss. They would be firm.

The following morning Sibyl rose early, dressing herself in a blue muslin and velvet spencer with fumbling fingers in her haste to be away from the house. When Annie scratched on the door, Sibyl swiftly crossed to let her in. The maid was astonished to see her mistress up and dressed, and apparently near ready to depart.

"I best get my things," Annie offered. "Where we be going?"

"Out," Sibyl replied absently. "Get ready for a voyage on a boat. We shall be gone most of the day. I shall need my net and collecting box, I expect. Do not forget the killing jar, either."

"A boat, miss?" the maid replied in a distressed voice. "Oh, lawks! A boat, you say? I niver been on no boat afore."

"Quite safe, I assure you. Now go, while I sip my chocolate. Please do hurry, girl."

When Sibyl presented herself at the door to the breakfast room, she found her papa reading the morning paper. "I have been invited on a boat trip with Lord Buckingham today. Mama suggested I try looking farther afield for butterflies, so I am."

"Fine, fine, puss. You have the maid with you?" He glanced at Sibyl, taking note of her proper dress. She was a pretty thing when wearing blue.

"Annie waits by the door. I shall see you later."

Only after he had heard the door close did Lord Eagleton recall his dear wife had said they were to discuss Sibyl's forthcoming marriage with her today. Ah, well, tomorrow would do as well, he figured, and settled back to read about what was going on in Parliament.

Lord Buckingham's carriage drew up just as Sibyl exited the front door of Cranswick House. He seemed taken aback to discover the lady seemingly waiting for him on the steps, so to speak.

"Miss Eagleton, I am gratified to see you so bright this morning. Stafford informed me you had the headache last evening. I feared it might upset your plans for the day."

"Not in the least, sir." She willingly stepped up into the carriage, then saw to it that Annie and all the paraphernalia were settled across from her.

"Good," was his only reply to her cheerful words. He signaled his driver and they set off toward the river at a fast clip. "Dashed early. Had a devil of a time getting myself up this morning."

Sibyl wondered if she was supposed to pin a medal on his chest for heroic behavior. "Well, when one will stay up late, one does pay for it later, they say." Still, she was determined to make the best of the day. Surely it might be possible to learn to like Lord Buckingham—just a little?

She pinned a smile on her face that faded a bit around the edges when they reached the pier. Annie paled visibly.

There were other boats in the area, one-masted boats with a boom to the mainsail. Papa had said they were called hoys, mostly because people hailed them by calling "ahoy" to bring the boat to shore when they wished to be picked up. He had also said they were dreadfully slow boats, and often dangerous, relating tales of fearful voyages.

To her eyes, the steam packet looked no more entrancing. Why had she not checked out the boat first, before agreeing to this trip that she really did not want? Living in London must be making her soft in the head.

A sign revealed that the fare was fifteen shillings or twenty shillings per person. She supposed the amount depended on the service you wished.

They climbed down the steep pier, then onto the boat. When she felt it sway beneath her feet, she swallowed rather hard. She had not known many boat trips. Somehow, she felt this would not be a promising one, even if she did find more butter-flies. Suddenly she wanted to toss the collecting box over the side and flee to the safety of her room.

Robert, why do you have to marry someone else? she wondered. But, knowing there was little use in railing against reality, she again smiled gamely and settled down on a wooden bench.

The boat was not what she had expected, being full of strange sounds and peculiar odors. There was a rolling movement as the waves slapped against the hull and the river made itself felt. The noise from the steam engine was rather alarming. Since no one but herself, and of course the frightened Annie, seemed to take it amiss, she said nothing, but rather stared at the activity along the river.

As they proceeded downriver, she was caught up with the sights along the banks. Wherrymen darted along in their tiny boats, seeming unmindful of the larger steam packet. Billings-gate could be observed from a safe distance, but even here the scent of fish might be detected. Farther on, she was fascinated by the view of a yard with a vessel under construction, while next to it was another that looked ready for launching. There were larger ships from foreign ports off-loading their goods, mostly to the smaller hoys, and some of the flat-bottomed barges. Her papa had said new docks were desperately needed to facilitate the handling of shipping. She could see it was true. Cargos of rice, silks, spices, and precious woods teased her imagination.

The breeze was fresh, and for that she was thankful. Sibyl was almost beginning to enjoy the trip when she observed Annie had turned a horrid shade of pea green.

"Best get her flat on her back," said one of the seamen. "Follow me."

Below deck the air reeked of various distasteful smells. The noise from the engine throbbed even more loudly here. Annie's eyes looked fit to start from her head. A sudden roll of the boat had her sinking flat onto a bench, her feet pointed toward heaven as though she fully expected to be there soon.

"Go on deck, miss. I'll be fine as fivepence here, I will," Annie declared bravely. It was clear to Sibyl she would rather die than have Sibyl waiting on her.

In a quandary as to what she ought to do, Sibyl decided she had best get to fresh air before she too succumbed to the roll of the boat.

"A case of mal de mer," Sibyl reported to Lord Buckingham when she joined him along the railing.

"Mercifully, this trip will be vastly shorter than on one of the hoys," he said in his superior manner.

It was most likely not the way a lady ought to travel, she thought. Robert probably would not have taken her on this boat. Yet it was not without novelty. Shocking speed, of course. She clutched at her bonnet as a spray of water hit her. The breeze was stiff; her spencer offered little protection.

"Could we get off any place we wish, as on the hoy? Or must we continue to Gravesend?" Of a sudden she wanted to know if it might be possible to change one's mind.

"Why would you wish to get off, Miss Eagleton? Unless you see a butterfly from here?"

He laughed, and Sibyl noticed that it did not ring true. She studied the man at her side. "Where are the other passengers on the boat? I just realized that I see no one else around us."

"Because," he declaimed grandly, "I have hired the boat

exclusively for us. It would never do to be required to share it with just anyone, you know.''

''It is exceptionally kind of you to do this for me. Why?'' Little suspicions nagged at her.

He did not answer her immediately. Rather, he studied the side of the river where rushes grew against steep grassy banks. Gulls dipped and wheeled about the boat in great numbers, their harsh cries a strangely disquieting sound.

''Because, Miss Eagleton.''

They neared Greenwich and Sibyl again wondered if she ought to leave the boat. But where would she go? Foolish girl, she had to be the most empty-headed female in all of London. Addle-pated, that is what she was. Her brain had become scrambled.

Then she observed that Lord Buckingham's arm had slid about her. She looked up at him in alarm. ''Sir?''

''Can you not see? There are some swells coming toward us. Brace yourself, my dear Miss Eagleton.''

Sibyl found that by planting her feet firmly on the deck as the sailors did, she managed very well, indeed. ''I believe I am fine now, thank you.'' She shifted to ease away from him, then found his arms clamped about her in an amazingly tight grip.

''Your maid is not here.''

Puzzled at this non sequitur, she frowned, then shrugged. ''True. She is suffering below. Sir?'' she repeated, not wishing to create a scene.

''Ah, Miss Eagleton, I believe I once made it clear that I wished to speak to your father, pay my addresses?''

''But after you found me in Lord Stafford's arms, you changed your mind.''

''True,'' he reflected, ''I did for a time. But, one must do what one must. You have a fine dowry, a pretty face. I believe we ought to get along well enough.''

''But, I do not love you, sir.'' Sibyl gave him an alarmed glance. Had the man taken leave of his senses? Or had she invited this by agreeing to make this journey with him? She wished Annie was at her other side.

''What has love to do with marriage? You may find that later if you please, after we have an heir to my name.''

"I am very sorry, my lord. I fear I have wronged you by accepting your kind invitation. You misread my feelings." She tried valiantly to keep her voice steady. How she wished there were other passengers on board.

"Surely you are not such an innocent . . . Your mama indicated . . ." He reached out to take her face in his hands, studied her for a moment, then claimed her lips in a kiss. Compared to Lord Stafford's, it lacked a good deal. However, it was not totally repugnant. Just unwanted.

She turned her head away from him, breathing rapidly, pushing against him with her hands. Swallowing some of her distress, she backed away from him. "You, sir, are not playing quite fair. I expected an innocent trip. You are turning this into a seduction, or at the very least a compromise."

"What the devil!" His exclamation was not at all what she had expected to hear. She turned to look behind them at whatever had caught Lord Buckingham's notice. Another boat was overtaking the packet. A light yacht skimmed along the surface of the river, its sails billowing in the wind, the man at the helm seeming bent on a race.

"So you know that boat, sir?" She wondered at the vexed expression on Lord Buckingham's face until she looked more closely at the yacht.

"Stafford," Lord Buckingham declared, even more vexed than before.

"And Lady Wayford as well, it seems," Sibyl added softly. Her words were torn away from her by the wind, but Lord Buckingham had heard one word. An awesome frown distorted his brow.

"Aurora? With Stafford? Impossible."

Sibyl did not need to reassure him that Lady Wayford was indeed on that yacht. Anyone with eyes in his head could see that. She wore a flaming poppy pink pelisse with a cap tied on her head. Not assisting in any way with the management of the boat, she leaned against the railing near the front, looking utterly furious.

In the stern, Lord Stafford could be seen, grim and determined. He wore a fisherman's jersey above his pantaloons and boots, looking an utterly disreputable character, yet very welcome to Sibyl's eyes.

A seaman approached Lord Buckingham. "Sir, the captain respectfully requests to see you, if you please."

Sibyl watched as Lord Buckingham left her side and went up to where the captain stood. A terse conversation followed. Lord Buckinghaam seemed much distressed.

"What did the captain want?" she asked when Buckingham returned.

"Wants to put to. Says the other boat is crowding him." Buckingham rubbed his chin in frustration.

"Will we?"

"I said we might as well. No point in damaging this boat. I do not want to pay the costs, in any event."

Sibyl thought that if Lord Buckingham truly loved her, he would defy the other boat and sail out to sea or something equally romantic. Lord Buckingham was not a romantic, quite obviously.

The engine's awful racket became greatly subdued as the packet slowed to a stop. Sibyl heard the canvas flapping in the other boat as it tacked across the bow of the packet. It must be nice to skim along the river with only the wind to whip the sails, the slap of water against the bow.

She waited, watching, wondering what was to happen next. She could not blame the captain for not wishing to run his ship aground. But what on earth was going on in Lord Stafford's mind, to do such a thing as this?

Lord Buckingham had marched over to the side of the boat when Robert suddenly appeared. Sibyl shrank back against the railing for a moment, then gasped when she saw Lady Wayford coming on deck directly behind him.

Taking a step toward the others, she froze as Robert drew his fist back, then knocked Lord Buckingham clean off his feet. His lordship staggered up, then came at Robert, arms flailing, looking mad as a hen in a puddle.

A crack to Buckingham's jaw sent him reeling against the railing where he teetered for a moment, then went over the side of the packet.

"Montague!" Lady Wayford screamed. "What have you done to him, you brute? Montague, take care! We will save you, my love." She called to a sailor, then fluttered about the side of the ship, alternately reassuring Lord Buckingham he would be saved in a trice and berating Robert for hitting Montague too hard.

Sibyl's eyes grew round as an owl's. When Robert came to her side, she gestured toward her ladyship, and said, "Did she say what I thought she said?"

"She did. We decided it was time and enough that we each got our heart's desire. What I have endured to get to this point no one would believe."

Sibyl suddenly found herself swept off her feet and carried across the deck. "What are you doing?" she screeched. An appeal to a nearby seaman was out of the question. They were laughing far too hard to do anything useful.

Without ceremony, she was swiftly brought down the side of the packet and dropped to the deck of the yacht.

"Have you lost your senses?" she yelled at him as he dropped to the deck not far from where she stood, defiant and proud. It might be romantic to be captured like this, but her maid was on board the packet! She was all alone with Lord Stafford.

"As I recall, you said I was as straight-arrow as they come." He looked wicked, rakish, and infinitely handsome as he stood braced against the roll of the boat. "Honorable, trustworthy, steadfast, true-blue. Have I missed any?" He had ticked off the points on his fingers.

She stared at his hands, fascinated with the strength in them. "Oh," she gulped, "none, I am sure." Then she approached him with wary steps, trailing behind him while he hurried to the stern of the boat.

He was ignoring her. Ruthlessly. Why had he captured her if all he was going to do was sail down the river?

The packet boat appeared to be a hive of activity. She could see Lord Buckingham being hauled up to the deck, dripping water all over the place. Lady Wayford hovered about him with a blanket. The seamen had stopped laughing and were busy at their appointed tasks. Soon the faint sound of the steam engine being put to full throttle was heard. At last, all Sibyl could make out was the splash of pink, Lady Wayford's pelisse.

"Are you going to speak to me?"

"Are you ready to listen?"

"Of course. Now, what was all that about? Why the exchange of ladies? And give me no nonsense about your heart's desire.

I heard you tell George that you planned to marry soon. It is not with me, for you have never said a word about it. I thought you to marry her.'' She sniffed, with little effect, for she lost her footing and fell to the deck with a thud. Feeling much abused, she retreated to the railing.

"Aurora? Never. She and Buckingham will make it legal now, I suspect. They were once very close to marriage. I had to keep her away from Cranswick, for Mother's sake. She was desperate for more money and another title. And, I also had plans for you, dear wigeon.''

They skimmed along the river for some time, passing several towns and villages, and now diverted to a narrow passage of water. Sibyl digested what Robert just said, a growing hope within.

"When are we to arrive in Gravesend?'' They were nearing a marshy area, devoid of habitation as far as she could see beyond the sea wall.

"Gravesend was the last town we sailed by, my love. This is Canvey Island.''

She stared out across the marshy land. "There is nothing here.''

"But us.''

"Why have you done this, Robert? If there was a scandal over a mere kiss, what will there be over an abduction? By boat, yet?'' She clasped her hands before her, pleading with her eyes that he somehow make everything right.

"There was nothing in the least 'mere' about that kiss. In fact, that is when I decided I would marry you. Only, there was the little matter of my title. It seems to me that you are rather adamantly opposed to them.''

He had let down an anchor and the sails, and now the boat was still, with only the gentle rustle of the wind in the rushes to be heard. A gull squawked in the distance.

Sibyl watched with apprehensive curiosity as he neared where she stood. "That was because of Lord Buckingham.''

"I rather hoped that was the case.'' He inhaled the scent of the sea mingled with lily of the valley, and grinned.

"Now what?'' her voice seemed very tiny, lost. The wolfish grin that had crept across his face intrigued her.

"We are to be married, my love. With your parents' blessing,

I might add. I have the required special license, which cost me a bit of time, not to mention money. But all is worth it.''

Gambling on her feelings for this man, Sibyl dared all. "I love you, you know.''

"I rather hoped you did, for I love you too, my little pea-goose.'' There was nothing to be done at this point but seal their future with a kiss.

Sibyl decided that either Robert had much improved, or the breathtaking kiss that had caused such commotion had been only practice.

At that point, shouts were heard. Several men scrambled atop the sea wall, waving their arms about.

Sibyl looked up at Robert, a question in her eyes.

"I expect they will drive us to town, most likely in a smelly old wagon, my love. But there is a church in Canvey where a clergyman will marry us. Then we can return to our boat and sail wherever we please.''

She chuckled, nestling close to him. "Not the castle, I think.''

"We shall go there next.'' He thought of the plunge bath with longing, then picked up his little love and began the trip to Canvey church.